AMBEREYE

What Reviewers Say About
Gill McKnight's Novels

"Angst, conflict, sex and humor. [*Falling Star*] has all of this and more packed into a tightly written and believable romance... McKnight has penned a sweet and tender romance, balancing the intimacy and sexual tension just right. The conflict is well drawn, and she adds a great dose of humor to make this novel a light and easy read."—*Curve* Magazine

"When an unlikely cast of characters sets out for a lesbian romance in Gill McKnight's *Green-Eyed Monster*, anything can happen, and it does! In this speedy read, McKnight succeeds in tantalizing with explosive sex and a bit of bondage; tormenting with sexual frustration and intense longing; tickling your fancy and funny bone; and touching a place where good and evil battle it out. With love vs. money at odds, readers ponder which will win, thanks to McKnight keeping the stakes high and the action palpable. "—*Just About Write*

By the Author

Falling Star

Green Eyed Monster

Goldenseal

Erosistible

Ambereye

AMBEREYE

by
Gill McKnight

2010

AMBEREYE

ISBN 10: 1-60282-132-1
ISBN 13: 978-1-60282-132-3

This Trade Paperback Original Is Published By
Bold Strokes Books, Inc.
P.O. Box 249
Valley Falls, NY 12185

First Bold Strokes Printing: January 2010

CREDITS
EDITOR: CINDY CRESAP AND STACIA SEAMAN
PRODUCTION DESIGN: STACIA SEAMAN
COVER DESIGN BY SHERI (GRAPHICARTIST2020@HOTMAIL.COM)

Acknowledgments

With many thanks to Cindy Cresap—remember, a stray semicolon is really just a wink for the editor. Roll on your next hundred.

Dedication

For Karen the meerkat.

CHAPTER ONE

Jolie Garoul slammed her car door and headed toward the elevators, her heels clicking sharply on the concrete.

She stepped in, punched button three, and then glowered at her image in the smoked mirrors. A tall, gaunt figure glowered disinterestedly back. Her mouth was already a tight, angry line, her eyes fierce and unhappy, and the day had barely begun. But Jolie Garoul had no time for appearances. There was work to be done. Deadlines with not enough hours in the day to meet them, endless meetings with total idiots, and lazy-ass, incompetent employees who wanted coffee breaks and regular hours and generally got in the way of an efficient office.

If that report is not waiting for me as promised, I'm gonna fly down to Florida myself and rip Malcolm's lying tongue out. I wonder if the patch for Release 12.7 is ready? When can we run that? I need to see Williams. We can't have a delay like last time. People were idle, sitting around on their fat backsides getting paid for squat.

The elevator doors slid open, and she moved onto the office floor of Ambereye, Inc., en route to her little corner of the Garoul business empire. She could hear laughter from the small staff kitchen and smell a rich coffee roast. The clock read 7:33 a.m., but already employees were coming into the office in dribs and drabs, heading for the kitchen and their morning caffeine fix. *Twenty-seven minutes and you're all mine. Better hope that coffee wakes you the hell up.*

Then she noticed the balloons pinned to the cubicle closest to her office. It had always been purposely left empty. A recognized buffer zone, a deliberate and necessary no man's land between her office and the rest of the workforce. No one wanted to sit there, and Jolie preferred it that way. It meant she didn't have to look at any of them as she worked through the latest load of incompetence dumped on her desk. Much more inspiring to sit and stare gloomily at the abandoned hardware and dust bunnies cluttering up the empty cubicle than look at her employees. Except this morning the cubicle was cleared out and cleaned. A top-spec computer was sitting on the desk along with a brand-new state-of-the-art ergonomic chair. Nicer than her own. Much nicer.

She glared at the new hardware and the executive chair. What did it all mean? With a scowl she mashed the padded headrest in her hand and wheeled the luxury seat into her own office, casting a last disdainful look at the balloons. *See they're keeping their brains on strings these days.*

Seconds later, a well-aimed kick sent an older, tattier chair spinning out of her door on whizzing castors. It crashed haphazardly into the cubicle and toppled over the brand-new wastepaper bin.

❖

Hope Glassy slammed her car door and trotted happily toward the elevators. Once there, Hope punched button three and anxiously assessed her image in the elevator's smoked mirrors. *It looks damned good.* She reassured herself again. *Nearly impossible to tell.*

The doors pinged open, and she headed directly to the kitchen where she knew she'd find her friends. Every morning Candace and Michael huddled over their coffee before the day truly began. Already she could hear the murmur of voices she recognized. It sounded as if Sally, Deepak, Nadeem, and a few others had joined them. *God, it's good to be back.*

Michael's cheery voice rang out as soon as she appeared in the doorway. "There's our girl."

"Hey, prodigal. I missed you." Candace rushed to wrap her in a massive hug, even though she'd visited Hope at home only last week. "You came back for all your sins."

Candace's big, hearty laugh was joined by a chorus of welcomes as Hope was hugged by the dozen or so friends who'd gathered to meet her.

"Guys, look. I brought Krispy Kremes. Who loves ya?" Hope

placed the box on the counter. It was ripped open before she could blink.

"They still don't feed you around here, or what?" she said. "Even the zoo provides snacks for its inmates."

"You've got to be kidding. You get a snack here, and ole Jollyface counts how many times you chew before swallowing."

"What zoo? Are they recruiting?"

"Yeah, the monkey house, you're as good as in."

"That's where we got him from."

As in most offices with a small crew, they were a tight team, sharing each other's highs and lows. Their humor and camaraderie helped to get them through a tough workload and a tougher schedule. Despite all the moaning, everyone loved their job and wouldn't wish to work elsewhere. Ambereye Inc., for all its size, had a cutting-edge reputation in games software development, and it carried a certain amount of prestige to be a part of its universal success.

"Save me a chocolate sprinkle," Candace commanded the unruly scrabble before turning her full attention to Hope. "You are looking a million dollars, babe. You can't believe how happy we are to have you back."

Hope had a fair idea. Candace had replaced her as personal assistant to Andre Garoul, the CEO, after Hope had gone on sick leave. She had returned earlier than expected because Ambereye had won another important contract and was gearing up for busy times ahead. Andre had been dropping hints for weeks now about how much they needed her. So now she was back and excited to see her colleagues, but she was still unsure of where her new position would be. Andre hadn't been very clear on that point.

"I'm raring to go. So tell me the latest news. Any idea where they're going to put me?"

"Mmm, maybe it's better I leave the best bit to Andre," Candace said. She reached for her reserved doughnut. "How's Tadpole?"

It was a pretty lame segue, and didn't fool Hope for one minute. Combined with the covert, sympathetic glances she was getting from her colleagues, her suspicions began to rise.

"Tadpole is doing just fine. What's going on here?" She brought the discussion about her pet dog to an abrupt end and got straight to the point.

"Come on. Spit it out." Her eyes narrowed with suspicion. She was not going to be distracted.

"Well…" It seemed Candace had been subliminally delegated to break the news to her. After all, she was Hope's buddy as well as her replacement. "Okay. So, Andre made me his assistant in your absence. But you know all about that."

"Yes." Hope nodded. Andre had visited her at home several times. He was a good friend to her, much more than a boss. But then he was a wonderful guy to work for, period. Apologetic about the reshuffle, he'd explained that a big project had just landed on his desk and he needed Candace on board from the get-go. He'd promised to squeeze Hope into an interesting position that would fit around her new part-time hours. He was bending over backwards to get her into the office as soon as possible.

"It makes sense since I'm only coming back part time. So, what's the problem?" She frowned over the rim of her coffee cup at her friends. They were looking decidedly shifty, and no one wanted to look at her.

"What? What is it? You're freaking me out here. Guys?"

Candace stepped up to the mark. "Okay. Well, word is, and it *is* only rumor, that you're the new PA for Jollyface."

"What?" Hope exploded. "Andre never told me that. I was talking to him just last night, and he never once mentioned it. Are you sure?"

"Yup," Michael muffled through a mouth of lemon filled glaze. "We even put balloons up in the Bunker—I mean your new cubicle. And Andre got you a new PC, and a real fancy chair as a special treat."

"As a special bribe, more like." Hope was aghast. Jolie Garoul, aka Jollyface, was a walking nightmare.

"And it's bulletproof." Sally tried a joke, but only managed to underscore the problem. Jolie Garoul had more moods than an orchestra pit.

"I don't get it. Jolie never has assistants. I assumed she never wanted one," Hope said.

"It's this new project. They've had to reshuffle the workload. I think everyone's more or less doubled up with no extensions to deadlines. It's all hands on deck for your new department."

"Well, I suppose it's only for four days a week until this project's over." Hope was determined to look on the bright side. "If we're busy, then I'll have to go where I'm needed most. Hey ho." She gave her brightest, most upbeat smile, resolute that all would be well. Hope had been itching to get back to work for weeks before her doctor would allow it. This was what she had wanted. *Careful what you wish for.*

"Ah, your parents named you well." Michael dropped a huge meaty hand on her shoulder, almost buckling her at the knees.

"Easy there, big boy," Candace said. "We only just got her back."

None too dainty herself, she flung an arm around Hope's waist and maneuvered her out of the kitchen and toward the balloon-adorned workspace. Hope was glad of the slow pace; her balance could still play tricks on her.

"Come see your new PC. You got the sexiest monitor *and* chair," Candace said.

"Hope." Andre Garoul descended on them from his office suite at the far end of the floor, a huge ribboned vase of roses in his arms. "Hi, darling. Great to see you back in the trenches. Just in time for the big push." He towered over her, dazzling her with a huge, happy grin that lit up his dark good looks.

"More like the big pushover." She accepted the bouquet pressed into her arms. "Is it true I'm working for Jolie now?" She peeped over the topmost blossoms. "These are absolutely beautiful, by the way."

"Mmm, well. Yes. I really need you to, Hope." His charming smile stretched a little thin, and a flash of desperation lit his eyes.

"Why didn't you say something at dinner last night?" They walked on together, the rest of the welcome party slowly peeling away to their desks as the workday began.

"I was scared you'd be a no-show."

"You know I'd never let you down, Andy." She used his homey name. "But I can't believe you welched out of telling me. You're such a yellow belly."

"I'm such a yellow six-pack," he corrected her. Several paces from her new booth, his pager began to hum on his belt.

"Hang on." He unclipped it and squinted at the screen. "Oh, hon. I've got to go. My call from Phoenix came through early. Look, I'll drop by later, okay?"

He was already backpedaling, eyes huge with apology. Hope shook her head and smiled ruefully at him. He'd been saved from her scolding by his heavy workload and uncanny luck.

"Later," she said.

Tipping the vase and its fragrant contents at him she mouthed, "Thank you" and turned to her new desk.

"Now, that is one nice computer," Hope mumbled to herself, placing her flowers on her desk. She realigned the chair and picked up the toppled wastepaper bin. She slid her bag under her desk and sat down. She wriggled in the seat, not as impressed with the so-called fancy chair as she was with her hardware. Next she checked the drawers, pleased to see Candace had stacked them with pens, paper, and a stapler. All the odds and ends that saved a tedious trip to the stationery cupboard. She wiggled in her seat again. *Wow, this is not my idea of luxurious. In fact, it has a serious butt groove thing going on.*

Hope clicked open her compact and checked her makeup and general appearance in the mirror. *Okay, looking good.* Satisfied, she gathered a pencil and spiral notebook, and with a calming breath, rose and marched over to her new boss's office. She rapped gently on the open door before entering.

Jolie Garoul sat behind her desk, slashing open mail with the vicious enthusiasm of a cutthroat; her silver letter opener glinted evilly. Hope noted the handle was styled with an elaborate wolf's head. It looked expensive and antique.

"Good morning, Ms. Garoul."

Eyes as black as midnight, and as soulless as a shark, looked back at her. With a quick flick they took her in from head to toe, assessed, judged, and rudely dismissed her, all in one uncomfortable instant. Hope flushed and struggled to hide her discomfort and annoyance.

Clearing her throat, Hope said, "Is there anything I can do for you?"

"Huh?"

"Is there anything I can help you with?"

"Yeah. Who the hell are you?" The question was cold and snipped, and came at her with all the personality of a bullet.

CHAPTER TWO

H ope stood frozen for a moment. *Never mind who I am, why am I even here talking to this Class-A bitch?*

"I'm Hope Glassy. Your new PA?" *I've been with the company over seven years. Don't pretend you don't know me.*

"What?"

"Your new personal assistant—"

"I know what a PA is," Jolie snapped.

"Do you know what manners are?" Hope came back at her coldly. "If so, I suggest you use them."

She swung majestically on her heel to leave the office and head straight to Andre's so she could throttle him with her bare hands. Momentarily, she lost her depth perception and staggered, grabbing at the door frame. Steadied, she rose to her full five foot three inches and as confidently as possible, considering she'd almost landed on her face, stalked to her desk. She slid into the uncomfortable seat and rested her head in her hands until her heart rate settled.

Shit. Her mind in a whirl, she tugged at her bangs. *Shit, shit, shit. This is impossible. I can't do this. I can't blow my top every time she acts like an ass.* She'd be in cardiac arrest before lunch.

❖

She's drunk. Jolie sprang to her feet. *A drunk has just wandered into my office. Wonderful.* She glared through the door to the cubicle that once upon a time had been empty, and therefore as restful as a field of opium poppies. Now it was full. Full of a…a bad-tempered PA, with a drinking problem.

It's not even eight thirty, for God's sake, and she's loaded. Jolie stomped to her door. Andre would have to resolve this. He was the one who'd brought the lush a bunch of flowers, so he could be the one to fire her.

Before her, her supposed PA was also on her feet and heading in the direction of Andre's office.

Oh no, you don't, Lushy. I'm gonna tell Andre all about you first. Lengthening her stride, she swerved to the right-hand aisle so she did not have to directly follow on the heels of her supposed assistant all the way to her brother's office.

❖

The right-hand side was Hope's good side. She could see Jolie Garoul striding purposefully down the far aisle with obviously the same destination in mind.

Oh no, you don't, you ill-mannered harpy. I'm going to be the first to rip Andre a new A-hole! You can talk to it after I'm done. And immediately she sped up to a neat little trot, her head start putting her in pole position.

As Jolie and Hope headed into the final straight, heads were popping up from all over the office watching the stilted walking race toward the CEO's door. It was obvious there had been an altercation.

Nadeem sprang to his feet as Jolie pounded past his cubicle. Hastily he grabbed at a paper. Flapping it in the air like a one-winged seagull, he called out, "Ms. Garoul, I have a question about the design schema."

Jolie faltered, staggered almost. Her body screamed at her to continue with its ever-increasing momentum—she sensed she was winning—while her mind was immediately engaged with a possible work problem.

Then she realized Nadeem was, in fact, waving a Krispy Kreme napkin at her and her opponent was at that precise moment barreling up to Andre's door. Nadeem had tricked her into losing the race! She felt the general sigh of relief around the office that she'd been waylaid. *They're all on Lushy's side, ungrateful pack rats.* She glowered at Nadeem, the little backstabber.

"I thought I told you to never, ever, talk to me before the nine a.m.

meeting. Never. Not even to tell me the building's on fire." She glared at him coldly. "What are you to do if the building's on fire?"

Nadeem quaked before her. "Fax you," he mumbled.

"What?"

"Fax your office to tell you there's a fire."

"And why?"

"Because I am not allowed to talk to you before the nine a.m. meeting, Ms. Garoul."

"And why?"

"Because I annoy you."

"Good. So, Chicken Little, I'll look forward to your report on the schemata falling, where you will no doubt highlight in minute detail what your mistimed alarm relates to. *And* I expect to see documentation."

Over his shoulder she could see a lot of arm action through the glass panels of Andre's office. The drunk had her back to the door and was animatedly waving her hands in the air as drunks tend to. *I knew it. Rabid little gin sipper.*

Andre, facing her way, had his hands up in a pleading, placatory fashion. *Maybe she's got a knife. That'll teach him.*

Deciding there was no point loitering, she returned to her office, slamming the door behind her so hard the glass panels rattled. She was well aware that the minute she turned her back, Nadeem would begin receiving thumbs-ups and back slaps. *Let him be the hero of the hour,* she huffed. *Until nine a.m.*

❖

"What do you mean she must have forgotten?" Hope said. "I swear, Andre, I don't know which one of you I'm going to throttle first. Did you even tell her?"

"Of course I—"

"The truth." Hope knew him too well.

"Well, it may have been a tail-ender…at a meeting, and she may have left a little early." He shrugged as nonchalantly as he dared.

"What?"

"Hey, it's in the minutes. She had plenty of time to read those and get back to me. Plenty of time. Until this morning."

Hope slumped on the black leather couch opposite his huge desk. "Andre, are you mad? She hates me."

"Don't be silly, she doesn't even know you."

"Somehow that doesn't help."

"I mean, she won't hate you once she gets to know you and sees how super efficient you are. Then she'll love you."

Hope snorted at this.

"Okay, okay. Look, Hope, this is a seriously massive project. I need Jolie to pull it together on time. And whether she believes it or not, she needs help. She needs a right-hand guy she can trust and lean on. If she continues at this rate, she'll go pop one of these days. And she's my annoying twin sister, and I don't want that to happen to her. Look, I'll get her to settle down." He was practically on his knees. "Please just give it a chance. I'm sorry she was so underprepared and got in a snit. You have to admit it's not like Jolie. The underprepared bit, I mean."

Hope frowned grumpily at him, but the firm set of her jaw was already softening from when she'd first stormed into his office. He knew he had won, but he also knew he had to charm her into believing it was a gracious concession on her part. He'd known Hope Glassy since before he'd opened the doors of Ambereye. They had worked together for another software company, and were the best of friends. She had danced at his wedding with none other than his own groom.

In fact, years earlier she had introduced him to the man who was to become his life partner. Godfrey Meyers was a friend of Hope's from the Sandpit's pool team. The Sandpit was an infamous gay bar in Portland, and Godfrey and Hope were a mean mixed doubles team back in the bad old days. Andre had been dragged down there one night to yell support in a cup match. He had met Godfrey's electric blue gaze over the pool table, and that was that.

Now he looked at Hope, saw her flushed cheeks, her upset that her first day back was going so wrong, and he felt incredibly guilty. He had in no way underestimated her ability, but maybe he had been too hasty to set this amount of stress on her shoulders. Why the hell couldn't Jolie just react like someone sane? What was the matter with her? Didn't she know she was looking a gift horse in the mouth? She was lucky to have Hope on her team, even part-time. Lucky.

He looked at Hope's left eye. Because he knew her so well, he could tell, could see the difference in the set of the eyelid, the strange luster of her iris. He knew *he* was lucky to be sitting here looking at her at all. His guts constricted. Hope glanced up and caught him looking at her eye. Her cheeks reddened but she held his stare.

"We're lucky to have you, Hope. It's going to be okay. I need you and Jolie needs you. She just doesn't realize it yet."

❖

"I don't need her. I don't need anybody," Jolie bellowed at him. "Are you suggesting I can't cope? That I can't do my job? Who the hell is she, anyway?"

"For God's sake, woman, calm down." Andre struggled not to yell back. "No one's suggesting anything of the sort. You need a PA. *I* need a PA. We are embarking on a major project and there can be no slipups. You need someone watching your back, picking up the slack—"

"What slack? Are you suggesting I'm slac—"

"The slack in the noose around your neck, but you're too thick-skulled to notice it." He did snap this time. "You were at the meeting when Hope transferred over. It's in the minutes. Suck it up."

She glowered at him, but he could see the cogs grinding away behind her eyes. He knew she wanted this project to come together even more than he did. He knew having a PA was slowly making sense to her, but would she overcome her personal issues? Jolie didn't want anyone near her. She was like a junkyard dog with a bone, but she had to learn to share…and to trust. Her office was her bolt hole, her place of safety in a world that sometimes confused and threatened her. If he hadn't made her get out into that world and use her considerable brainpower for the good of their software company, Andre swore Jolie would have happily scrabbled an even bigger hole to sit in and whiled away her life. She had a den mentality all right, but had nothing but work to fill it.

Stress ruled every waking minute of her life, and from the dark rings around her eyes it played a major part in her sleep patterns, too. She didn't give a damn about anything but Ambereye's success.

Andre hadn't lied to Hope; he *was* worried about Jolie's health. It had been months since he'd last seen her smile. The workforce disliked her with a passion that actually broke his heart, but she got results and they had a grudging respect for that, if nothing else. Deep down he was certain Hope Glassy could turn things around for his stressed-out, burned-down sister. He was gambling on it.

With a sniff Jolie stood and made for the door. There was no time left to argue, the deal was already done. She accepted she'd missed her opportunity for protest. He'd slipped one past her at a hyperbusy moment. Andre's sneaky methods annoyed her, but he was usually astute, and she trusted his opinion. Maybe he knew something she didn't about the upcoming project, or this PA person?

"So, who is she again?" Her hand rested on the door handle and she glanced back at him. Andre looked genuinely surprised.

"Hope. Hope Glassy." He looked confused when the name didn't register with her. "Jesus, Jolie, she was my assistant like, forever."

Annoyance bled into his voice and she felt color stain her cheeks. It irritated her to be judged because she didn't immediately recognize the name. In fact, she still didn't. Jolie paid little attention to things like that. Facts and figures were her companions. She reported to Andre alone and had little time for anyone or anything else. People disinterested her.

To keep him happy, and his acid tongue in his mouth, she feigned recognition. The PA did look *vaguely* familiar. Nodding slightly, she grunted something that sounded like a confirmation and left, shutting the door behind her with a sharp click.

CHAPTER THREE

Hope held her hands under the hot air dryer in the ladies' room and examined her reflection in its chrome surface. She knew she looked shaken, and she was. Her talk with Andre had calmed her down, but now she was annoyed at losing her cool. Especially over a moron like Jolie. The woman was a hard-assed nut.

She took a long, hard look at her face. She looked okay though she felt tired, and it wasn't even midmorning. That did not bode well.

"Okay, you came here to do a job, so go out there and damn well do it." She gave a pep talk to her reflection in the dryer. "To hell with Jolie Garoul."

Another deep breath and she swung open the door and marched to her new cubicle. She knew her job inside out; in fact, she was excellent at it. She was also well respected and liked in this workplace, and she was not going to let her rude, boorish boss take all that away from her. She'd already lost enough confidence and self-esteem to last a lifetime. Now she was beginning to build it all back up, and no one was going to demolish her. No one.

Hope was back at her desk when Jolie returned. She seemed intent on organizing her new space and kept her head averted, ignoring Jolie's presence. Jolie hesitated and took another quick look at her new assistant. Andre insisted she knew her, but Jolie couldn't place her at all. She was pretty enough, dressed in a smart business suit that did not manage to hide her curvy figure. She was short by Garoul standards, but then many people were. Her hair tumbled to her shoulders in waves of rich chestnut that shone in the overhead lighting. Jolie's gaze lingered on shapely legs and a nicely rounded posterior. *Now that's a lot of little person.*

Uncertain what to do next, Jolie passed by into her own office, sure she had just been snubbed.

Huffy little thing, ain't ya? Ms....What? Already Jolie had forgotten the name. What had Andre said? Ho...Haa...What? Glassy was the surname, of that she was sure. She flicked one last disdainful look at her PA. *Well, Ms. Hoohaa Glassy, you better be as good as people say you are or I'll have you for breakfast.*

Moments later Jolie had lost herself and the rest of her morning in the complexities of a flowchart.

"Ahem."

I'll have to duck out of the two thirty if I'm to make that teleconference with the East Coast. Damn, have I got those times right? Jolie's mind was crunching twenty-five hours into the clock.

"Ahem."

Jolie looked up from her scheduler at the persistent distraction. Her new assistant hovered before her desk, clearing her throat to get attention. Jolie arched an eyebrow. *Now what?*

"I'm going to make coffee. Do you want some?" A perfectly shaped eyebrow was raised back at her.

"Huh?"

"It's eleven. Coffee break."

"Huh?"

"Coffee break?"

Jolie stared at her. *She's sidling off on a coffee break already?*

"Cream, sugar?" Her PA sighed, as if she had embarked on a task of Herculean proportions. "How do you take yours?"

Jolie was more than surprised at the question. She actually had to think about how she liked her coffee. She'd never had time for coffee in the workday before.

"Black," she said, flooded with suspicion and uncertainty at this strange turn of events.

With a nod, her assistant headed for the door.

"Strong," Jolie remembered something else about the way she liked coffee. "And bitter," came as an afterthought.

"Now there's a surprise."

Jolie's keen hearing picked up the exasperated mutter. *Yup. That is a surprise,* Jolie agreed in wonder. She watched her PA's swaying walk all the way to the kitchen door. *That's never happened before.*

But then she'd never had an assistant before. Bemused, she returned to her scheduler.

❖

"About your scheduler."

It was early afternoon, and she was back, this assistant person. Hovering over Jolie's desk with more questions and an obvious agenda.

Well, maybe not that obvious. What does she want now? Jolie scowled at the interruption.

"What about my scheduler?" Jolie said.

"I'll need access to it."

"What? Access to my scheduler?" Alarm crept into her voice. Jolie was unused to sharing her workspace. She simply sat in her office at the far end of the floor and calculated diagnostic facts and figures down to nine decimal points. Then she told the rest of the workforce what they could and couldn't do—and to get on with it double quick. No one came to annoy her, no one was stupid enough to enter her private den. Now this PA person was walking in and out of her door like it was some sort of sports stadium turnstile. And asking for things, like her scheduler, and her time and attention.

"Why do you want access to my scheduler?" Jolie could feel her heart rate quicken with anxiety. She hated change, and that's all this little person did. *Change things, all the time, all over, and she's only been here...what? Five hours?*

Her PA's body seemed to inflate, as if halfway through a massive sigh she had changed her mind and held on to the breath.

"Well," she began delicately, "as your *assistant* it means I know where you are and where you need to be. What meetings are scheduled, on a daily, weekly, monthly basis, and what documents you'll need readied for them."

Hope could swear Jolie Garoul was actually squinting at her, like some sort of organic lie detector.

She underscored her raison d'être for being in Jolie's office in the first place. "It's so I can *assist.*"

She watched as Jolie began to slowly circle her heavy silver pinky ring. A nervous habit, it seemed. Hope surreptitiously examined the rotating ring; it was a wolf head with inlaid yellow diamond eyes. A little too rock and roll for Hope's taste, but an expensive bauble nonetheless.

"Okay." Jolie relented, the scowl never leaving her face. "I'll open up my calendar for you. What's your e-mail address?"

Hallelujah. Hope had thought she'd have to hack into it. She was a little surprised Jolie was being so reasonable. Maybe it was the caffeine buzz? She noticed the coffee had been practically inhaled, and a slightly improved mood had followed almost immediately. *Aha, I've found your opiate.* She reached for the empty coffee mug, noticing as she did so the splendid black leather chair Jolie lounged in.

"Okay. Go check that you can see my calendar." Jolie's head dipped back to her monitor and the conversation was over.

Hope rinsed out their mugs and placed them back in the kitchen cupboard, very carefully as she could still misjudge the edge of a shelf or countertop too easily. She was feeling tired now. It had been a long day with an overemotional start and her head was getting achy. Looking back at the morning, she was a little embarrassed she had lost her cool so easily, but she had been so keyed up at coming back. Lord knew why. Everyone had been lovely, as usual. She had been silly to get so stressed out, especially with Jolie Garoul as her new boss.

Jolie wasn't a nasty person, more like an absolute workaholic, and as blinkered to the world as a Kentucky mare on the home straight. She had to remember that and try to be kind to the oddball she was now working for. But hopefully it wouldn't be too long before she smoothed out Jolie's rough edges. If there was one thing Hope excelled at, it was managing the managers. Hope knew she'd also need to work on her own self-confidence if she was to get her old upbeat self back. The last few months had been hard—her world had shaken apart around her, but she was on the way back. Determined to make this new start work.

Satisfied the kitchen was tidy, she returned to her desk. Once more she squirmed in the uncomfortable chair, frowning at the worn armrests. She recalled Candace's earlier claim that Andre had spoiled Hope with a top-of-the-range computer and executive chair. Well, the computer was fantastic. The monitor was nearly as big as her TV back home, but the chair? She remembered Jolie's sleek leather number. *Now that's a chair*— Hope stopped short and wriggled her bottom once more, as if to confirm the facts: the worn fabric, the bum groove, the squeaky castor. Then, exploding at her beautiful roses, she spat out in total disbelief, "That's *my* chair! That skinny-assed bitch has stolen my chair."

❖

The following morning Jolie Garoul stood at her desk looking in amazement at the steaming cup of black coffee and the pecan maple twist waiting for her. Well, she assumed they were for her. *Hard luck if you ain't, because you're mine now.*

She plunked down in her seat and, lifting the fresh Danish, sniffed it.

"Mmm." Her appreciation came out as a deep, happy growl. Tentatively, her tongue tip touched the sticky surface and a soft croon drifted from her throat. With a deep sigh of satisfaction she bit into it and reached for her bitter brew. The day was going to be perfect—if Nadeem stayed away from her.

On her way to the daily nine o'clock meeting, Jolie passed her assistant's cubicle. She rose to meet her with laptop in hand.

"Nine o'clock, room two, right?" she said.

Jolie blinked at her in confusion. "Huh?"

"I'll take the minutes." She tapped the laptop.

This was apparently an explanation for something. Jolie looked at the overflowing notebook in her own hand. Reams of loose papers sprung haphazardly from its edges. Inside was a mass of scrawled notes in scratchy biro. Minutes, memos, hasty diagrams, and doodles of dismembered coworkers made the notebook twice as thick as it was manufactured to be. She had crammed so much loose paper between the battered covers that the spine had popped ages ago. A good sneeze and it would disintegrate into confetti.

Much of the extra paper was meeting notes. Jolie hated taking minutes but trusted none of her lobotomy ward of a team to get anything right. At least not since Deepak got the buyer and seller mixed up in his last effort. Unpicking the mess he'd presented was like unraveling a cat's cradle. Never again, she had sworn to herself. She had sworn at Deepak, too, as colorful as a rainbow.

Her PA held her gaze with a cool, intelligent stare. She seemed unflustered, calm and collected. As if she was born taking minutes and formatting spreadsheets. Out of the blue, Jolie felt herself nodding in acquiescence as an itchy feeling called…trust…filled her.

"Room two," she said before she could dissect her rationale and refuse the help offered.

Before Jolie could even blink, she was being led to the morning meeting. All she could do was fall in behind and marvel.

I've got an assistant. The thought perked her up a little. *Or is that a sugar rush from the pastry? She's going to do the minutes, and directly onto a laptop.*

Maybe Andre was right and everything was going to be okay. As she moved to follow, the subtle sheen of top-quality leather caught her eye. It winked seductively from under the jacket draped across the back of her assistant's office chair.

That's my *chair! My sexy new chair.* It had been swiped out from under her, and she had been too busy chomping on pastries to notice. Jolie gasped. The Danish was a distraction. *Sneaky, scheming little—* Jolie's mind spluttered to a halt. She couldn't think of anything as underhanded and artful as her new assistant.

The day sped past with Jolie casting furtive glances through the glass of her solidly shut door. Ms. Glassy was obviously not the obsequious little helper Andre had presented her as. Oh no. She was a malefactor of Machiavellian proportions, and had to be kept under stealthy surveillance every minute of the working day. But if she thought she could outfox Jolie Garoul with her bare-faced larceny, then she had made a huge mistake. A *huge* mistake.

Jolie stewed all day and waited until her PA left for home. No loitering to tidy away the never-ending flow of paperwork for her. *Straight out the door with the rest of them.* Jolie huffed, glowering as her assistant shrugged on her coat and chatted with Candace before the pair of them left. Pacing her workload until the office floor was finally empty, Jolie slipped over to the cubicle and swiftly swapped chairs.

❖

On Wednesday morning her coffee and a cinnamon roll were waiting for her. A simple thing, but it cheered Jolie up immensely. Cup in hand, pastry halfway to her mouth, her bottom was inches off her chair before she realized it was her old one.

Midmorning she went to the water cooler. Michael Williams walked by with a lemon-glazed doughnut in a wad of napkins and gave her a grin. She was so startled the water ran over the rim of the paper cup and onto her shirt cuff. No one ever smiled at her.

"Glassy, can I have those minutes on my desk before twelve?"

"Glassy, did you collect those printouts?"

"Glassy, reformat these immediately." If prim, little Ms. Glassy was going to steal her chair, Jolie would be damned if she let her rest easy in it.

"This photocopy is too blurred. Redo it. And Glassy, get a few extra copies." *What was her first name? Ho…Ha…Hanna…Anna… whatever.* It was not as if she really needed to know it. Glassy was as good a name as any.

As usual, the duplicitous Ms. Glassy loped off for lunch with her crony Candace. Jolie couldn't rest. She nipped out and dragged the luxury chair back into her office, kicking the old one out into the cubicle. Content that the balance of power was restored, Jolie wandered over to Andre's office for a brown bag meeting. She liked these meetings Andre provided good sandwiches.

Nadeem and Sally were there, too. They smiled in greeting. She blinked back. It freaked her out. More people smiling at her? Was she was losing her mystique, her mojo, her mean streak? What was happening? Ever since her new assistant had arrived, things had begun to slip in strange directions. Whatever was going on, it was downright uncomfortable.

❖

"How's it going?" Andre fell into step beside Hope later that afternoon.

"She stole my chair."

"Great, I'll leave you both to it then." He swerved into the men's room.

Coward. Hope glared at the door. *If you want something done right round here, you've got do it yourself.*

❖

It was one of Hope's early days and she'd already left by the time Jolie returned from a meeting across town.

Part-timer. Jolie glowered at the empty cubicle as she returned to her office, her mood soured by the time-wasting meeting with a third-party supplier. Nobody ever cooperated with her. She hated all their suppliers. They were next to useless.

She stopped short when she noticed the coveted chair sitting back in Glassy's cubicle. *Son of a—* Jolie could barely believe her eyes. She snatched the headrest and rolled it away. Thunk. It jerked to a sudden stop. Tugging at it again, it refused to budge another inch. She craned her head to see what was stopping it, and her eyes popped. It was attached to the desk leg with a chain and padlock.

That's it. She's a lunatic. She's got to go. Andre's got to get rid of her.

For the rest of the afternoon she sat in her office, glaring through the doorway at the leather chair tethered to her PA's desk, fuming.

The next morning she huffily tried to ignore the fragrant coffee and the glazed pastry waiting for her. They were nothing but humble pie. They sat on the desk before her, sweet and steaming, tantalizing her, tempting her.

"Humph." She settled into her ratty, old chair. It fit like a glove. No funny smells of "newness." No super-fast castors that overshot the mark when she glided over to the filing cabinet. No flat, slippery seat cushions to beat into submission, and the correct ass shape.

Sulkily, she reached for her caffeine and sugar fix. This old chair was a classic. The new one was too shiny. Too poseur. Jolie bit into the apple raisin, her nostrils flaring with pleasure. *She can keep the stupid chair. I don't care anyway.* "Mmm…apple…"

❖

"So, how are things working out?" Andre asked between bites of his shrimp salad. They were in his office going over paperwork on their Wednesday working lunch.

"She stole my chair."

Andre tried unsuccessfully to suppress a smile at Jolie's rather immature declaration. He recognized this competitive side of Jolie from their childhood.

"I know. The whole office is talking about it. And for the record, it was her chair first."

"She's driving me mad."

"And how exactly is she doing that? Is it her timeliness, efficiency, hard work, dedication…what?"

They sat in silence. He refused to give in first. Jolie glared and chewed her salad, looking over his shoulder out the window. Still he waited. Finally, she relented and answered.

"No."

"Okay. Because from my point of view, you seem to be freed up from the minutiae you used to obsess about, leaving you time to obsess about the more important stuff. I see that as a *good* thing."

Jolie gave a reluctant grunt of acknowledgment. She knew his words rang true. Her new PA was exceptional. Papers and reports were on her desk before she even knew she needed them. Her scheduler was streamlined. Jolie had become extra efficient because her assistant oiled the cogs of her working day.

"I also see you've got more time to eat the cakes she brings you," Andre said. "In fact, that little move has made you slightly more bearable to the rest of the staff. A stroke of pure genius. But then that's Hope's forte, those clever little touches. It elevates what she does from a job to an art form."

"Huh?" Jolie looked over at him utterly mystified.

"The doughnuts and pastries, doofus. The ones you cram in your cakehole every morning, remember? Hope brings in a box every day and leaves them in the staff kitchen. They're for *your* team from *your* office. Don't you know anything?"

"She does that?"

"Sure. Why do you think people have been smiling at you recently?"

"Dunno. Thought they were goading me, to see which one of them I'd swing for first."

Andre shook his head and gave a despairing sigh. "Ah, Jolie, all the more reason for her to stay. Get used to it."

❖

Jolie was in a good mood, and it lasted into the evening. Things were definitely better at work. Her department was easily staying abreast of the schedule rather than lagging behind playing catch-up. This wedge of extra time was now added to the contingency buffer for the myriad of little things that always went wrong, despite everyone's best efforts.

By ten thirty that night, her high had turned into something else. Blood beat through her veins in a wild and ancient rhythm. Her skin prickled, and every organ inside her body seemed to tighten in anticipation. Everything about her was taut and humming with excitement. Her apartment was suddenly claustrophobic, cluttered with odious smells and itchy unnatural materials.

She threw on some casual sweats and drove a good hour or more out of the city into the quieter country roads that intersected the farmlands and vineyards. From there she followed well-known, dusty back roads, some no more than dirt tracks. Eventually she arrived at a favorite spot, under an old black cottonwood tree. She pulled the Jeep over and shut off the engine.

Her running shoes crunched quietly on gravel as she stepped out and stretched, breathing in the sharp night air. Her spine and shoulders popped and she relaxed. A cool wind rattled a welcome in the branches above her; she stood, head tilted, listening. Nearby, she picked up the rustle of mice in the grass, frogs croaking in the irrigation ditch, and the rasp of wings in the cottonwood. An owl had arrived, locked on its prey. Perhaps the mice? Farther out in the fields the musk of a fox caught her nose, but it had scented her, too, and was wisely retreating.

Certain she was alone, Jolie disrobed and stashed her clothes on the car seat. She crouched nude in the long grass and looked at the overcast night sky. She was content, assured. She needed this. The first stab of pain, as usual, caught her unawares even though she'd been waiting for it. It drove the air from her lungs with its ferocity as her spine hunched and contorted. Feet and hands popped and crunched simultaneously. These hurt the most, as the dozens of little bones twisted and extended. The nails began thickening, curving into cruel hooks. She raised her head to the heavens in an agonized cry that partway turned into a mournful howl. She no longer saw the storm clouds; instead, the night sky was suffused with a muted amber glow. Her jaw cracked, gums seeping blood and saliva as savage teeth pushed through the soft tissue.

It was a perfect night for hunting. There was no moonlight to catch the shine of her dense black fur or the predatory glint of her eye. Stealthily, she crept through the long grass and scented the air, easily picking up the fox's cooling trail. Gleefully, she began the hunt.

CHAPTER FOUR

Hope's second week wore on. She was very tired by Friday, but then she expected to be. Most lunchtimes she left the building with Candace, and they went to a little bistro a block down. It felt good to get out of the office for a while and sit with her friend, gossiping and giggling.

"You seem to be coping okay," Candace said.

"Yeah. But, boy, am I glad it's the end of the week. I'm exhausted."

"I meant with ole dragon knickers. You seem to have a handle on the situation."

"Well, she's an odd one. No doubt about it. But she's a hell of a hard worker, and I think she just expects everyone to be as committed as she is. And for the record, I don't know what she has embroidered on her underwear. Could be dragons, could be bunny rabbits, for all I know or care."

"She's the 'I work, therefore I am' type. A real flatliner outside of the office. Now there's a surprise," Candace said dryly, stirring her honey Frappuccino.

"She is definitely a workaholic," Hope said. "You know, despite that weird stealing my chair episode, I actually get where she's coming from—"

"And it ain't the One Stop Chair Shop."

Hope smiled. Candace was still frazzled at the tug-of-war over the chair. The entire floor had witnessed it. In fact, it had mesmerized Hope's colleagues for days. Deepak had even opened a bet on it.

"Candace, relax. I got the whole chair thing under control."

"I know. I won five bucks." Candace pinned her with a stern stare. "So what's still bugging you? I can tell, you know."

Hope shrugged and pushed her apple juice carton away. "Just another of her little idiosyncrasies I've got to figure out. And I need to do it before today is over."

Candace bristled with concern. "What do you need to do, sweetie? Tell me and I'll help."

"It's no big deal. I'll figure it out for myself. Outwitting Jolie Garoul is hardly rocket science." Hope caught herself smiling secretly. She had to admit she did enjoy her little tussles with Jolie. Their relationship was lurching along, and Hope was confident she would soon have Jolie behaving in a civilized manner.

"It is a big deal if she's annoying you. You know there'll be a long line behind me to smack her if she upsets you."

"Deep breaths there, Candace. I do not want, or need, anyone smacking at my boss. I can do that all by myself."

"Okay, sorry. So, what is it you have to figure out?"

"How to get her to use my first name." Hope sighed, feeling even more tired than before. When it came right down to it, Jolie Garoul was a strange creature indeed.

❖

Jolie sat clicking her pen. She had several minutes in which to do it because she had finally caught up with her workload. Her assistant's super processing of Jolie's working week had finally accumulated in this little oasis of calm. Jolie was dismayed at this unappointed twenty minutes of idleness in her schedule. She sat and blinked at her monitor, totally lost.

This is scary. Maybe the clocks are wrong. They weren't. She checked her watch against the computer clock and the wall clock several times. Who knew a minute could be so long? *I'd go mad in prison, sitting around all day doing nothing.*

"Ms. Garoul, I'm heading home now. I finish early today, remember?" her PA called through from her desk. Jolie scowled. Her assistant seemed to take a lot of time off.

"Glassy, did you update that spreadsheet and send it out? And I need you to tidy up a few memos before you go." She decided to play a few delaying tactics. After all she had time to spare and was bored. Glassy continued to shrug on her coat and then came into the office with a pencil and pad.

"Yes?" She hovered over Jolie's desk, hiding her annoyance well. "I sent the spreadsheet out with a covering e-mail just before lunch."

"And they all know to add their departmental figures and return it before end of business today?" Jolie handed over a sheaf of scribbled papers. "Can you organize these memos before you go, please?"

"Yes. The e-mail tells them to update the sheet for you." Hope quickly shuffled through the memos. Jolie was just being ridiculous; these were not important and could easily wait until Monday. One caught her eye. "This says, 'Don't go to prison.' What's this about?"

Jolie blushed furiously and snatched it away, throwing it into the bin.

"It's not important. And you'll collate all the figures first thing on Monday?" Jolie was fussing now that her little time-wasting game had been busted. Hope refused to be fazed. The real issue was that Jolie wanted the figures collated that afternoon as soon as they arrived, rather than wait until Monday morning for them.

"I'll have them on your desk before the morning meeting." Hope knew Jolie was huffing because she wanted to peruse the figures over the weekend and then chow down on her department heads first thing Monday. But other than that little quirk, there was no real rush and the figures could easily wait until next week. Jolie had to learn to let go, especially on Friday afternoon.

"Anything else before I go?" As Hope spoke she spied her new stapler sitting on Jolie's desk. *Here we go again. What am I to do, superglue everything down? The woman's a freakin' magpie.*

Jolie scowled even more, her eyes roamed the room. Hope knew she was trying to think of some other reason to hang on to her for a few more moments. Just then a pop-up alert bounced onto Jolie's screen reminding her of an update meeting with Michael Williams. She visibly brightened.

"Nah. You can go, Glassy." She dismissed her without even looking up.

Hope hesitated, and then decided to go for it.

"Did you just call me Glassy, or Glasseye?"

"Huh?" Jolie peeped up from her screen, frowning at the odd question.

"Did you call me Glassy, or Glasseye?" Hope said again. She had Jolie's full attention now. Jolie blinked at her, kind of stupidly, Hope thought. Jolie Garoul didn't have many fallback positions if a conversation or situation did not go in the straight line she expected it to. Her social skills were pretty limited, too.

"Glasseye is my nickname. So I wondered..." Hope let the sentence tail off. She got another huge blink. Finally, Jolie took the bait.

"Nickname?" she said.

"Yes. Glasseye...because I have one." With perfect timing Hope tapped her prosthetic left eye with her pencil.

Jolie started in her chair as if an electric current had just zinged through it. Her jaw dropped and her eyes widened. She visibly paled.

Hope went in for the slam dunk. "It's why I was off work for ten weeks. I needed to have my left eye removed after they found a melanoma."

Jolie's ruddy tan turned chalk white, making her eyes blacker than ever. Her shocked gaze fixed on Hope's face, dancing from one eye to the other, back and forth, in some sort of compulsive twitch. She'd obviously had no idea.

Let's see you call me Glassy again, big gal. "Well, I better be on my way. Have a nice weekend, Jolie." Hope gave a megawatt smile as she used Jolie's first name for the first time.

"Hmm-mmm..." Jolie's voice struggled to surface. "You too, Ho...Ho...Ho..."

C'mon, Santa. You can do it. Hope encouraged her with an even brighter smile.

"H...Hope." Jolie grabbed at the name with a puff of relief.

There ya go. You can remember it when you have to. Hope beamed approval. The lesson had been learned and would never, ever, be forgotten. It was not as scary as Hope thought it would be. Well, at least not for her.

Happily humming, Hope entered the elevator a few minutes later. She turned just in time to see Jolie hightail it across the office floor to her brother's door. She looked considerably agitated. The elevator doors slid slowly closed on the little tableau, and Hope broke into a chirpy whistle.

❖

"Choroidal melanoma. It's an eye cancer," Andre said bluntly. "And it's very rare to have to undergo enucleation. Only about six percent of people have to have the eye removed. Unfortunately, Hope fell into that group. Her melanoma was a large one, and was too close to her optic nerve. They told her radiation would only delay the inevitable, and there was always the threat that the cancer could spread into her socket. After weighing up the options, she made the call all by herself."

He was worried at his sister's response to this news. She had blasted into his office like an express train out of a tight tunnel, genuinely upset.

"She's been exceptionally brave," he added unnecessarily, but he wanted Jolie to realize and appreciate the exceptional caliber of Hope Glassy. He had witnessed her brusque behavior toward Hope these past two weeks and it annoyed him that Jolie still couldn't see how essential Hope was to both her and the project. Never mind that Hope was a perfectly lovely person to work with. If someone like Candace had been teamed with Jolie they'd both be in straitjackets by now, and Andre would be gargling Valium.

"Shit." Jolie sat opposite him, her initial shock turning to anger. "Why didn't you tell me?" She twisted her wolf head ring frantically.

"I did. I told you ages ago. When she had the operation."

"You said your *friend* was having an oper— Oh."

Andre raised his eyebrows as the penny finally dropped. "Hope is a close friend of Godfrey and I. She's been my buddy for over twelve years, Jolie."

"Oh."

"Yes, oh. And wait for it…she has worked at Ambereye since its startup. Okay? Gonna fall over?"

"Well, I never saw her before." Jolie became increasingly angry and flustered.

"Unless a person reports directly to you with a file at least five feet thick and an éclair in their pocket, I don't think you'd notice anybody."

"The éclair jibe's unfair," she said, still fiddling with her ring.

Andre looked on sympathetically as she struggled with her ignorance of Hope's situation. He was waiting for the surliness she always hid behind to propel her from the room in an offended huff. That was her usual way of dealing with emotional discomfort—run from it in anger. Jolie was not an emotionally complex person. She had only two options open to her: coping, and not coping. What he was seeing today was new behavior. Jolie was trying to accommodate this new information about Hope. That had to be a step in the right direction.

I bet she'll never forget who Hope Glassy is from this day on, he mused. Hope was a genius at handling Jolie. He should have teamed them up years ago.

"So…is there anything I need to do around her?" Jolie asked gruffly. "Anything special?"

Andre shrugged, surprised at this turnaround. He'd expected Jolie to be sulking in her office by now, not sitting here asking what were, for her, sensitive questions.

"She told me she didn't need anything. Just not to creep up on the left side, as it startles her. She puts mirrors around her cubicle to help with that."

"Oh. That makes sense. I thought she was snubbing me that first morning, but I must have been outside of her peripheral vision." Jolie seemed pleased with her conclusion. She stood to leave but hesitated.

"One more thing. If anyone calls her Glasseye within my hearing, I'll fling them out the nearest window."

Andre frowned at this. "No one has ever called Hope that as far as I'm aware." He stared at her in confusion.

"I'm just saying." She was awkwardly defensive. "Nickname or not. I don't want to hear her called that. So warn your staff, or the monkeys around here will be flying ones."

He was still staring after she left. What the hell was she going on about? Nicknames? He'd have to check it with Hope. But it amused him how Jolie was now so overprotective of her PA, when only weeks ago she'd been screaming at him for appointing her one at all. Strange how the territory changed.

❖

Early Monday morning, Jolie found Hope already at her desk collating Friday's end-of-week figures, as promised. She approached cautiously, trying not to clumsily overcompensate for Hope's curtailed field of vision. She was also uncertain how frostily she'd be welcomed.

"Good morning," Hope called over her shoulder without looking up from her monitor.

"Humph." Jolie grunted, and ducked into her office. There, her eyes alighted on the Danish pastry and coffee sitting on her desk. Her shoulders relaxed. She had been tense all weekend without really realizing it until now.

Some part of her had been worried she had been irredeemably insensitive to her assistant. She liked the young woman. She liked her a lot. She was efficient and hardworking, and seemed in sync with Jolie's own work habits and moods. Even after a few weeks, Jolie did not want to lose that synchronicity over a social gaffe she'd not even known she'd made. *It's Hope, not Glassy. And not Glasseye! Just Hope.* She sat at her desk. Hope was a nice name.

Munching on her breakfast, as she had come to think of it, she took a surreptitious look through the office window at Hope Glassy. She noted things about her that hadn't registered before, like the little mirrors strategically located around Hope's desk to help her see people approaching on her blind side. The careful way she moved around the office, each step calculated and deliberate. *She must worry about falling or tripping.* Jolie frowned at the thought. She didn't want Hope to hurt herself. It must be hard to adapt to such a life change. Nevertheless, Hope always had a big, bright smile that engaged others effortlessly, along with her cheerful voice and happy laugh. Hope was a popular person, a likeable person. She connected with people on some strange level that was alien to Jolie.

Sipping the dregs of her coffee, Jolie sat and watched as every single member of staff passed by Hope's desk on their way in, and offered her some sort of comment, or joke, or smile in greeting. Suddenly Jolie realized she was smiling right along with them.

Chapter Five

The next few weeks were very productive. People were shouted at, deadlines met, new deadlines drawn up, reports were presented and dismissed as utter rubbish. But Jolie Garoul's project crept along on track, and therefore the world kept spinning.

Wednesday morning she came over to Hope's desk, deliberately approaching from the right-hand side, to ask after a PowerPoint presentation.

"It's done. And I've printed you out a copy so you can add notes in big, red, angry marker pen. Here." Hope clamped the sheaves together with the new stapler she had bought for herself. A plastic wolf's paw, a novelty stationery item, more toy than tool. She'd noticed Jolie's interest in wolves early on, like the silver letter opener and the Wolves of the Americas desk calendar and mug, not to mention the chunky ring she wore on her pinky.

The bait worked. Jolie fixated on the pop and crunch of the toy as her draft copy was stapled together. Her jaw relaxed and her lips pursed into a soft, round *O*. Hope watched all this in her little mirrors with a small smile.

"Where'd you get that?" Jolie nodded at the gray plastic paw, trying clumsily to hide her covetousness. "Do they have them in the stationery cupboard?"

"This thing? No, it's just a cheap stapler I picked up at Wal-Mart. I seem to have lost my good one." Hope handed over the papers and shut the wolf paw away in her top drawer with a decisive click. Jolie watched it disappear.

"Mmm, the chrome one? I think it's sitting on my desk. Hang on." She bounded into her office with a few long strides, returning almost immediately with Hope's original stapler.

"Is this it?" she mumbled, handing it over. "You must have left it there."

Hope raised an eyebrow at the blatant, awkward lie. Jolie's cheeks reddened but she said nothing further, just stood and waited.

"So it is. Thank you." Hope opened her top drawer and placed this stapler in beside the plastic one. She felt Jolie's eyes glued to her every move. Jolie continued to hover, even after collecting her papers.

"You've got two now."

"Mmm." Hope nodded, leaving the drawer partway open so both staplers peeped out tantalizingly. She turned her attention to her next job. Jolie watched her intently for a few seconds more before turning slowly away.

Hope counted to three, then, just as Jolie's back was fully turned, she murmured, "Unless—"

"Huh?" Jolie spun back round far too quickly, her face eager and hopeful. Hope smiled again; it was like shooting fish in a barrel. Malleable, stupid, doofus-type fish.

"Unless you want the wolf paw one?" Hope reached in her drawer and lifted out the piece of plastic junk.

"Hey. Can I?" Jolie accepted it gratefully, her eyes shining like a kid's on Christmas morning.

"Of course. I don't need two staplers, and I prefer my old one." Hope smiled and handed over the coveted item.

"Thanks. Saves me a trip to Wal-Mart." Jolie grinned and disappeared into her office with her new treasure.

Hope watched her go, shaking her head at such an easy play. There was a childlike quality to Jolie that Hope suspected was seldom seen by others. She had a sort of awkward charm that when it did surface, which was rare, Hope found totally intriguing. No two days were ever the same when you worked for Jolie Garoul.

Sliding the drawer shut with a contented clunk, she hoped she was securing her chrome stapler in its proper home once and for all. *She's attractive when she smiles. Let's hope that toy keeps her Velcro fingers out of my cubicle for at least a day or two.*

❖

Andre noticed slight changes in Jolie. Her step was lighter, her posture less tight. She moved around the general office with a fluid grace, her sphere of comfort for once bigger than her own four walls where she usually hid. And her eyes sparkled. It seemed she was enjoying herself, rather than being buried alive in that cesspit of stress she was practically addicted to. He needed to investigate this new phenomenon further.

He dropped by her office on impulse late Friday afternoon. "Jolie, what are your plans for tonight?" She shrugged.

"Thought I'd go over the finances. Why?"

"Ptooie to that. Come over for dinner. Godfrey says he's got a nice salmon from the market." He was rewarded with a bright smile. A rare reward indeed.

"Okay. Do I need to bring anything?" she said.

"A crisp white."

"What? Tablecloth?"

"No, an unoaked Sauvignon, smart-ass." Walking back to his own office, he shook his head in amazement. Jolie was actually joking with him. And on a workday.

❖

"So, what do you make of our Hope?" Godfrey fussed over the serving dishes. "These vegetables have been basking in a lemon and chive marinade all day. Then slow roasted for twenty minutes before adding the salmon fillets."

"You make it sound more like a beauty spa than a kitchen." Andre poured the wine.

"The love comes out in the taste. Of course, to know that, you'd have to chew," Godfrey responded primly. His spouse and sister-in-law were notorious hogs.

"So?" Looking for interesting dinner conversation he turned his attention back to Jolie, who was overloading her plate, as usual. But then Andre was piling his high, too. Godfrey sighed at their juvenile competitiveness. Another of their family traits, along with dark good looks, a passionate temper, and that other thing decent people don't mention over dinner—lycanthropy.

"What do you make of Hope?" he said again.

"She bought me a wolf paw stapler," Jolie said. Godfrey's brow creased and he shot a quick look at Andre, who grinned complacently back.

"A stapler? You remember what we told you about strangers and candy? Well, the same goes for shiny things." Godfrey clucked, looking for an opening to winkle out what he really wanted to know.

"She gives me candy, too. Well, pastries and doughnuts. With coffee," Jolie said proudly, between mouthfuls. "And the coffee's always just the way I like it."

Godfrey flashed another questioning glance at Andre, who sat grinning smugly across the table. Andre seemed happy to let Jolie speak for herself, letting her dump herself neck deep into one of Godfrey's verbal ambushes.

"Wow. Somebody knows how to look after their boss." Godfrey responded to Jolie's enthusiasm appropriately. Hope had obviously realized early on, as he had, that the Garouls were best managed well fed. "And what nice things do you do for her? Remember, she has been very ill."

Jolie's fork hesitated and she frowned. Andre grinned.

"Here it comes," he murmured.

"I let her have my new chair." She glared over at Andre as he choked, grappling for his water glass.

"Here." Godfrey handed him a clean linen napkin before turning his full attention to Jolie. "I heard about the chair, dear. That's not really giving, now, is it? That's more like surrendering." Jolie blinked at him. "I mean, have you gone out of your way to show her how important she is to you? How much you appreciate her work and effort? Hope's been exceptionally brave. Every few months she has to go for scans to make sure she is still cancer free. But she insisted on returning to work as soon as possible when she heard Ambereye had landed a massive project. *Your* project, by the way. I hope you are showing her your appreciation with lots of praise and attention and, of course, little treats." He raised his eyebrows at her in gentle reprimand.

"My team gets doughnuts…every day," Jolie said a little contritely. Godfrey's eyebrows rose even higher as he held her gaze. Across the table Andre laughed into his napkin.

"Okay, maybe Hope does that, too," she mumbled, throwing a warning look over at Andre.

"You need to add some sugar to your spice, hon," Godfrey said. "I've known Hope for years, and she's such a gorgeous person everyone wants her. You need to bind her loyalty to you and treat her right. Or else she'll be back in Andre's office after this project's over…" He allowed his words to taper off, watching Jolie's alarm register first, before landing his killer blow. "And you'll have Candace."

The alarm spun off into shock, quickly followed by red-faced anger.

"No." Jolie threw down her fork in disgust. "Hope's mine. You can't have her." She glared at Andre.

"It's up to her, Jolie. After this project, Hope can make up her own mind." Andre gave an elegant shrug. "If she wasn't on sick leave when we started, you wouldn't have had her at all. I love working with her—"

"*I* love working with her more." Jolie thumbed herself in the chest. Again Andre shrugged but said nothing.

"Well, let's hope it's mutual, and you'll have no worries. We've got homemade apple pie for dessert. Coffee anyone?" Godfrey closed the discussion now that Jolie had gotten the message.

❖

Hope was perturbed. Jolie had been in a massive sulk all week. Work went on as usual, becoming even more streamlined as they grew used to each other's methods. Hope congratulated herself on housetraining her new boss in record time, considering Jolie was half feral when she got her. But recently, every time she looked up, Jolie was staring mournfully at her through the glass-paneled door which had stayed firmly shut all week—an indicator, Hope now recognized, of Jolie's more morose moods. She seemed out of sorts with Andre, too.

Jolie had canceled her working lunch dates with Andre, a big deal, as food and work were her two favorite things. She had also screened his calls all week until he eventually walked across to her office to talk to her, whereupon she immediately had something important to do elsewhere, and left him standing.

"Okay, what's going on?" Hope stood at Andre's office door. It was late Thursday afternoon and she was on her way home. It had been a long, hard day and she was looking forward to an evening date with Godfrey. Andre looked up.

"She's huffing at me."

"Duh. Why?"

"Last week, I happened to mention over dinner you were coming back to work for me once this project's done. So she stomped her dainty size twelves, ate all my food, and hasn't spoken to me since."

"Ah, I think I see a pattern here. First my chair, then my stapler, now me. She has a fetish for office accoutrements. Don't tease her, Andy, I could well end up locked in her filing cabinet, only allowed out to take minutes and memos."

"And fetch cookies," he added solemnly.

"Yes, let's not forget my fiendish secret weapon. Worked on you, too, remember?" She smiled, and with a little wave good-bye, headed for the elevators.

Andre watched her leave. With an assessing gay man's eye he examined the sexy, hourglass body walking away from him. Hope was a good-looking woman. She was not a classic beauty, but her warmth and positivity gave her an attractiveness that lured in suitors—of both sexes, much to Hope's vexation. She was a walking honey trap, but only had treats for the girls.

Andre knew that in a parallel universe, where both of them were straight, he would have pounced on her. Years ago, when they'd first met, he'd had that wolven super sense that she'd be the perfect mate, if only he were that way inclined. It blew him away, as he got to know her better, to find out she was gay herself. In that other universe they'd have had a dozen cubs by now. His instincts told him Hope would be an excellent mother and a loving partner.

Was she even looking? How much had her operation affected her confidence? Did she want a love life? He so wanted Hope to find the happiness she had inadvertently brought him, both as a friend and as the person who had introduced him to his true mate, florist extraordinaire Godfrey Meyers.

Hope and Godfrey were meeting up later that evening, and if anyone could get her to open up on the love topic, it was Godfrey. He would have to prime Godfrey on what to ask before he left on his date. The elevator doors dinged, and Hope disappeared from his view for another day.

Before Andre could immerse himself back into his work, Jolie strolled by, obviously on her way home, too, judging by the coat, briefcase, and scowl.

"Jolie," he called out impulsively. She looked like she was going to pass on by and ignore him, but after a slight hesitation went into his office. She stood rather than sat down, as if to keep a prim distance and underscore some private point.

"Look," he began, trying to put the proper look of contriteness on his face. "I didn't mean to upset you. I don't really understand what's going on here. A few weeks ago you were in here yelling at me for appointing you an assistant. Now I'm getting the cold shoulder because she might move on?"

"You're turning this into a popularity contest…and I'll lose. Hope's a good worker. I get on just fine with her. Have you any idea how weird that is for me?"

With an angry puff she turned to the door. "She can go after this project's done," she said curtly over her shoulder. "I don't care anyway."

For the second time that day Andre found himself thoughtfully examining a woman in exit. Everything about Jolie perplexed him these days. She was still cranky as ever, but over the weirdest things. Like giving up Hope.

In fact, before the question of Hope moving teams came up, Jolie had been sort of…chilled out, relaxed even. At first he thought it was because the project was rolling along splendidly. But could it be more than that? Could it be…*Hope and Jolie sitting in a tree? Ha ha ha, hee hee hee.*

He smiled. This was something he just had to pursue. He reached for the phone, connected to an outside line, and dialed.

"Hello, the Enchanted Florist, Godfrey speaking."

"Hi, baby, it's me. I need a Miss Marple. Would you do some snooping for me this evening?"

❖

Jolie and Andre had their own dedicated parking bays in the parking lot. Moping along toward her Jeep Rubicon, Jolie glumly cursed a world that played favorites. And in particular her fabulously popular brother. She was surprised when she passed Hope sitting in her Ford Focus. *Thought she left ages ago?*

Hope's head was bent, her lower lip caught between her teeth, brow creased in concentration. Something was bothering her. Jolie hesitated before drifting over. As she got closer she could hear an ineffectual clicking from the Ford's engine.

"Trouble?"

Hope looked up and opened her door. "Yeah. When I turn the key it just clicks."

"Did it try to start when you first turned it over?"

"No. It's not the battery. I had the car serviced when I was off work, and they put a new one in. It just went click from the get-go."

"Probably the starter," Jolie guessed.

"Well, whatever it is, it's nearly six o'clock now. I won't be able to get John over here at this time of day."

"John?"

"My mechanic. The guy who looks after my car. I'll take the bus and call him first thing in the morning. He'll come out and collect it for me tomorrow. He's great like that."

"Ah." Jolie nodded. For a moment she thought Hope was talking about a husband or boyfriend. For some strange reason she was glad she wasn't. "Where do you live?"

"Sellwood." Hope began collecting her coat and bag. "I better get a move on. I'm meeting Godfrey later—"

"I can give you a lift," Jolie blurted.

Hope looked at her in surprise. "But you don't live near me?"

"Not too far. I'm in Lake Oswego."

"Oh. Not too far at all, except the traffic is crazy at this time and it will double your journey to drop me home and then head back."

"I'm in no hurry." Jolie had decided this was what she was going to do. She was going to be helpful and friendly. Whatever it was popular people like Andre did, she was going to do it, too…for Hope. Jolie was going to add some sugar to her spice.

"Come on. It's no trouble." She strolled over to her Jeep as if it was a done deal.

Looking a little surprised, but at the same time grateful for the lift, Hope followed.

CHAPTER SIX

"I didn't know you could drive."

"I've been driving since I was seventeen."

"No. I mean…well, I mean…" Jolie's words dried up. She was worried she was being rude.

"Because I only have one eye? I can drive fine. I just have to look twice, and be a little more careful. Which isn't a bad thing, now is it?" Hope sat at a slight angle in the passenger seat so she could face Jolie with her good side as they talked.

"Does it hurt?" Jolie braved the question she had asked herself at least a hundred times since finding out about Hope's prosthetic eye.

"I get headaches. And the eye socket can get dry and irritated. I'm not looking forward to summer and the high pollen counts. I've always had problems with hay fever. Next year will be brutal."

"Can you cry?"

"Oh yes. Believe me. I can cry." Hope smiled to herself. Jolie had no idea how close she had come to bursting into tears that first morning over her acidic new boss. "The tear ducts work perfectly."

They drove on. Hope watched Jolie scratch around in her mind for a topic not health related, obviously too embarrassed to ask any more personal questions. Her heated cheeks showed she was trying her best to be sociable. Hope looked away with a small smile. It was comfortable sitting here in a luxury Jeep. She didn't need Jolie to force a conversation. Heaven knew she had a good handle on Jolie's taciturn nature after several weeks working with her and didn't really need her straining for the social niceties now.

Out of the blue Jolie blurted, "Godfrey?"

"Excuse me?" Hope couldn't follow the sudden topic shift.

"Godfrey. You said you were going to meet him later? Are you having dinner or something?" Jolie sounded relieved to have latched on to something pertinent.

Hope smiled at the attempt at small talk. Combined with the offer of a lift home, Jolie was trying to override her earlier huff-fest. Hope appreciated the effort at cordiality.

"We promised ourselves ages ago to take a night class together. We wanted to try ballroom dancing, but after the eye operation I don't have the same balance. Well, not yet. It will improve over time, I'm told. So we decided on classic movie studies instead. We both love the oldies."

"Black-and-white movies? Real old ones?"

"Yeah. I love them. Especially the weepies."

"You know, I can totally see Godfrey sharing a box of tissues with you."

"Turn right here. Then left. It's about thirty yards." Hope directed Jolie as they got closer to home. "There, mine's the one with the yellow door."

Jolie pulled up before a pretty little house with a bright yellow door and neat planting around the front step. It could have belonged to Doris Day, it was so bright and cheerful. *It's just like her.* Jolie sat and admired the neat paintwork and well-kept yard.

Hope collected her bag and slid out of the Jeep, calling over her shoulder, "Come in for a cup of tea before you head back."

She slid her key in her door lock. "At least you'll miss the worst of the traf—" Jolie was towering over her shoulder. She had left the Jeep and gotten to the doorstep in seconds flat. "—fic. Oh. You were quick."

"I like tea." Jolie didn't need to be invited in twice. Part of her was curious to see inside Hope's pretty little home. She was unsure why, but she felt compelled to get to know more about Hope Glassy.

"Okay. Follow me, then." Hope pushed open the yellow door and entered. She dropped her bag on the hall floor and shrugged out of her jacket.

"Sweetie, mommy's home," she called out, hanging her coat on the hook.

Jolie froze. Hope had a kid?

A yapping and a scurrying of paws answered the call. A small dog came barreling round the corner and hurtled toward Hope's feet. His body was a long, cylindrical roll of ginger fur. One ear was part cocked, the other crimped and flattened to a fuzzy skull. He had a long whiskery muzzle, short legs, small beady eyes, and a whole lot of love.

"Here's my boy." Hope reached down and scooped up the squirmy bundle. Jolie looked on aghast. A grumpy teenager seemed much more preferable.

"What's that?"

"This is Tadpole. Tadpole, say hello to Jolie."

"But what is it?"

Hope blinked. "Tadpole…my dog." She became defensive and hugged him a little tighter as he nudged her neck and tried to deliver kisses on her chin.

"Dog?" Jolie snorted derisively. "What breed of dog?"

Hope bristled. "He's bichon frise."

Jolie just looked at her.

"And dachshund."

Still Jolie stood silent.

"And some other stuff…"

"Like rabbit?" Jolie looked pointedly at his bizarre, floppy ear.

"He's nothing like a rabbit."

Hope brewed a pot of tea and they settled into her bright, comfortable living room. Tadpole curled up on her lap, his head on her belly. His half-closed, contented eyes were riveted on Jolie.

Jolie glared back at the little weasel. Her eyes narrowed as she watched his ratty little head rise and fall on Hope's stomach with each breath. His claim of ownership was unmistakable and totally confident, and Jolie took great exception to it. Every way she turned these days, her tenuous hold on Hope was being challenged.

Hope chatted away, formulating some of her ideas for a team morale boost. "…so? Do you think that sounds all right?"

"Uh-huh." Jolie was deep in a staring contest with Tadpole, and grunted appropriately at the pauses in Hope's monologue. Tadpole yawned rudely in her general direction and stretched out his stumpy little legs, the epitome of a relaxed canine in his own den. He was giving out a clear message; he was the top dog in this house.

"It will be great for morale," Hope prattled on.

"Uh-huh." Jolie was livid. Her nostrils flared. *How dare this little ball of ginger crud diss me?* Where she came from, he was less than a hors d'oeuvre. *I'm gonna eat him the minute her back's turned.*

Tadpole twitched in alarm as he picked up her predator vibes.

"Are you even listening to me?" Hope asked.

"Uh-huh. Yeah." *And use his tail bone as a toothpick.* Tadpole burrowed deeper into Hope's lap.

"With gift vouchers and maybe…" Hope paused mid-sentence, noting Jolie was lost to her, eyes glued firmly on Tadpole. She understood totally. He was adorable, and Jolie was probably a dog lover and had fallen head over heels for him. Tadpole was so cute and handsome; everybody fell in love with him.

"Okay, I'm glad we agree. I'll start organizing it after the Thanksgiving break." She smiled happily.

"What's that?"

"The Christmas staff party. My, look at the time. I have to get ready. Godfrey will be here soon. And I've still to feed this little fella. Don't I, Taddy?"

Tadpole waved his tail like a victory flag as they escorted Jolie out.

"Thank you so much for the lift, Jolie."

"It's okay. Thanks for the tea."

"Drive safe." Hope waved.

The yellow door clicked quietly shut.

"Look at your happy tail. You liked her, didn't you? Good boy." Hope tickled Tadpole's mismatched ears before heading to the kitchen to feed him. "She's not so bad once you get to know her."

❖

The city streets spun past Jolie as she headed home to Lake Oswego. But she barely noticed the traffic; she was on automatic, her head full of her visit to Hope's house. It was a lovely home, and she'd felt at ease there. Usually Jolie was stiff and awkward in new places, but not Hope's. Hope's place was comfortable and cozy, suffused with her scent. Hope had a pleasing scent. It still clung to the fabric of Jolie's passenger seat. She inhaled it deeply and examined it again. Her tongue tingled.

Jolie was excited by the visit but was unsure why. Even Hope's jealous little squirt of a dog hadn't soured the experience. What was his name…Rathole? Something daft like that. Well, he'd just have to learn, along with Andre, that Hope was hers.

Pfft, males. They were so stupid and possessive.

❖

The Philadelphia Story was tonight's classic movie, and Godfrey and Hope dropped into a little bistro near the college for a light supper before class.

"Next week it's *Now Voyager.*" Godfrey reached over and grabbed Hope's forearm. "Oh, Hope. I can never thank you enough for suggesting this. It's the evening class of my dreams."

Hope laughed. "Well, you're hardly going to get that bad boy of yours into a movie theater. He can't sit still a minute."

"Tell me. A roller coaster is more his style." Godfrey sighed. "Yet another cultural gulf between me and my man."

Hope giggled at his theatrics.

"So…" Godfrey continued. "*The Philadelphia Story.* What do we think?"

"We think it's wonderful. Anything with Katharine Hepburn is wonderful."

"Of course. You know, you sort of remind me of her."

Hope exploded in a loud guffaw. "Yeah, stick thin with no chest and good at golf? I don't think so—"

"I mean her attitude, silly."

"Oh, thank you. I see you as a young Robert Redford."

"Why, thank you, too." He preened. "I want the whole world, outside of our mutual appreciation society, to know it."

"We are the only appreciation we need."

"Body wise I see you as a young Dorothy Lamour. But with our Kate's toughness and irascible spirit."

"Ooh, I like that. And I'm already a friend of Dorothy. I loved those cheesy *On the Road* movies." She raised her glass and clinked with Godfrey in a toast. "Here's to On the Road to Recovery."

"Chin-chin," he said. They took a sip of their sprizters.

"Here's to On the Road to L'Amour." Godfrey offered up his toast with eyebrows raised suggestively.

Hope laughed. "I think I'm more parked up than on the road to love at the moment."

"I refuse to believe that. A vital young woman like yourself? Why, you ought to be out there on the freeway of love. In the fast lane, breaking all the speed limits with your hardtop all the way down."

They both dissolved into giggles.

"A hardtop all the way down would be lovely." Hope sniggered into her wineglass. Godfrey swiped at her arm, giggling along with her.

"No, seriously." Godfrey sobered first. "Is there no one out there who catches your eye?"

"My good eye or my bad eye?"

"Touché. Now you have an eye for all types."

"To be honest, I'm not in the mood. It's the last thing on my mind at the moment."

"Well, of course. You've been through a lot."

"No. I haven't been through a lot. I'm still slap bang in the middle of it. In three months I get another scan. It's scary to wait all that time to find out if I'm still cancer free. And then it has to happen all over again three months after that. And again, and again. How can I bring a burden like that into someone's life?"

"It will be okay, Hope. You're a fighter." Godfrey leaned in and gave her a peck on the cheek. "Anyone would be blessed to have you in their life. And I should know."

"Thanks, Godfrey. But seriously, the last thing I need right now is a relationship. All I want to do is see how much of my old self I can recoup. Some mornings I wake up and if it wasn't for my job and the day-to-day structure it gives me, I don't know what I would do."

"Same as you do very morning, Hope. Get out of bed and go live life to the fullest. You have a wonderful life because you are a wonderful person. And you are very much loved. Never forget that." Godfrey was stern now.

Hope smiled. He was right and she was being far too maudlin. Time to snap out of it. "I do have good things in my life. I have you and Andre, and the best bunch of friends imaginable. I love my job and the people I work with—"

"And you have the best boss in the world."

"I assume you mean Andre."

"Whom you can twist round your little finger." Godfrey wiggled his pinky.

"Now I know you mean Andre."

"No. I mean the Klepto Queen."

"Jolie?" Hope gave a loud, unladylike snort.

"Careful lest she steal your heart," Godfrey whispered with B-movie melodrama.

"You're such an idiot. Twist her round my finger, indeed. If you had any idea of the amount of energy I put into outmaneuvering her on a daily basis. Why, it could fuel a rocket."

"Well, she is a rocket. She's a serious good looker."

"She's some sort of explosive device. But I think I found her defuse button."

"Mercy."

"Shut up, Godfrey. Get your mind out of the dirt."

"Dirt helps my unsavory thoughts grow and blossom. Don't diss it, dish it." He wagged a finger in lecture at her. "Seriously, what do you think of her?"

"Jolie? I think she's a lunatic who needs a vacation, in a resort for lunatics on a faraway lunatic island—"

"Ah, Lunatic Island, the jewel of the Lunatic Sea. So exclusive." He sighed. "She'd be happy there."

"We're not being fair." Hope stifled her laughter. "And I'm being mean. She's actually okay, despite all the weird stuff. She's very hardworking, and she knows the business inside out. I guess she's just a little socially awkward."

"But do you like her? What do you really think of her as a woman, not your boss? I know she can be a little intense."

"Intense! I had to bribe her to get my stapler back."

"Bribe her?"

"I had to go out and buy a novelty stapler to tempt her into letting the other one go. It's like psyching out Tadpole. Only easier."

"You had to buy a stapler?"

"No, not really. I've set up a petty cash account for her office. It pays for the doughnuts and pastries and I'm hoping to organize a team event around Christmas. The morale is very low, and this is too important a project to fall apart over something as easily fixable as team spirit."

"You really do look after her, don't you?"

"It's my job. And I want her to do well. She's my boss and she reflects back on me, and my performance. Not to mention my end-of-year bonus."

"If you say so."

"What do you mean by that?"

"I mean aside from all those business-type things, I think you like her."

Hope mulled this over as their food arrived. "Yes, yes, I suppose I do."

CHAPTER SEVEN

Jolie turned onto Tacoma and then the Sellwood Bridge, crossing the Willamette toward home. Sliding into her private parking space beneath her apartment block, she eyed Andre's Lexus LX sitting in the visitors' bay. Minutes later she opened her apartment door to be greeted by the mouthwatering smell of garlic bread.

"What are you doing here?" she called as she dumped her coat and bag in the cloakroom before moving through to the open plan living room and kitchen.

"Thought I'd swing by and make you supper." He was fussing around her stove, a mammoth flowery oven glove on his hand. "Where were you? The lasagna's almost ready."

"What if I'd had other arrangements and wasn't coming home? You can't just waltz in here and try to make up by cooking me my favorite meal, you know."

"I can't? Wow, all the more for me, then."

Jolie ignored him and went over to her wine rack and selected a robust local red. "Pinot noir?"

"What year?"

Jolie snorted. "Snob. Two thousand four."

"A perfect vintage for my cooking."

"For your heating up, you mean. I can see the wrappers in the trash can."

"One more word out of you and I shall collect my peace offering and walk. Now pour me a glass. Where were you, by the way? It's not like you to go AWOL between here and the office."

"I dropped Hope home."

Andre's eyebrows shot up. "What? Is she okay? Is she feeling unwell?"

"Relax. She's a lot better off than her car. The starter's gone. A guy is coming out in the morning to tow it." She grinned, and he calmed down.

"And you drove her home." He noticed her smile. She smiled a lot when the subject of conversation was Hope. Smiled, or scowled. Either way, Hope had an effect on her.

"Yes. She had to meet Godfrey for their night class. Don't think I don't realize why you're here. You hate being on your own. This has nothing to do with being sorry at headhunting my assistant."

"I see I've been found out. And I'm not going to poach her. I wouldn't break up a winning team." He sipped his wine. "This is a tiny glassful."

"You're driving. It's all you're getting." She settled on a high stool at the kitchen counter and watched as he served. "We *are* a winning team. I like working with her. She's competent."

"Yeah, one small bundle of red-hot competence. Gotcha." He winked and she glared back at him, immediately defensive.

"She knows Ambereye inside and out, and all our contractors and clients as if they were family. The other day she got a delivery date moved forward by two weeks just by *talking*. They'd never have done that for me, no matter how much I threatened."

"Wow, talking. That *is* a skill. I can see why your office needs her."

"I do…I mean, my office does…need her. So…hands off."

"Received and understood." He produced a store-bought green salad from the fridge with great aplomb, and perched beside her to enjoy their impromptu meal together.

"She likes old black and whites," Jolie said out of the blue. Andre looked at her questioningly. "Classic movies. That's the class she's taking with Godfrey."

"Thought they were going ballroom dancing?"

"No, dopey. She can't do that. At least not yet. Her depth perception needs to adjust over time. And her balance is still a problem. That's why she sometimes goes woozy if she moves too fast."

"Ah." Andre nodded wisely. He was surprised Jolie knew all these facts considering only a week ago she hadn't even known Hope was partially sighted. She must have been reading up on vision impairment somewhere. It was obvious she was interested in Hope, but how and to what extent? And did Jolie even realize it? That was another issue. "You like her, don't you."

"She's okay. Like I said, she's a good worker—"

"I don't mean work."

She looked over at him, perplexed.

"It's all right, Jolie. She's a really nice girl, is all." Something in her eyes alerted him that she hadn't worked out what was happening yet. Hastily he backpedaled. "I agree, Hope's brilliant at her job," he finished lamely.

Jolie nodded, still digesting his earlier comments.

"Yes. She is nice. Everyone likes her. *I* like her," she said, sounding pleased.

Andre watched her quietly. It hurt him to see such an intelligent, capable woman so awkward with her emotional self. But Jolie always had been a late developer that way. She had hidden behind his gregariousness all her life, content with her own company and space. And for a wolven, there was nothing wrong with that. Nothing wrong at all. Except he sensed she was no longer happy or at peace with her choices. Had quietly outgrown the singular future she had carved for herself. She needed a mate, a life-bond. It was programmed into her, but Andre was unsure how clearly she understood the bloodcall within her that was growing daily.

He shook himself out of his reverie and moved on to family news. "I called Mom earlier. She says all's well in Little Dip. Leone's made a great recovery and Connie's coping well. And the almanac will go to press right on time."

Jolie perked up. The news caught her full attention. "Great. Our project couldn't be better timed. When's Marie coming up?"

"That's just it. She may not if Connie still needs her."

"Huh? But I have my actuals and forecast ready for the meeting."

"Well, Mom said Marie is toying with the idea of holding the meeting in Little Dip over Thanksgiving." Jolie looked stunned at his news. "It's a great idea if she goes with it," Andre continued. "Most of the board will be there already for the holiday, so it can be a sort of mini company meeting. Of course, that would be ideal for Godfrey and me. We're taking the following week off to go skiing. It's no bother dropping into Little Dip for a few days before heading off. It's practically on our way."

❖

Back in the bistro, Godfrey and Hope were finishing their meal. The conversation moved on to the upcoming holiday.

"Any plans for Thanksgiving?" Godfrey asked.

Hope shook her head. "Andre says you two are going skiing?"

"Yes. I'm looking forward to the break, but not the skiing. I'd rather be *après* than *en piste*, anytime."

"I'm looking forward to the break, too. Just me and Tadpole snuggled up at home, and a lot of peace and quiet." Hope sighed happily at the thought of it.

Dessert arrived and Godfrey began to probe as delicately as a surgeon looking for buckshot. He knew he was pushing it, but he was under strict instructions from his better half to bring home the bacon. Andre was plotting, and nothing would deter him when he got in meddle mode.

"So, Jolie gave you a lift home? That was uncharacteristically kind," he said.

"If we lived in Stepford I'd be suspicious. But I reckon Jolie has a sweet side she keeps hidden deep down in the molten core of the seventh level of hell."

"She's attractive, though. Don't you think?"

"Of course she is. Andre and Jolie are both gorgeous. But personality-wise, they're the yin and yang of twin world."

"True, but demanding as she is, at least you got yourself a little nine-to-five eye candy, eh?"

"Please. Look at her long enough and you'd end up diabetic. She's a lot more demanding than her brother. Perfectionist, meticulous, preposterous. And at least Andre doesn't swipe my stuff."

"You've obviously never baked cookies and turned your back for a split second."

"But they work so well together. Look at the global success Ambereye is today. And in just under seven years."

"Andre says it was the best decade to launch into games software development."

"He's very astute, very aware of trends and issues, and even industry politics. Whereas Jolie works in a total microcosm."

"True. They've matured well as a business team. They complement each other beautifully."

❖

"You lazy git. You're taking a whole week to go skiing? A whole week?" Jolie exploded.

"Yes, fathead." Andre defended his holiday plans. "When was the last time you had a vacation? Huh?"

Jolie looked at him blankly and he plowed on. "Three years ago, that's when. You need a break, too. And that's why you'll be going up to Little Dip with me. You, and your actuals, and your forecast."

"I can't just—"

"Can."

"Can't."

"Can. And I told Mom you would. So there."

"You can't do that. I've—"

"Did."

"You're a pain in the ass."

They lapsed into silence as they spooned a third helping of ice cream into their dishes. Eventually Andre broke the silence.

"I'm looking forward to visiting Little Dip again."

Jolie nodded fervently.

"Me, too."

❖

The next day Jolie found herself behaving in an uncharacteristically thoughtful way. She knew Hope was using public transport, so she decided to take it upon herself to bring in the team pastries. Rather than going straight to her office from the parking lot, she took to the streets, speed-dialing Nadeem's desk.

"Nadeem, I'm outside Cookie Heaven, what do I ask for?"

"Jolie?" he squeaked. "Is that you?"

"No, it's the Donut Fairy. Of course it's me. What do I ask for? Hurry up, man, I haven't all day…Okay, got it." Click.

She pushed open the door and walked up to the counter. "Can I have a dozen stud muffins, please."

A short while later she stomped onto the floor. The general tittering immediately ceased as all eyes watched her scowling progress to her office. Entering, she glared at the pastry waiting for her on top of her desk...mocking her. Hope emerged from the staff kitchen, two cups of steaming coffee in her hands.

"What's that?" Jolie huffed as Hope joined her and handed her a coffee.

"A stud muffin, apparently." Hope tried to suppress a grin behind her cup, but Jolie caught it and huffed even more. Even Hope was laughing at her.

"I'm gonna kill the little bastard."

"Too late, he went home sick before you arrived. I think he was in deep trauma that he actually had the nerve to joke with you."

"He'll be in a deep grave when he limps back in."

"Well, another way to look at it is it's the best morale boost your team has had in months. You might as well turn your lemon face to lemonade," Hope said, and watched as Jolie processed her point.

"Doesn't it mean anything that Nadeem tried to share a joke with you? When was the last time anyone did that? Candace says he nearly crapped himself when you hung up on him. He never thought you'd just barge off like that," she continued, anxious for Jolie to understand the lightheartedness of the moment. No harm had been intended. Jolie growled, a deep rumble that made Hope tingle all over. But she could see Jolie's tension begin to dissolve as she accepted that it was simple jokiness gone awry.

"Go on. Call him on his cell phone before he grabs the bus," Hope gently urged. Jolie sulkily shuffled papers and ignored her. "Go on," she pressed again before leaving Jolie's office.

No sooner was she back at her desk than she saw Jolie reach for the phone with one hand and her pastry with the other. She could just about make out Jolie's muted words into the receiver. "Hello, stud muffin, get back in here at once. There's a cowardy custard bake with your name on it." Click.

That's my girl. With a satisfied smile Hope started her working day. She was glad she had helped Jolie cope with a possibly embarrassing situation. It would have destroyed their precious team morale if Jolie had knee-jerked into a massive huff. Jolie had no contingency plans for events like this morning. She would have assumed the worst, that she had been made the butt of some office prank. Hope was beginning to realize there was incredible insecurity at the core of Jolie's behavior. She had a small comfort zone that consisted mainly of her office. Anything outside of that was greeted aggressively. Now that she understood more about the complex woman who was her boss, Hope felt more inclined to help and guide her. What she had said to Godfrey the previous evening was true. She did like Jolie, and did want this project to work out for both of them. Loyalty was a natural emotion for Hope, but suddenly she was aware of a new feeling underlying that: protectiveness. She cared for Jolie Garoul a little bit beyond the office door and a five o'clock home time.

CHAPTER EIGHT

Later that afternoon Andre popped his head into Jolie's office as she and Hope labored over a stack of reports.

"Hey, gals, is this where the stud muffins is at?" he said.

"Sorry, we're all out. Just us babe biscuits left." Hope giggled.

"You're so funny. What do you want?" Jolie looked up scowling; the interruption was not welcome if he'd only come to gloat.

"I just came to tell you that the board meeting is a definite for Little Dip. I'm afraid I won't be there for the first few days, Godfrey's mom's sick and he wants us to stick around, so we'll be delayed."

"What? You can't. You're the company president. You have to go."

"What's wrong with Mrs. Meyers?"

Jolie and Hope spoke at the same time, expressing separate concerns.

"You're the VP, so you can stand in for me for at least a few days. She's having a hernia operation and Godfrey wants to be here for her until his sister flies in." He answered both in turn with his most handsome of smiles, the one he reserved for when he was dropping someone in it. "We'll follow you both to Little Dip straight after."

"I can't do this all by myself!"

"I hope his mom gets well soon."

Again, Jolie and Hope spoke over each other.

"Yes, you can because Hope will be with you. I'll tell Mrs. Meyers you sent best wishes." And again Andre answered each in turn.

"Oh? That might work."

"What! I've got plans for Thanksgiving."

This time it was Jolie who sounded happier and Hope who blustered in alarm.

"Yes, it will work perfectly," Andre assured Jolie, and then turning to Hope, said bluntly, "No, you don't. You told Godfrey you were staying home alone, like a big fat loser."

Jolie frowned. Andre seemed suspiciously well rehearsed for this three-way discussion.

"Okay, it's all sorted. Hope goes, too." Jolie was suddenly very relaxed with the decision. It felt right in her gut.

"I can't go." Hope pouted, looking very put out.

"Yes, she does. Yes, you are." Andre was still adroitly multi-tasking the conversation.

"And you'll address the board as soon as you arrive?" Jolie had her mind on business while Hope obviously still clung to escape.

"I can't go. What about my dog? Who will mind him?"

"Your dog?" Andre seemed surprised he had overlooked something.

"Tadpole.

"Rathole."

Both spoke simultaneously yet again.

Hope turned to glare at Jolie. "It's Tadpole," she snipped.

"Close enough," Jolie muttered, far from contrite.

Andre looked confused. "You bring him with you, of course. The little guy will love a trip to the mountains."

Both women frowned as if Andre's logic missed some crucial point, but neither could quite point out where.

Hope seemed surprised she had overlooked Tadpole's enjoyment of an excursion to the mountains. "It would be ideal for him," she murmured, mostly to herself.

Jolie wondered that the little rat weasel ever set foot out of doors, useless lapdog that he was. Fresh air would probably blow the top of his stupid head off.

Taking advantage of the temporary lull, Andre, like any high-level, top quality manager, took the opportunity to duck out.

"Gotta run. Candace has the details and will deal with any queries. Okay, guys, nice to chat." And he was gone.

"I can't believe he just did that to us." Hope looked after him.

"And everyone thinks I'm the bastard," Jolie muttered.

Secretly she was relieved Hope would be assisting her with the important presentation Andre had just dumped on her. The information she had collated was much more than needed, but she was confident in her projections. Now her report had to be manipulated for optimum content, and it was good to have another senior representative from the firm there to help. Hope knew this project almost as well Jolie did. She would be a great asset and would be well compensated for her time away on this business trip. Yes, all in all Jolie felt very relaxed with this new executive decision.

Best of all, she'd see her folks, and maybe after the work was over she could run free for a few days in the safety and seclusion of Little Dip. Her wild side had been restless of late. She wasn't sure why. Usually she had a firm handle on it. But recently she felt the heated thrum of her blood and the tingling in her body that screamed for her to change, and hunt, and bite. She so wanted to bite something...anything. Yes, she was heated. Her wolven side was high, and it was only the new moon. Suddenly Jolie was looking forward to the visit to Little Dip very, very much.

Hope was not so sure. A few days in the mountains sounded lovely. But since her operation, her recuperation had been divided between home and the office. In both areas she felt at ease and in control. Forays to the mall were always in the company of Godfrey or other friends, never alone. Heading for the hills was a major undertaking, and a big challenge. Yet she found herself looking forward to it, much to her own surprise. She needed to be braver. She used to appreciate breakaways to the mountains, and Godfrey often warbled on about the beautiful Garoul valley in the Wallowa Mountains. This would be as good an opportunity as any to gain more confidence in the great outdoors, and truth was, she was curious to see Little Dip for herself.

Tadpole would love a break in the forest. He loved it when they went away on small adventures, and she didn't want to kennel him during such a busy vacation period. He would have the best fun with Jolie. Maybe an adventure was just what she needed. Her confidence was blooming and Hope felt good, more like her old self.

She slid a sideways glance at Jolie, who sat twisting her pinky ring, a dark and hungry expression on her face that made Hope's blood run hot and cold all at the same time. A rush of sexual attraction hit her belly as if she'd just drunk a quart of scalding water. Hope was well enough versed in the lowdown dirties to remember this molten, stifling heat for what it was—lust. She was utterly dismayed that her hibernating libido should finally lurch from its slumber only to attach itself onto the first big hunk of dark, brooding sexiness it saw. Like a newborn chick, straight out of the egg of stupidity. *Typical. If something's going to be bad for me, I'm the first in line.* And Hope knew women like Jolie Garoul were a sexy and wicked addiction.

❖

"Well, in some ways it sounds pretty cool. A paid-for vacation in a beautiful, privately owned valley. *And* Tadpole gets to come along, too. Downside is you gotta help with an important presentation, but it won't be much…" Candace let her words tail off as she sipped her latte, looking at Hope with sympathetic eyes.

"Go on, just say it."

"You'll be accompanying Jolie on the way there and back again, and it's one long, long road trip."

"Well…" Hope was momentarily lost for words. "It'll be okay. She's fine, you know. She drove me home last night and came in for tea and we got on okay. And anyway, we'll be talking about work."

Part of her felt bad that Jolie was still seen as such an ogre. But then again everyone's eardrums were still ringing from the meeting they'd just surfaced from. Jolie had gone apoplectic when informed a database restore had been missed and they had to roll back the next release much further than intended. The extended regression test would now take more time than planned. Heads were rolling like bowling balls before they'd all managed to scrabble from the room.

"Over four hundred miles. Six, maybe seven hours, once you hit those back roads. A whole day locked in a car with her yakking nonstop about work." Candace shook her head. "Ain't enough pay in the world to make me do it. Andre sure knew what he was doing teaming you two up. No one else would have lasted an hour with her, and here you are, still hanging in there."

"It's not that bad, really. I don't need a shrine." Hope batted away Candace's doom and gloom. She was very much enjoying her work, despite the morbid warnings of her colleagues. Her little tussles with Jolie had taken the impetus off her own anxieties. They had helped ground her in her new concept of self. Dealing day to day with Jolie Garoul had brought her a challenge and at the same time built her self-esteem. Jolie had even introduced plain good fun back into Hope's life with her ludicrous attempts to outwit her over chairs and staplers and the like. No two days were the same; everything around Jolie was fluid, furious, and fast.

Plus it was nice to have a sexually attractive boss who never once used her sex appeal as a corporate weapon. Even Andre could turn on the charm when he wanted something. But it never seemed to occur to Jolie that she could exploit others that way. Hope found it strangely refreshing that Jolie didn't act like that. In fact, she respected her for her straight-ahead approach to business, even if it did sometimes turn into a full-ahead charge.

"I'm telling you, Candace, she's not as bad as she seems. Her bark's much worse than her bite."

"She's biting now?" Candace grinned as Hope's cheeks blazed. "Oops. Did I hit a nerve?"

"Stop being silly."

"Only if you stop being red. Spill. Do you like her, you know? As in *like* her?" Candace's eyes sparkled with mischief as she leaned in for the juicy bits. She loved to tease.

"I told you, stop it. You're only doing this because you're bored." Hope knew Candace could be merciless in this mood.

"I suppose she is handsome, in a forged in the fires of hell way. That might explain your heated look?"

"Look, it's just a little flush I get from time to time. My medication can bring them on. Okay?" Hope felt bad about lying but was in no position, or condition, to share any half formulated theories on how Jolie Garoul was affecting her—or not, as the case may be. The jury was still out, and Hope felt perfectly justified in blaming her medication for any hormonal surges she had around Jolie. Her libido was obviously drugged to the point of stupidity. It was not to be left alone with heavy machinery or Jolie Garoul. The outcome could be disastrous.

"Okay." Candace gave her a sly look but let it rest. Mercifully she changed the subject. "So, did the garage guy fix your car yet?"

"No." Hope was suitably miffed. "He can't come and tow it until late this afternoon. I'll have to get the bus home. Hopefully, he'll have it ready for me by Monday afternoon."

"Thanksgiving's next Thursday. I'm taking all next week off. And Andre has Tuesday as his last day. Just so you know."

"Well, Jolie was talking about leaving on Wednesday and spending Thanksgiving in the valley. The meetings begin first thing Friday. Andre is due up the day after, and I think Jolie and I will be coming back on Sunday."

"My, what a fun-packed holiday weekend."

"I'm sure there'll be time for a little R and R. Hopefully Jolie will be my guide and show me some of the things she likes best about Little Dip."

❖

"You're late tonight." Jolie paused at Hope's desk. The rest of the office had emptied over an hour ago as the weekend officially started. Hope looked up from her monitor.

"I'm catching the bus tonight and thought I'd go a little later and miss the Friday crush."

"I'll give you a lift. Why didn't you ask?" Jolie was genuinely hurt. She could tell from Hope's scent that she was fatigued.

"Well…" Hope said. "I guess I didn't want to take you for granted. And I knew you were busy. You're usually the last one out on a Friday."

"I'm done now. Grab your bag and let's go." Jolie ducked back into her office and for some reason she couldn't fully qualify, closed down the open spreadsheet she'd been working on and shut off her computer. It could wait. All of it could wait. She grabbed her coat and car keys. Hope didn't need to be on a bus twice in one day. Jolie snapped her briefcase shut. Hope was still recovering from her illness, and was a very important member of her team, as well as crucial to the business.

And therefore she's crucial to me. Because of the business. So I must take care of her. Justified, she allowed herself to feel a little upbeat at the thought of driving Hope home again.

❖

"I'd offer you some tea, but I really have to walk Tadpole. He didn't get his evening walk yesterday, what with the car breaking down and night school. It's not really fair on the little scamp." Hope turned to Jolie as they drew up before her yellow door. "Unless?"

"What?" Jolie asked, a little disappointed that her time with Hope was over so soon. She had been looking forward to maybe having a cup of tea in Hope's cozy home.

"Unless you'd like to come for a walk, too? The park is only five minutes away." Hope asked hesitantly.

Jolie's spirits soared. What a brilliant idea! A walk with Hope and whatshisface…in a park. Jolie liked the big city parks. She liked being outdoors, and walking, and being with Hope. The thought caught her unawares but an instant re-examination of it made her certain. She *did* like Hope and enjoyed being around her. Jolie relaxed into the idea. It felt surprisingly okay.

Even as Hope spoke, she wondered why she was asking. True, she did have to give Tadpole his walk. It was unfair not to stick to the routine he knew and depended on. These last few months her illness had thrown his tiny world into chaos, and he had been more upset than her on occasions. It was important that they both got back into their comfortable groove again. But why on earth was she inviting Jolie along? It was ridiculous to think she would even consider walk—

"Okay."

"Huh?" Hope blinked as Jolie leapt out of the car and stood patiently at her house door, waiting for her to catch up.

"Yeah, let's go for a walk in the park. What a nice way to end the week."

"Well, good, then." Hope joined her, mystified, but pleased at Jolie's eager acceptance.

❖

"Jolie—give him a chance!" Hope called in perplexed frustration. They had moved down to the park and Jolie and Tadpole now stood about twenty yards before her, each eagerly waiting for her to toss the Frisbee. She was not sure how it had started, but now both seemed to be in open competition to catch the damned thing, and Tadpole hadn't won once. Jolie had snatched the Frisbee unerringly out of the air on every occasion, no matter how much Hope had tried to favor Tadpole in her throw. It was uncanny how lithe Jolie was. She moved like a cat, arching her back and snapping her fingers around the spinning plastic disc with minimum effort. A big, sleek, sexy cat, sensuous and extremely disconcerting to watch. Hope felt that unwelcome flutter in her belly again and forced it down as she tossed the Frisbee straight to her dog. It sailed in the air and then dipped before—Snap! Jolie gracefully swooped and claimed it. Poor Tadpole; he managed to look both very excited and dejected at the same time.

"Well, that was fun." Hope looked at Jolie glowing beside her, then down at her exhausted, panting dog. They stood outside her front door as she turned the key in the lock. "I bet you're dying for a big, cold drink of water, aren't you?" she cooed at Tadpole.

"Please." Jolie was completely energized. It had been ages since she'd had so much fun. *That was fantastic. I need to go to the park more. Maybe I can talk Hope into letting me come with her and Rathole again.*

❖

"Mrs. Meyers is doing fine, Mom. Godfrey and I should be there for Saturday." Andre shrugged the cell phone to his other shoulder and tucked it up under his ear.

Half listening to his mother, he groped for his lost car keys in his discarded trouser pockets. He was already late for his badminton lesson, his mind more on his backhand volley than the conversation.

"Yeah. Jolie and Hope are coming up late on Wednesday... Hope?"

He located the keys and headed for the door, grabbing his kit bag on the way. "Hope is her number one gal, Mom. I don't think Jolie could get through a day without her. Look, Mom, I've got to go. I'm late for an appointment...Of course you'll like Hope. What's not to like? She's as sweet as a cupcake...Okay Mom, gotta go. Bye...Love you."

Click.

Without a backward glance or another thought, Andre was out the door.

CHAPTER NINE

D id you see the way I backed him into a corner like the stinky little ratboy he is." Jolie growled in satisfaction as they settled into their cab. It had been a long, tough meeting on a long, hot day and it was good to finally escape the stuffy confines of their supplier's office building and head across town to Ambereye, Inc.

"You got his back up, all right," Hope said, looking out at Powell Boulevard. She was still a little frazzled.

"It's like hunting sheep."

"Herding sheep," Hope corrected quietly.

"Right. Herding." Jolie threw her a sideways look.

It had been one of the most bizarre business meetings Hope had ever attended. At first the supplier had been awkward, trying to pin Ambereye to unmovable dates with penalizing small print. He obviously thought he had the upper hand and held no kind regard for Jolie Garoul whatever. Jolie had sat quietly, letting him deliver his slippery spiel. Hope had noticed her knuckles slowly whitening, her fathomless eyes sparking with an energy Hope found unnerving in its intensity. Jolie seemed to vibrate with a controlled mix of anger and excitement.

"I loved bringing that jerkwad to his knees. He was as tasty as pie." Jolie sighed contentedly and relaxed back into her seat.

"Easy as pie."

"Whatever."

When the project manager stopped to draw breath, Jolie had pounced. She knew the contract inside out and had evilly embedded several time bombs in it when it was first drawn up. Now she was happy to detonate each and every one under him. In less than fifteen minutes he was sweating, spluttering, and obviously outmaneuvered by a master tactician. It was clear he had no clue about what he had actually signed on behalf of his company. Jolie was gleefully crucifying him before his superiors when Hope deftly stepped in to powwow and move the deal forward to a favorable conclusion. She had poured so much oil on troubled waters it surprised her environmental agencies hadn't been alerted. But it had worked. Ambereye got the amendments it wanted, and for free. Another coup.

"You were too soft on the bastard," Jolie said. "You should have let him squirm."

"Do you want to work with them again?" Hope asked. "It's all very well you showing what a pompous waste of salary he is, but his bosses are the ones to get rid of him, not you." She tried to make light of it. "Anyway, where would you hide the body?"

"I'd swallow it." Jolie grinned in satisfaction as the cab drew up outside Ambereye, Inc.

"I'm dying for some coffee. Want a cup?" Hope peeled off toward the staff kitchen once the elevator doors opened. Jolie grunted a confirmation and went straight to her office.

❖

Minutes later, Jolie appeared in the kitchen with the dirty cups she'd found abandoned on their desks. Hers was a Wolves of America one, and she refused to use anything else. Hope's mug was a souvenir from Provincetown. Taking it to the kitchen, Jolie wondered if it meant Hope was lesbian. Looking at the girls in bikinis dancing around the rim, it was kind of obvious. She shrugged off the thought; she had no idea where it came from and couldn't give a damn. It was none of her business, and of no interest to her, either. Not at all. Hope was simply her employee, and a damned good one. After today's performance, Jolie knew they were a great team. Not so much good cop/bad cop as redeeming angel and hell spawn. Hope was the perfect balance for Jolie's aggressive approach. Jolie tore the opposition apart and Hope appeared with the tourniquet of peace. This project would be unstoppable with them both at the helm. Ambereye was on to another winner and Jolie was floating on clouds of contentment.

"There they are. I was looking in the dishwasher for those." Hope took the cups from Jolie and began to rinse them in the sink. "Would you get the cream for me, please? This carton's empty. There should be some in the fridge."

Jolie opened the refrigerator beside the sink and squatted to hunt for a carton on the lower shelf. Crouched by Hope's legs, she noted her scent was much stronger this close. Much stronger. Hope was menstruating. The earthy musk flooded Jolie's senses, sending her reeling. Saliva flooded her mouth, her skin prickled, and her tongue actually itched. A low, soft growl rolled from her throat before she could stop it. Sexual arousal slid through her guts like mercury, hot and heavy, and it completely threw her.

"What's wrong?" Hope asked leaning in close behind her, mistaking the growl as Jolie's typical frustration at something she wanted not being at her fingertips. "I can see it from here. Second shelf, right at the back."

Jolie's nostrils flared as she drank in even more of the bloodsweet perfume. It called to her. She wanted Hope, right here on the floor, naked and bloody. Her mind reeled with lust. She wanted to cover Hope's breasts and belly and throat with deep red bite marks. Taste her, eat her, lick her clean—the crimson of her tongue flashing over Hope's pale marble skin.

Jolie snatched the carton and slammed it on the counter. Without another word she fled from the kitchen. Her cheeks flushed and her hands were trembling so much she rammed them into her pockets. The strong wave of primal energy galloping through her almost made her stagger. She knew Hope was exasperated at her for blowing the morning's camaraderie, but she had to get away before she growled and scratched and bit. Hope's scent had blown her apart, sent her plummeting back into her wolf side without warning. Jolie had never experienced such strong longing, and her only cure was to remove herself from the source of temptation immediately.

For the rest of the afternoon Jolie kept her office door firmly closed. Hope was confused and a little hurt at this mood swing from the shared victory of the morning to that afternoon's shutout. She was very conscious of the dark, enigmatic looks Jolie flashed her way every time her back was turned. She caught every unsettling one in the little mirrors strategically placed around her desk. Jolie Garoul was burning holes through her, and Hope didn't know why.

❖

It was never the wisest thing, to run in the cities, but many wolven did. Sly and stealthy, they were seldom, if ever, noticed. The alarmed barking of domestic dogs soon fell mute. Even the fiercest dog did not wish to draw this predator's attention. Cats hid and watched from a safe vantage point, and humans were always clueless, as they should be.

One by one, street after street, yard after yard, Hope's neighborhood fell silent. The earlier onslaught of barking had quieted as suddenly as it had begun. Now streets sat eerily silent under the new moon peeping out from behind scattered rain clouds.

Hope puttered around her kitchen, cleaning up after supper and chatting away to her dog. Her kitchen blind was open, and light spilled out onto the tarmac path that skirted her house, shining on the oily black surface still slick from an earlier rainfall. Tadpole was restless; he paced around the small kitchen floor, staring uneasily at the door, then the window, then the door again.

"Do you want out, Taddy?"

He quickly slithered into his basket and curled up tight.

Outside, in the boughs of a neighboring honey locust tree, a liquid shadow crouched. Jolie's gaze was glued to Hope's every move as she dried her dishes and stacked them away in the cupboard, emptied the sink, wrung out the dish sponge, and watered the potted plants on her window ledge.

Jolie's ears flattened as she picked up Hope's quiet humming of a popular tune. She stretched her lips over her muzzle of sharply curved teeth and ran her tongue over their smooth surface, savoring an imagined delicacy. She devoured the curve of Hope's neck, the pale flesh of her forearms, the flush on her chin and cheek as she worked in her kitchen.

Jolie sat there, immobile, transfixed, until the light was snapped off, plunging the room into darkness. She waited, hesitant. Then with a deep, satisfied growl, she gracefully leapt a full twelve feet from the tree limb to the ground and simply melted into the night.

❖

Jolie pulled into Hope's driveway at nine o'clock on the dot to be greeted by a barking Tadpole. He was out doing the morning circuit of his doggy kingdom, especially sniffing around the neighbor's honey locust tree.

"Quit yapping, you mad ferret, or you'll be my new exhaust muffler." Jolie growled.

"Hi, there." Hope appeared smiling at the door, bag in hand, "Taddy, stop that racket at once," she said. "Here, could you take this for me?" She passed a sizeable tote bag to Jolie, who stashed it in the trunk with her own.

"Is that all?"

"No. That's Taddy's. It's got his food and bedding. I have another one for me." This time she passed out a much smaller bag.

"Mmm," Jolie mumbled, not at all amused that Hope so obviously put the small dog's needs before her own. Jolie still thought the kennels would be the best place for the mutt. Lots of excitement there for him.

She put Hope's bag in beside the others, then picked up the runt and popped him in the trunk, too. Jeeps were great for transporting dogs, if you absolutely had to, she decided. Satisfied, she snapped the rear door closed as Hope locked up her house. Settling into the passenger seat, Hope looked behind her, on the back seat, and in the rear foot wells.

"Where's Tadpole?"

Jolie nodded to the back as she started the ignition. "He's in the trunk."

"What? Oh no. Taddy always travels up front on my knee. He loves to look out the window."

Jolie was as appalled as Hope, but for a very different reason. Sullenly, she went to retrieve him. *Now I gotta drive with him looking at me*, she huffed to herself. She handed the dog over to Hope and glumly climbed back into the driver's side. All packed and ready to go, they pulled out heading for Sellwood Bridge and the I-84.

❖

Every thirty miles or so it seemed they had to find a byroad or service station for Tadpole to toilette, sniff, and strut some. It was okay at first, as Jolie could buy Hope some bottled water or magazines. Try and act out the "little treat" tip that Godfrey had given her. She found she liked buying small things for Hope. But soon there was nothing else to do but sit and wait while Hope escorted the little piddle machine to the nearest bushes.

They were going to be late arriving. Not that it mattered, but Jolie was excited now. She could barely wait to show Hope around after business was over and done with. The opening presentation speech still cast a shadow she couldn't quite forgive Andre for.

On one occasion Hope needed to go to the washroom herself, and left Jolie to oversee Tadpole's exploration and watering of the service center greenery. Not amused at her babysitting duties, Jolie strolled behind as he zigged and zagged, and ducked and dived, following his nose through dirt and grass, until he finally surfaced practically under the wheels of a Mack truck. Luckily, Jolie had noted his blind meander into the path of danger and swooped to pluck him clear before he became a fur coat for a Michelin tire.

"Oh my God!" Hope had exited the washroom to witness Jolie's heroic rescue of her pup from under the wheels of an impossibly large truck. "Oh, thank you. Thank you."

She flung her arms around her. Jolie stood frozen, with the wriggling Tadpole in her hand and Hope's arms wrapped around her waist. It had been nothing to her to extend her arms and stretch her compressed energy into a whiplash lunge. The truck had been reversing slowly; all she'd done was put on a spurt of speed and snatch the little runt out of the way. Now she found herself unexpectedly swamped by Hope in a warm, sweet-scented hug, which totally dismayed her.

"I saw it all. You saved him," Hope mumbled emotionally into Jolie's shirt front. The softness, the enveloping comfort was astounding. Jolie didn't expect to feel good things when people touched her. Usually she wanted to fight and flee, in that order. Now she held her breath and gently relaxed her back muscles as Hope's arms encircled her. She became acutely aware of Hope's ample breasts squeezed up against her ribs, and went a little light-headed. Her cheeks flushed, her ears burned, saliva flooded her mouth, and her teeth tingled in longing. She didn't know what to do with this feeling, how to contain it, control it. Hope smelled delicious and scary all at the same time. Before, in the staff kitchen Jolie had walked away—no, run away, flustered and excitable. Now she was trapped by Hope's embrace, swimming in her.

Hope's scent was home and sex and bloodcall all wrapped into one. Jolie had never experienced this sensation before. She knew what bloodcall was, an indescribable urge to select a mate for life. She had heard of it and seen her brother and cousins fall to its power one by one. Was this bloodcall? Was this it? Was it? Her anxiety levels soared.

"He's so silly sometimes. Thank you so much, Jolie." The arms tightened in one last surge of gratitude before Jolie was released into the cold, cold world.

"Mmm, here, have him." She shoved Tadpole into Hope's loving arms, begrudging him the hug, but pleased to have a buffer zone and a little breathing space. She realized she hadn't been breathing at all. No wonder she felt light-headed.

"I'm going to go to the shop," she muttered and darted through the sliding doors into the service station. Inside it was cool, and ordered, and she felt immediately more centered. She stood looking around her. What was she in here for? To escape Hope, or herself? On the fresh produce counter she saw expensive, out-of-season strawberries and bought a carton on impulse. The smell reminded her of Hope's shampoo, a welcome distraction from the scent of her skin, her body, her humanness.

"Here." She handed them over as she slid back into the Jeep. Hope was already strapped in the passenger seat. Tadpole sat upright on her lap like a sentry, glaring out the windows in all directions.

"Strawberries. I love strawberries." Hope beamed, rummaging for a plump one. Jolie smiled, pleased with her gift. She watched as Hope sank white teeth into the succulent scarlet, and started at the bolt of raw energy that shot through her. It ricocheted from her brain to her chest, to her belly, and finally settled her groin with an uncomfortable buzz. She swallowed hard and looked away, turning the ignition savagely.

It was a strange day; the farther she drove from Portland and her usual life, the deeper Jolie slipped into unknown territory. This was becoming a dangerous journey for her. Blood rush thundered in her head and her hands were shaking. Her pelt felt too close to the surface. She had to cling hard to her self-control today, even if it took every inch of her claws to do it.

❖

"So, tell me about Little Dip." They were halfway into the journey and Hope was cheerful and relaxed. Tadpole slept in a ball at her feet, and the weak November sun shone through the windshield. Hope felt warm and cozy and curiously excited about this unexpected Thanksgiving trip. "Godfrey says it's a beautiful and secluded spot. 'Mysteriously hidden away in the Wallowa Mountains.'" She quoted him. "He's such a big Nancy Drew. How did an entire valley come to be in your family?"

"Um, well, it's been with the Garouls since pioneer times, really. Yvette Garoul came over from France and worked as a fur trader in the Northwest. She laid claim to Little Dip and it's been in the family ever since." Jolie shrugged. "I've heard the story a million times growing up. It's no big deal."

"Wow, a fur trader, how unusual for a woman. But I suppose anything went in those days, it was all a matter of survival. Hundreds of years later and it's still with the same family. Does anybody live there full time or is it just for holidays?"

"Aunt Marie and her partner Connie have retired there, along with my mom and dad. Though they still keep a home in Portland. Every so often Mom has to get out of the backwoods, as she calls it, and go shopping." Jolie grinned thinking of her mother's jaunts back into her version of normality. When her mom and Andre would hit the boutiques and malls on a massive spending spree, that seemed to placate her mother for another several months.

Jolie was more like her father in nature. She liked the outdoors, the solitude, and plain, old-fashioned hard work. They could spend an entire weekend clearing a fallen tree, or just fishing in companionable silence. It seemed right that each twin should complement a parent so perfectly.

"So they actually live in the valley in their own cabins?"

"Yes. Most of the cabins are for family vacation use, but a few are more robust and are long-term homes. My cousin Leone is building one right now for herself and her partner, Amy. Amy's an artist and Leone's a publisher. They can work from home a lot of the time, so they might as well live somewhere they love." Jolie nodded at the logic of it and wished she could move into a similar arrangement. It must be bliss to live outside of the city in the quiet and safety of the valley, to be free to behave naturally. And with a loving partner who understood the truth about the Garoul family and accepted their wolven side. She knew it was an accomplishable dream; she had seen the reality of it time and time again in the people closest to her. Her parents were her template.

But somehow, even as a very young child, Jolie had the suspicion it was not for her. She was too odd, too awkward around strangers. There was no other half out there. No one was distorted enough to dovetail with her.

Growing up as twins, she and Andre had often been assured of their individuality. But when her parents told her she was one of a kind, Jolie suspected what they really meant was that she was a solitary animal.

A deep and unexpected sigh slid out of her chest.

"Are you tired of driving? Do you want to stop for dinner, and maybe I can drive a little afterward?"

Jolie was touched that Hope should care. "No. I can drive. But I do need to stop soon for some food. There's a restaurant another couple of miles ahead if I remember right."

She perked up at the thought of sharing dinner with Hope. Then she frowned almost immediately. There it was again, that stupid, fluttery feeling. It disconcerted her. Why was she feeling like this? Why Hope? Hope was not mate material. Hope was a work colleague, one who had no interest in Jolie that way, whatsoever. And as for bloodcall…Jolie wouldn't know a bloodcall from a wakeup call. She was just being stupid and whimsical, and she didn't know why.

"I'm really looking forward to meeting your family. Even if we are here to work. The mountain air will do me a world of good." Hope's lilting voice filled the vehicle and Jolie found herself hanging on every word.

Meeting your family. That was the hook! That was what she was doing—she was acting out a fantasy. Garouls always took their chosen to the valley to meet the clan. Jolie was unintentionally falling into the prescribed pattern for the younger Garouls with their would-be life mates. By taking Hope with her to Little Dip, her psyche was instinctively reacting to this part of the mating ritual. She was wallowing in a newly awakened desire for a mate. After all, she wasn't getting any younger, and there'd never been anyone remotely suitable until now— No! Not even now.

Relieved she had finally analyzed what was going on in her subconscious, Jolie stole a quick sideways glance at Hope. She felt drawn to Hope because she was a very attractive woman, because Jolie respected her, and because they were traveling together to a place Jolie loved, to meet people Jolie adored. It was all just nonsense playing out in her head that she could rationalize away.

Except she couldn't quite as easily rationalize away her body and its strange, traitorous behavior. In the confines of the vehicle, Hope saturated all her senses. Jolie was bathing in her, consumed by her. Her hands began to shake again, and her throat dried up until swallowing was painful. The diner sign appeared, indicating they needed to turn left a half mile up ahead. Gratefully, Jolie followed the instructions. She had to hang on until they reached Little Dip. Then she could shed her human skin and run free, burn off this unwanted sexual energy and be calm again. She would shake out these knotted and cramped muscles, free the wolven, and find new resolve for her human side. Then she would throw herself into work, as usual, and everything would be all right.

❖

"We've given you your own cabin," Patrice Garoul said on her third round of a series of ever-tightening hugs. She had begun with Jolie the moment she'd stepped out of the Jeep. Then she'd hurried around to hug Hope as soon as she slid out from her side.

"It's wonderful to meet you, Hope."

"It's wonderful to be here, Mrs. Garoul."

"Call me Patrice, and this is Claude, Jolie's father." Claude gave Hope such a warm bear hug she felt sure a rib would crack.

"We've missed you so much. You look tired, sweetie." Patrice fussed over Jolie.

"I'm fine, Mom."

Wow, how welcoming. Hope was overwhelmed at the friendliness and warmth of Jolie's parents, given their taciturn daughter.

"Did you have a good journey? Were the roads clear? You can never tell this close to the holidays. Any more news on Mrs. Meyers?" This barrage of questions all came from Patrice, and all within three minutes of their arrival, followed by, "Have you had dinner? Would you like some coffee before unpacking?"

"Yes. Yes. No. She's fine. We had dinner about an hour ago, but coffee would be great." Jolie humorously answered her mother's string of questions.

"Mrs. Meyers is recovering well. Godfrey says the doctors are very pleased with her, and she may be out of hospital before the weekend." Hope politely filled in the relevant details. Patrice squeezed her forearm and beamed at her.

"You go and get settled and I'll put the kettle on the stove and cut some cake. Don't be too long now." She spoke directly to Hope, leaving Jolie and Claude to unpack the Jeep.

"So, what's been happening, Dad?" Jolie passed him a bag to carry.

"Need to dig out the drainage ditches on the old logging road. Big cedar crashed in the north end. Should give more than enough firewood for next winter."

"I'll have free time after Andre arrives. I'll help you cut it up." Claude smiled under his whiskers. "I've been saving it for your visit."

Jolie smiled back at him. The tree felling would be the time they shared together, father and daughter, when they could talk; really talk, away from the snooping of her mother, Marie, Andre, and all the others. And maybe she could ask him about bloodcall, and life bonds, and how did you know when it was time to take a mate? And all the other things that made her head and stomach spin like a tornado.

"Where's Tadpole?" Hope came over to join them, lifting the bag full of his stuff.

"Dunno. Here, give me that." Jolie took the bag from her. "Did he even get out of the car?"

"Taddy?" Hope found him stuck under the passenger seat. "What are you hiding under there for? Come out, you silly goose. We're here… in the forest, and it's beautiful. Come and see." She trailed him out and nursed his trembling body in her arms.

Tadpole was going into anxiety overload. The minute the car doors opened and the scent of a hundred werewolves filled his quivering nostrils, Jolie reckoned he had decided to live under the car seat forever. Much to her annoyance, he burrowed deeper into Hope's cleavage and refused to be set down.

"He must be tired from the journey." Hope fell in behind Claude and Jolie as they set off on the quick jaunt to their cabin.

"What sort of animal is that?" her father asked Jolie discreetly. "A dog?"

"No." The response was clipped.

"Oh my goodness, this place is just stunning. Look at the trees. They're gigantic. And the air is so fresh," Hope exclaimed. "It's so beautiful."

"I love this time of year, too," he said. "It's as if nature's getting herself in order before the real snow arrives. There's a calm dignity to it."

Jolie stole a glance at her father. She knew exactly the sentiment he described, but was surprised to hear him try to explain it to Hope. Hope did that to people. They made an extra effort around her because she shone it back tenfold. Suddenly, it meant a lot that her father obviously liked Hope, and was putting himself out to make her feel welcome. And her mother, too, had seemed to form an immediate attachment. Jolie felt proud of Hope. *God dammit, it's the old prospective mate thing again.* She winced at the ease with which she had tricked herself.

"Here you are." Claude pushed open the stout wooden door of the chunky little cabin, set back from the creek. "Nice and peaceful out here. Your mom thought you'd rather be here than in the compound."

They stepped directly into a cozy living room. He switched on a lamp, as winter dusk was falling quickly, though the light from the blazing wood stove already illuminated the room as well as blasting out welcome heat. He set the bags down just inside the door.

"Your mother filled the fridge." He nodded to a door off to the right, which Hope presumed led to the kitchen. "The fire's been lit all day so you should be warm. This cabin has propane, so the radiators will be warm in the morning, and it heats the shower, too."

"It's beautiful. It's the most gorgeous cabin I've ever seen. Just like in the movies." Hope was in awe.

Jolie stood and watched as Hope spun slowly around, agog at the simple rustic charm of the log cabin. Beamed ceilings and varnished log walls reflected the soft glow of firelight. Thick native rugs adorned the floor and couches. And beautiful watercolor paintings covered the walls. The central fireplace housed a cast iron wood burner that blazed away merrily. It was a picture-perfect log cabin. In fact, Jolie could see how Hope thought it belonged on a movie set.

"I'll tell your mother you'll be down in say, thirty minutes? I think

Marie may pop over to say hello and have some coffee, too," her father said.

"Okay, Dad. See you soon." Jolie closed the door after him to keep the heat in. She turned to see Hope already on her way to investigate the kitchen while Tadpole, a little braver now that he was indoors, began sniffing out all the corners. Jolie smiled and looked around, seeing the cabin through Hope's eyes. Yes, it was a cozy little home. Two people could be very snug in here. *Damn. Stop it.*

Angry at her fluffy thoughts, she bent to retrieve Hope's bags to take them to her room...to her...to where? Jolie hesitated, her brow creased. The bedrooms. She glanced around again. This cabin. She'd stayed here before, hadn't she? About a year ago, and this cabin was— *Oh my God. This is the love shack!*

"Jolie?" Hope came back into the lounge, her exploration complete. "Why is there only one bedroom?"

CHAPTER TEN

Jolie froze for a split second. Then she thawed with a big, stupid blink. *Shit. Mom and Dad think we're a couple.*

Panic and embarrassment washed over her in huge waves of icy water. She felt exposed. Her fantasy had been exposed and was now held up for her own private ridicule. She was a fool and a failure and… and upset. Incredibly upset, but she couldn't understand why. It was just a mistake, just a misunderstanding. Hope must never find out about this mess. It would embarrass her terribly.

"Because," she managed to croak through a tightening throat, "because…" She spun her silver ring as she cast around fretfully looking for rescue. She noticed the couch. "Because that is a bed settee," she said, pointing at it with great aplomb.

Relief flooded her. It was indeed a bed settee; she had slept on the lumpy bed of nails only last Christmas. Always the single adult, Jolie often found herself shoehorned into the weirdest corners when space became cramped during the busy holiday seasons.

"Oh? Is it comfortable?" Hope moved toward the couch.

"You're having the bedroom. The couch is for me," Jolie declared sternly. There was no way Hope was going to sleep on that sack of rats.

"Okay. If you're sure, but I really don't mind."

"I mind. I love that couch." Her words came out more clipped that she intended.

"Okay. It's all yours, then." Hope held her hands up in surrender. She looked confused. "I wasn't aware we were competing for the precious couch."

"Good. Because it's mine."

Jolie brushed past her, carrying Hope's luggage into her newly allocated bedroom. Her stomach sank at the conversation she needed to have with her parents, but it had to be made clear. Hope was not, and never would be, her mate.

❖

"Let me help you, Mrs. Gar—Patrice," Hope said as she followed Jolie's mom into the kitchen. Claude and Patrice's home was much bigger and more personalized than the holiday cabin she and Jolie were sharing. Hope loved sneaking little peeks at the photos on display of the twins at various ages, and the paintings on the wall, and the impressive book spines. Art and literature were obviously important to the Garoul family. It was not surprising; Hope had heard Andre talk proudly about the Garoul Press, the family's core commercial interest for generations. He saw his own software company as an offshoot of it.

"The cups are in the top cupboard." Patrice pointed, happily plating a slab of cake she'd evenly sliced up. "Tell me. How did you and Jolie meet? She's been very secretive about you."

Hope clattered about collecting cups and spoons. "We met through Andre."

"Oh." This news seemed to please Patrice, so Hope elaborated further.

"Yes. I started out with him and he passed me on to Jolie. He said she really needed me…she was ready to go pop."

"Oh." Patrice sounded a little less confident. Hope sensed her concern.

"Don't worry. I figured Jolie out real quick. The trick with her is something hot and sweet first thing in the morning. Preferably on her desk."

Patrice's mouth worked but nothing came out so Hope continued, "I've warned her over and over, one day her sticky fingers will mess up important paperwork, but she never listens. Shall I take in the coffeepot?"

"Yes. Yes, please," Patrice murmured.

"Hope, this is my sister, Marie. Jolie's aunt. She's dropped by for coffee." Claude introduced her to another tall, attractive woman. It amused Hope that a family resemblance could be so strong through both the males and females. The Garouls were really just slight variations on a theme. Their spouses differed a lot, but the Garoul gene seemed to thunder through the bloodline, producing more tall, dark, and handsomes than a fortuneteller's tent.

"Hello." Hope shyly shook Marie's hand, impressed with the understated authority but friendly warmth exuding from the woman. Jolie had explained on the way down that Marie was a retired physician and president of Garoul Press and held a controlling interest in Ambereye. Although retired from the day-to-day running of the publishing house, she was still active in a boardroom capacity until her eldest daughter, Leone, eventually took over.

"It's lovely to meet you, Hope. I'm sure you'll enjoy your stay with us."

"I'm enjoying it already."

Over coffee and cake, the conversation remained rooted firmly in the valley and its familial history. Hope was fascinated with the pure romanticism of it and had a hundred and one questions Marie and Claude were only too happy to elaborate on.

Jolie watched from her armchair, mystified at the ease with which Hope relaxed into her family. It was a seamless transition from a city desk to her parents' couch.

She examined Hope closely: the ready, contagious smile, expressive hands mapping out her thoughts and ideas in the air around her. The light laughter, the bone-deep happiness. Hope was sunshine; she was fresh and wholesome. Joie de vivre shone out of every pore. Was it because her brush with cancer made her appreciate life more? Or had she always been an infectiously upbeat person? Jolie found herself wishing she'd known Hope from before. Seven years they had shared the same office roof, and Jolie had never once noticed her. Now she was glued to her every movement. The irony wasn't lost on her. *I'll have to tell Mom and Dad soon that she's not my partner.*

She glanced up and her dad winked at her approvingly, a big smile on his face as he guffawed at some comment Hope had made. It was going to be an excruciating conversation. How the hell did it get this mixed up? She sighed, conceding it must have been something her parents had subconsciously wanted for her; otherwise, why jump to such a mistaken assumption? Now she was going to disappoint them hugely.

She excused herself and went outside for some air. A resurgence of her old teenage angst was beginning to suffocate her. Annoyed at her own ridiculousness, she sat on the porch step and rested her chin on her knees.

"I like your girl."

Her father's big boots appeared beside her. She looked up; he towered above her.

"She's not my girl," she said. "She's my PA."

There was a pause and then the boards creaked as her father lowered himself to sit beside her.

"There's been a mistake," she continued unhappily.

"Oh. I wondered."

"Wondered what? How someone like me could be with someone like her? She's gorgeous and I'm a freak...even by our standards."

"That's not what I meant at all. And stop pouring that self-pitying crap in my ear. Why, she's just been telling everyone in there about my daughter the hero, who threw herself in front of a monster truck to save her dog."

Jolie snorted. "It was hardly heroics. And the damn dog looks like roadkill anyway."

"Well, it told me a lot."

"A lot of what?"

"A lot of something. Like the way she waited till you were out of the room to tell us. And the look on her face as she spoke. She's proud of you, hon. It meant a lot to her. But she's shy, too. Maybe 'careful' is the better word. Yeah, careful."

"She was proud? Of me? Are you sure?" Jolie frowned, mulling it over suspiciously.

"She was proud, all right. My whiskers were quiverin'." She grinned at his old werewolf super-senses joke. He swore he could detect the truth through his whiskers. It had reeled so many confessions out of her and Andre over the years that it had become part of their family lore.

"Why is she being careful?"

He shrugged. "I'm thinking this is new for her, too, and she's gotta get used to it. Seeing you differently, I mean. You're her boss, and now you're something else, a sort of out-of-office hero-type thing…"

"And you're not disappointed? I mean, I never once said we were together."

"It's okay. You'd never disappoint me. Never have, never will." His hefty arm wrapped around her shoulders in a tight hug. They sat quietly for a few minutes, content to listen to the breeze in the trees, lifting a myriad of scents from its feathered caress.

"You know, you're kind of halfway there with that girl. I think you should consider changing the nature of your relationship." His deep voice rumbled through the silence.

"I don't think that's on Hope's agenda, Dad."

"You're the boss. I thought you drew up the agendas." With a slap on her shoulder, he stood. "Come on. It's getting late. Dinner's tomorrow at four and we have to meet at Marie's early."

"How many will be there?"

"About fifteen. The board members and their families. I like this idea of gathering in the valley for Thanksgiving and then getting all the meetings out of the way real quick."

Jolie knew her father hated going back to the city for any reason, and tried his best to avoid it. She wholeheartedly agreed with him on that. Why suffer the city when you could have Little Dip as the center of your world?

"Dad. Will you…will you tell Mom about the mix-up? And Marie, if that's why she came over. I just—" She broke off, choking on her misery.

"You leave everything to your pa. Okay?"

"Thanks, Dad."

❖

"Jolie?" Hope was trailing a couple of yards behind when she called out.

"Yes? You okay?"

"Mmm. Not really. I'm having trouble with this flashlight. I can't make out the path well enough, so my balance is all out of whack."

"Here." Jolie was by her side in less than two strides. "Put your arm around my waist and I'll guide us." She placed her own arm around Hope's shoulders and pulled her in protectively.

"Can I go the other side, so my bad eye is closer to you?" Hope shifted across and snuggled in again. She felt a lot more confident. Jolie's whole body heated her, and minuscule quivers of delight ran like quickfire through to her bones. Hope wrapped her arm tightly around Jolie's waist. It felt heavenly, they fit together so well.

"You've got no flashlight, so how come you can see where we're going? You must have fantastic night vision," she said to distract herself from her giddy thoughts more than anything.

"I've been up and down this track a million times." Jolie shrugged.

"I enjoyed this evening. Your parents are lovely. And your aunt Marie is amazing to talk to, especially about First Nation medicine. I actually have one of her herbal books. It was as a present from Andre when I was first diagnosed."

Jolie thought this over. "You and Andre are great friends, aren't you?"

Despite the rational question, Jolie felt a pang of jealousy deep in the pit of her stomach. Hope nodded, her cheek scraping against Jolie's coat where it covered the side of her breast. Jolie's temperature soared another hundred degrees and she had to force herself to concentrate on the conversation.

"So why have I never met you before?"

"You have, countless times, at work, in meetings, even at parties."

"Parties?"

Hope laughed. "Well, no one can say you're easily impressed. We even spoke once at a Christmas do at Andre and Godfrey's, about two years ago."

"We did?"

"Yes. Not for long, though. I think you assumed I was just another of the boys' fag hags—"

"I'd never have thought that."

"It's no big deal. Two gorgeous gay men like that have lots of straight female friends."

"And you're not?" Jolie swallowed around the question, so it came out sounding thick and strangled.

"A fag hag?"

"No. I mean…" Jolie was flummoxed. *How do you do this?*

"Straight?" Hope carried the conversation effortlessly. "No, I'm not straight."

"Oh." Jolie gave an involuntary sign of relief.

Hope smiled. "And you?"

"Me?"

"Yes. Seeing as how you're asking, I thought I'd ask, too."

Jolie's face scorched. For the first time in her life she blessed the lack of moonlight. "I'm the same as you."

"That's nice," Hope said. The trail suddenly widened and the front porch of their cabin opened up before them.

"Look. We're home." Hope sounded very happy.

CHAPTER ELEVEN

Jolie squirmed and thumped and shuffled, but nothing made the damn couch any more comfortable. It was past three o'clock in the morning, and she was getting madder by the minute, which was not the best cure for insomnia. The valley played this trick on her often. If she had been alone, or with other Garouls, she would have changed to wolven form and prowled the forest, howling and hunting. It didn't seem appropriate to sneak away somehow, with Hope sleeping so close. Plus she knew she would only be running from her thoughts and unsettling feelings, rather than trying to work through them and purge her overstimulated system.

Glaring at the wood beams, she tried to organize those thoughts. She already knew what was troubling her—Hope Glassy. Tucked up safe and sound in the bedroom, just one thin wall away. Jolie ran her father's earlier conversation around in her head for the umpteenth time and tried to pick out the bits that caused her the most consternation. Well, all of it, really.

Carefully, she broke it down. She was upset at feeling stupid that everyone thought Hope was her partner. She was upset because she was secretly pleased everyone thought Hope was her partner. She was upset because she had to admit to herself that someone like Hope would never be her partner, despite what her dad thought. She was upset at the situation no matter which way she looked at it. She didn't understand how her life had become such a morass of contradictory emotions.

In the middle of all this morose deep thinking, exhaustion finally tricked her into a fitful sleep.

Hope was in bed with her. Naked and ripe. So deliciously luscious, all softness and curves. Jolie wanted to bite her…

She lay on top of the gorgeous, yielding body and buried her face between sweetly scented breasts, licking and nipping every inch of the succulent flesh. Pinned under her weight, Hope slowly opened her thighs for her, and Jolie was accepted into the most beautiful place on earth. Her belly brushed against Hope's. She so wanted to bite her. Hope spread herself wider, and Jolie sank deeper, nestled against Hope's dark sex. Jolie growled with lust. She was going to bite her. Her scent was everywhere. Her scent belonged to Jolie…

❖

Hope and Tadpole awoke almost simultaneously. Hope shot bolt upright in bed, Tadpole's good ear mimicked her by sticking straight up in the air. Both swapped a look of alarm.

"Do you hear that growling, Taddy?" she whispered. In answer he slunk under the bed. Ignoring him, Hope concentrated on the silence that now cocooned her, causing her to doubt her own ears.

Uncertain as to what had actually awoken her, she felt compelled to investigate. She felt relieved Jolie was in the cabin, too. It was not as if she was alone. In fact, it might be best to wake Jolie up and tell her.

Cautiously she slipped out of bed and padded barefoot into the small hall that led off the bathroom, kitchen, and finally into the living room. Wrapping her arms tightly around her body, despite the warmth of her flannel pajamas, she slowly pushed open the door. It was warmer in this room; the dying embers gave off a soft glow. She could make out the form of Jolie sprawled belly down on her makeshift bed, her blankets in a heap on the floor, feet dangling over the edge. But there were no more strange noises. Could it have been the wind rumbling under the eaves? Hope doubted it, but was at a loss to come up with a rational answer. She'd rather it was the wind than an animal prowling around outside. With no more noises to be heard, it seemed silly to wake Jolie. It was probably best to go back to bed.

Quietly crossing the floor, she tut-tutted to herself as she lifted Jolie's kicked-off bedclothes. Despite the winter night, Jolie was wearing cotton panties and a T-shirt for night attire. Guiltily, Hope sneaked an admiring glance at the long muscular legs and beautifully curved butt before carefully pulling the blanket over Jolie's slumbering form. Hope tucked it in gently, right up to Jolie's shoulders, as the room was already cool and the fire was dying down— With a snapping snarl Jolie whipped out a hand and grabbed Hope by the forearm, dragging her down onto the bed. Another savage snarl and Hope was flipped onto her back. Jolie's teeth fastened on the curve of her shoulder where it met her neck. A guttural growl vibrated through her throat and into every organ in Hope's body, liquefying her insides with pure terror. She screamed. Immediately Tadpole, who had bravely followed her to the door but no farther, fell into a flurry of distressed yapping.

Jolie's eyes flew open. Hope's taste was thick on her tongue. Her scent filled her head. Sweet blood sang to her through the thinnest membrane of flesh. It thrummed in a primal beat with the heavy throb in her sex. Every one of her senses pulsed in deep, urgent rhythm with Hope's heartbeat. It was union. It was delicious. It was terrifying. How had this happened? Her mouth was fastened on Hope's thumping pulse. It resonated through her. How had Hope moved through her dreams and into her bed? Was this dream magic?

"Get off me, you great lump." Hope whacked her across the ear and she ducked away to avoid another blow. "Jesus Christ, you scared the shit out of me."

"What are doing in my bed?" Jolie spluttered, dragging herself upright.

"I was putting your goddamn blankets back on you, and you grabbed me." Hope was outraged, her voice rising in anger. "Shut up, Tadpole. It's a bit late to start protecting me now, isn't it?" Immediately he flopped onto his belly and shut up. This allowed Hope to turn her thunderous gaze back on Jolie, who shrank backward a little.

"I'm so sorry," Jolie blurted, her eyes wide with apology and mild shock. She still had no idea what had happened. "I was dreaming about"—she blinked owlishly, groping for a way out—"pies."

"You bit me, you shit." Hope tenderly probed her neck. "Since when am I a pie!" She was far from happy with the explanation.

"No, I didn't really bite you."

"Liar. You did. Look." Hope pointed in the general area of a bright red mark. "Is it bruised? Have you marked me?" She was seething.

"No. No." Jolie shook her head fervently. "That's not a bite. Honest."

The relief she felt that the skin hadn't been broken was beyond all measure. A proper bite would snap bones. What the hell had happened? How did she wake up with her mouth around Hope's carotid artery?

"Oh, so now it's just a good-night kiss? Don't think this is the end of it, Jolie Garoul." Hope was crawling out of the bed, her face still a mask of fury. "If there's so much as one tooth mark on me in the morning, so help me to God, there'll be several boot marks all over your skinny ass."

With those parting words she stomped back to her room, leaving Jolie sitting completely astounded and confused in her rumpled bed. *What a bad-tempered little…little…* Jolie couldn't think of anything bad-tempered enough offhand. Hope's anger was a sight to behold. Who knew such a temper could lurk in a normally congenial person? She still had no idea what had just occurred, except that they had both had a lucky escape. Flummoxed, she fell flat onto her back and resumed glowering at the ceiling, looking for answers, the last thing she could remember doing before being beaten awake.

Desperately, she tried to dispel the sexual tension slithering through her bloodstream like a hundred baby serpents. Hope was a tang on her tongue, coating it with sensuous wants and desires. Her head was full of her. She wanted her. Wanted her so much she nearly bit her in her sleep?

This was dangerous, and Jolie felt weak. It dismayed her at how her wolven side had reached out and taken control. It had to be the valley, and all this talk of mating. She had to be careful around Hope. She had to measure time and distance away from her temptation, and come up with a formula that would save them both.

"Mom, I bit Hope last night," Jolie said. She had been unable to fall back to sleep and instead lay fretting about what had happened, what had nearly happened, and what would happen when Hope saw the bruising on her neck. Now she was up and about with the sole intention of making Hope a fantastic breakfast to try to placate her. It was the best she could come up with as a treat out here in the forest. She was sure Godfrey would approve. But to do that she needed eggs.

An oversight in the stocking of their fridge meant she had to go rustle up some, so she'd slipped down to her parents' knowing her mother would be in the kitchen even at this early hour. It was Thanksgiving, and the food preparations started early.

"That's nice, dear." Her mother fussed over the julienne carrots. Jolie blinked.

"I could have bitten deep. Broken skin. Drawn blood."

"We're not vampires, Jolie. Pass me that bowl. No, the yellow one."

"But, Mom—" Jolie began to protest, handing over the bowl.

"Sweetheart, you should know by now to be careful. Glad Wrap, please," her mother said. "You're too old for me to have to lecture you on humans and rough sex." Her voice was light and lilting, as if she spoke of these things every day.

"The eggs are in the refrigerator. Where *is* your father? He promised to fetch me herbs." Her mother flew out of the kitchen to hound her husband, leaving Jolie looking at the swinging door in total shock.

❖

"Hello? Anyone home?"

Hope opened the door in answer to the call.

Tadpole burst past her and dashed out to welcome the visitor. Hope smiled back at the friendly face of the young woman standing at the foot of the porch steps. She was of a similar height to Hope, and her mass of blond corkscrew curls seemed to buzz with the same energy that danced across her face.

"Hi," Hope said.

"Sorry to interrupt. Is Jolie there?" she asked before turning her attention to Tadpole. "Hello, you, who's a handsome fella?" She reached down and scratched his wriggling belly.

"Jolie's not here. But she won't be long. Would you like to come in and wait? I've just made a pot of coffee."

With a huge grin her visitor bounded up the steps and extended her hand. "I'd kill for some coffee. Hi, I'm Amy. I live with Leone, Jolie's cousin."

Hope took the hand and shook it warmly. "I'm Hope. I'm visiting with Jolie. And the one shamelessly prostituting himself at your feet is Tadpole. Come on in and I'll pour you a fresh mug."

❖

Though she had supposedly walked this track a million times, Jolie Garoul couldn't have recalled one thing about it that morning. She came from her parents' cabin with a carton of eggs and in a total daze. Her world was slipping into chaos. Her father had obviously not enlightened anyone as to the truth of her relationship with Hope. He must have his reasons, and until she saw him she had no idea what she was meant to say or do.

It panicked her that she had woken up to face the same mess she'd fallen asleep in. That she had awakened to find her teeth fastened on the subject of her erotic dreams. And that everyone in this valley, except her dad, thought that Hope was her chosen life mate. Everything was a lie. Except for her subconscious desires—they were red hot and true.

Jolie was beside herself with worry, and stress, and a million other things she didn't even have names for. What if she'd hurt Hope? It was obvious she wanted her, but she had to accept she couldn't have her. This was a business trip, nothing more.

Laughter and soft voices wafted from inside. Jolie frowned. Who could be visiting so early?

"This one is the south end of the valley viewed from Old Jack."

She entered to see Hope and Amy Fortune, coffee mugs in hand, examining the painting over the hearth.

"Amy." Jolie smiled a welcome. Her cousin Leone's mate was always a favorite with her.

"Hey, Jolie." Amy came over and hugged her. "I came by to see you and Hope invited me in for coffee."

"Amy was showing me her aunt's paintings. And those ones over there are her own." Hope signaled another wall of the living room. Her eyes sparkled. She had mentioned the delicate watercolor paintings when she'd explored the cabin on arrival. Now she had met one of the gifted Fortune artists. Jolie nodded, pleased that Hope was enjoying Amy's visit.

"I got some eggs. I was going to make you breakfast in bed but you woke up too soon." She was still uncertain how mad Hope was after last night's incident. Though she wore a high neck sweater, Jolie could clearly see the edges of a massive bruise and inwardly cringed.

"I saw your note, so I just warmed up the stove and made a pot of coffee. Would you like a cup?"

"Yes, please." Jolie turned to Amy. "Would you like to stay for breakfast?"

Amy shook her head, setting her empty cup on the table. "Thanks, but I better go. I'm on my way to Marie's to help with the dinner preparations. I'll catch you guys later. It was lovely to meet you, Hope."

"You too, Amy," Hope called back, before heading to the kitchen to get Jolie her coffee. Amy gave Jolie a good-bye hug.

"She's a keeper," she whispered in Jolie's ear. "*Love* the bite." And with a crafty wink she left.

CHAPTER TWELVE

"Huh?" Andre gawped at his mother as she fussed over the glazed ham.

"...and apart from that unusual conversation where I just know I misunderstood something about sex on Jolie's desk, I think she's a lovely girl."

"She *is* a lovely girl, Mom. Hope's worked with me from the start. What sex on a desk?"

"Ah. That explains what she meant by meeting Jolie through you. They're such a sweet couple. Your father just adores Hope." His mother still wasn't making any sense. "Andre, you're getting in the way. Happy as I am that you made it for Thanksgiving, I'd much rather have Godfrey in my kitchen than you. You're such a pilferer. Now shoo."

"Sweet couple?"

"Andre. Out."

"What sex on a desk, Mom?" His hand stretched out for a bread roll only to be slapped away.

"Out."

Bustled out of his own mother's kitchen, Andre hightailed it to try to find Godfrey and relay the crazy conversation. He was halfway across the compound when he bumped into Amy.

"Andre, great to see you got here. Typical of you to make it in time for dinner."

"Hi, Amy. I've just seen Mom. Now I'm looking for Jolie. What cabin is she in?"

"The one near the creek."

Andre hesitated. "The love shack?"

Amy nodded, a big smile on her face. "I dropped in for coffee this morning. They invited me to stay for breakfast but I had to go help Marie peel a mountain of potatoes." They continued across the clearing arm in arm. "I enjoyed meeting Hope. She's so perfect for Jolie."

Andre's mouth hung open. "They're a couple? Really?"

Amy frowned. "Yes. Why are you so surprised?"

Andre shook his head in disbelief. "It's just that it happened so quickly. Amy, who told you they were an item?"

"Mmm, I think it was Marie who told Leone. And either Patrice or Claude told her."

"Jesus. It must be true. Crap. I never saw it happening *this* fast. How the hell did she manage it?"

"Were they not together before this?" Amy looked confused now.

"They were sort of skirting around each other. Well, Jolie was. Sort of. But you know what she's like. Clueless." He tsked. "It has to be Hope. Never in a million years could Jolie have gotten it together to pounce." He was flummoxed.

"Well, I wouldn't go writing off your sister's fly moves, big guy. Hope had a serious wolfie love suck on her neck this morning." Amy giggled as Andre came to a stunned standstill.

"Oh, my God. It has to be Hope's doing. Hope's gone and hooked my big lovesick sister. Jolie's finally found her love teeth."

Laughing, they wrapped arms round each other and went in search of Godfrey to share the amazing news.

❖

"Godfrey. Wait up."

Godfrey turned at the call and broke into a wide grin as Hope came to meet him.

"Hey, baby doll." He gathered her in a hug. "Have you settled in? How are you liking it?"

"I love it. But Tadpole isn't so sure. I can't get him to leave the cabin, and usually he'd be in his element snuffling and grubbing about in a place like this. I'm worried he's ill."

"Oh, poor Taddy." Guiltily, Godfrey thought maybe it was a bad idea to bring the little dog to a werewolf den. "Take him to the vet on Monday. I'm sure he just needs a nerve pill or something."

They fell into step together and headed back to the compound.

"I'm so glad we got here in time for Thanksgiving." Godfrey gave her arm an extra squeeze in excitement.

"You got away early. When did your sister arrive?"

"She flew in on an earlier flight, so she's minding Mom now. It freed us up to get an early start on our vacation."

"And your mother's doing fine?"

"She's looking really good. She loved the flowers, by the way. Thank you for that."

"Good. I'm glad she liked them. And I'm glad you and Andre are here. I know Jolie is very nervous about the opening presentation. She's cool with her own facts and figures, but if it's outside her immediate sphere she tends to get jittery. Andre will take over now, won't he?"

"Yeah, he's brought his papers. He knew Jolie wasn't that happy, so we tried to get here on time. Hey, where are you staying? We're in the main compound."

"We're in this sweet little cabin down by the creek."

"Oh, I know that one. Its nickname is the love shack." They both giggled at that. "It's lovely down there," he continued. "Nice and quiet. I suppose there's so many coming for this Thanksgiving meeting they're squeezing everyone in anywhere they can. And it's going okay, sharing with Jolie?"

"It's fine. Except for the biting incident. I was way mad about that—"

"Biting incident?" Godfrey looked shocked. "What biting incident?"

Hope pulled down the neck of her sweater to show the large, dark bruise.

"Oh my God," he cried. "What the hell happened?"

"Jolie bit me. She—"

"Jolie bit you?" He looked like he was going to fall over.

Hope nodded enthusiastically.

"Yeah. She—"

"Jolie bit you?"

"Yes. She—"

"You mean she really bit you? Oh my God."

Hope frowned. Godfrey seemed to be having a real hard time with this.

"Yeah. I was mad at her last night, but this morn—"

"Jolie bit you last night?"

"Yes. She dragged me onto the bed and—"

"She bit you in bed? Oh my God."

Hope was getting annoyed at Godfrey's freak-out. It's not as if it was a sexual overture or anything. Jolie just dreamed as weirdly as she lived.

"It's not that big a deal," she said defensively.

"Around here it is."

She slapped his arm. "Stop being silly. It's not like that. Oh! Oh, wait till I tell you what happened on the way up here. Jolie leapt under a truck and saved Tadpole's life."

"Oh my God—"

"Please don't start that again."

❖

"She what!" Hope exploded.

"Well, that's what I was told," Andre said.

"What?" Hope's voice rose to near-hysterical levels with every word Andre uttered. "She said what?"

They were in Andre and Godfrey's cabin, where Andre's initial congratulations on Hope's new love interest soon evaporated under her pyroclastic reaction.

"Now, Hope, just relax and—" Andre tried to pacify her.

"Why would she say that? Why? Why? Is she mad? Is she absolutely mad? Has she lost it completely?"

"Take a deep breath—"

"Don't you deep breath me. Your sister has told everyone she's having an affair with her secretary. That's sexual harassment and so… so…seventies."

Both Andre and Godfrey stood before Hope, swapping concerned looks. If she vented any more, their cabin would be a sauna. She needed to calm down.

"Hope, honey." Godfrey tried this time, as Andre was unsurprisingly useless in the placatory department. "There's obviously been a misunderstanding. Jolie's not going to lie about something like that. Has anything happened to make her think you and her are…

involved?" He chose his words carefully. "Tell me once more about the biting incident."

Hope puffed in exasperation but complied with Godfrey's gentle request, forcing the words out in a heated rush.

"I told you already. She just lunged on top of me and bit my neck like freakin' Nosferatu—"

"Where were you when she 'lunged'?" Andre quirked a knowing eyebrow.

"On the bed," Hope snapped back defensively.

"You were in bed together?"

"No. Yes."

"So…You were in bed together?" Andre belabored his point.

"She was in bed. *I* was tucking her in." Hope's voice rose even higher.

"Why were you tucking her in?" Andre frowned.

"Because she'd kicked the blankets off and it was cold."

"Okay, so you were cold and you got out of bed to tuck the blankets back in?"

"Yes. No. *She* was in the bed. Not me."

"Because you'd got out to tuck in the blankets," Andre said.

"What did I just say? Are you even listening to me?"

"Now let's all calm down. Remember, it's a complicated scene for us to picture, sweetie." Godfrey tried to placate her. "You and Jolie in bed together, on your very first night here. It's just kind of hard to imagine."

Hope went a shade redder, if that was possible, and her mouth worked but no sound came out. Godfrey frowned at her. Between Hope's apoplexy and Andre's blundering, *someone* had to be the mediator if they were to get to the bottom of this. If everyone kept calm he was sure he could guide them all toward a simple and viable explanation.

"To be honest, sweetheart, you're not explaining things very well," he said gently, reaching out to stroke Hope's arm in support.

"You're telling me." Andre snorted. "No wonder Mom thinks they had sex on Jolie's desk—"

"What! What?" Hope flew into orbit.

"Oh my God." Godfrey gave up.

CHAPTER THIRTEEN

"H ey, sis. You home?"
Andre's holler drew Jolie into the living room. She'd been in the bedroom getting dressed for Thanksgiving dinner. Her job was to go down early and help set the dinner table.

"Here," she answered and came to see him, tucking her shirt into her pants. "You made it. Boy, am I glad to see you." She smiled in sheer relief.

"I bet you are. Don't worry, I'm here to rescue you from the opening presentation. Though how it can be any worse than your financial report I'll never know."

"Most of 'em doze off during mine. By the end of the hour I'm practically talking to myself." She shrugged, feeling a lot better at seeing his face.

"Oh, Mrs. Meyers says thank you for the flowers."

"Huh?"

"I thought as much. Hope sent them, didn't she? How's that going, by the way?" He nonchalantly wandered over and examined the bookcase.

"Mmm. Okay, I guess." Jolie didn't want to reveal the mix-up to him; she felt lacerated enough. Besides, she still had to talk to her dad and find out why he hadn't followed through on the damage control they'd planned. It was too humiliating if she had to do it herself, so she was inclined to hang on until she'd spoken to her father. "Hope loves the valley. She went for a stroll while I helped Dad stack wood. She'll be back soon if you want to wait."

"I knew she'd love it here. I hoped she would. But I'll catch her

later. Godfrey and I want to talk over something important with her."
He turned to her, eyes shining with excitement. "You'll never believe
it, Jolie."

"What?" she asked surprised at how charged he was.

"Well, Hope and I have talked about it before, off and on…but
now Godfrey agrees." He gave her his widest smile. It was so infectious
she found herself goofily smiling back at him.

"What?" she asked eagerly. It had to be good news, he looked so
happy. She picked up on his excitement, bubbling with curiosity.

"We're going to ask Hope be the biological mother of our cubs."

A loud buzzing filled Jolie's ears, as if a low-flying aircraft was
crash-landing in her lap. Tunnel vision reduced her world to a distant
pinprick of blurred light. Her blood pressure fell through the floor, then
bungeed straight back up to the top of her skull. She felt cold, hot, cold,
ill. She felt ill. Her guts heaved and churned. Yeah—ill. Very, very ill.

"Jeez, look at the time. I better go and get ready. See you at dinner,
sis." With a slap on her back, he sprang for the door, leaving her standing
there pale and sweating. Frozen in place, she found herself staring at
her ghostly reflection in the mantel mirror, her stunned black eyes the
only color in her chalk white face.

❖

When Hope returned from her walk Jolie had already left to help
dress the table at Marie's. It seemed every Garoul had a small task
to contribute to the massive family feast, whether it was piling up
firewood, or folding napkins, or willingly bearing the brunt of the food
preparation. Though that last duty seemed to be the realm of the more
senior female family members. It was definitely a matriarchal family.
Hope had seen that at once.

It was probably best Jolie had gone before Hope arrived. The mood
she was in, she'd have swung a fire log at her, boss or no. Hopefully,
later in the evening, she would take Jolie aside and reveal the trick
Andre had played on her as payback for not correcting the rumor mill
at once.

When he'd returned and described Jolie's face, all three had a
terrible fit of guilty giggling over pre-dinner martinis.

"I'm worried we're being too cruel," Godfrey, ever the ambassador of peace and goodwill, wondered aloud. "It might have been best to just confront her. In a reasonable fashion, of course," he hastily added. Hope still vented the odd little puff of steam when she thought about Jolie for any length of time.

"No. I really liked Claude and Patrice. Now I'm not sure I can look them in the face knowing they think I'm their daughter's bit of office fluff. Thanks to Jolie, this weekend has become embarrassing and awkward. Let her stew in her own lying, underhanded juices." Hope felt no such pangs of guilt. This was justified retribution, and Andre had hit the nail on the head with his counter-tease. She'd have loved to have seen Jolie's face for herself.

"Well, I'm going to tackle her about it after dinner. See what the big dollop was trying to pull, starting a story like that," Andre said.

"And tell her the having your baby thing was just a joke," Hope reminded him.

"Oh, I don't know. Maybe you should mull it over?" Andre raised his eyebrows hopefully. Godfrey snorted and Hope exploded into laughter.

"I swear," she said to Godfrey, sidelining Andre, "these Garouls just get stupider and stupider the closer they get to home turf."

Drying herself after a quick shower, she smiled ruefully as she recalled the weirdness of her first day in Little Dip. Then, noting the time, she moved through to the bedroom to dress for dinner.

"Okay, Taddy. Mommy's gonna go get you a big ham bone," she said. "And her name's Jolie Garoul."

Tickling Tadpole behind his good ear, she said, "Be good and guard the cabin until I get back. There's Mommy's best boy."

Freshly dressed in a smart new blouse and skirt, she stepped out, gathering her resolve for her first and perhaps only introduction to the Garoul family en masse. She wandered down to Marie's large cabin in the central complex, where she had arranged to meet the boys by the fire pit before they joined the rest of the family for Thanksgiving dinner. She was nervous about meeting the Garouls in general, and even more so now that she was aware they all thought she was associated romantically with Jolie. It still angered her that Jolie had allowed such a nonsense to color their whole visit here. Misunderstanding or not, Hope was Jolie's guest and employee, and it was up to her to make sure this rumor was squelched, not dither around making things worse. She was glad Andre's joke had knocked Jolie flat on her ass. She deserved it.

❖

Marie's cabin was the largest in the compound. A long table ran the entire length of the cozy room, bedecked with huge platters of festive food. Delicious aromas and cheerful laughter filled the air as the huge fire crackled merrily away. Hope, Andre, and Godfrey were happily greeted as they entered. Jolie had headed down earlier, as her contribution to the dinner was helping set up the huge table.

"Hope," Amy called, motioning her over to meet a tall, dark Jolie look-alike, "this is my partner, Leone, Jolie and Andre's cousin."

They shook hands greeting each other. Hope immediately warmed to the woman. She was very like Jolie in looks and stature, except more relaxed and outgoing than Hope could ever imagine Jolie being.

"Pleased to meet you, Hope." Leone smiled. "How are you enjoying your visit?"

"I love Little Dip. What I've seen of it is beautiful, even for this time of the year. After the presentation is over, I hope to see some more before we go."

"Oh, I'm sure Jolie will drag you all over it. Especially to her favorite fishing hole. We all love showing the place off to our guests. Patrice tells me you work with Jolie and Andre at Ambereye?"

"Yes, I've been PA to both of them."

"Aah, you're the one who keeps their inoculations up to date, then," Leone teased.

"It's actually in the job spec." Hope threw a surreptitious glance around the room for Jolie, but didn't see her. Maybe she was lurking in the kitchen doing her chore for the day.

"Hey." Andre came over to join them, catching the tail end of the story. "I'm way the better boss. I'm much more reasonable than my vice president. Where is she, by the way?"

"She was banished out back last time I saw her," Amy said. "Seems she's all fingers and thumbs today. She dropped a pie." They all winced.

"She can be such a klutz sometimes. Remember the summer of the bees?" Leone turned to Andre, who winced again at the memory.

"We spent an entire afternoon sitting up to our necks in the creek until the swarm left. I was terrified. I had bad dreams for years about that mad buzzing sound." He shuddered. "Jolie blundered into a hive and brought an angry swarm down on the rest of us," he explained to Hope.

"And don't forget the summer of the skunk," Leone said. "We had to sit in a tub of cold tomato juice then."

"And you still smell."

"Oh, grow up, Andre."

"Jolie was responsible for that, too?" Hope asked.

"Yeah, she brought bees and skunks down upon us like the plagues of Egypt," Andre said.

"Her name means joy…what a misnomer." Leone rolled her eyes.

"Ignore them. Jolie was a bit of a loner as a kid," Amy said to Hope. "She didn't join in a lot—"

"Because when she did all hell broke loose," Leone interrupted.

"Then there was that flock of geese that chased us for miles. I can't recall how she pissed them off, but, boy, were they mad," Andre said.

"She was just the quieter twin, and she had a big blowhard like Andre to follow. Talk about theatrics." Leone took the opportunity to get a dig back.

"It's not theatrics…it's a love of life."

"Never listen to them." Amy tugged Hope gently on the sleeve and they moved aside leaving the more boisterous Garouls to escalate their childhood arguments. "They wind each other up disgracefully at events like these. Jolie was a great kid. She just did her own thing a lot of time. I'll bet she's relieved Andre has appeared to do his share at the board meeting."

"I haven't seen her since breakfast. I'll go find her, maybe see if our schedule for tomorrow needs to be tweaked. You said she was out back?"

"Yes, straight through the kitchen, you'll see the door to the back porch."

"I'll catch you later." With a smile Hope left.

She found it hard to equate her taciturn boss with the clumsy child described by her peers. Then again, there was an emotional clumsiness with Jolie. Perhaps she had transcribed her earlier awkwardness onto other areas of her life? Or perhaps she was just a recalcitrant twin, content to let a monumental show-off like Andre plow the social furrow for both of them.

As she passed through the kitchen, Patrice looked over and called, "Are you looking for Jolie, dear?" Hope nodded. "Tell her to come back in, her banishment is over. I've cleaned the floor, and dinner's about to be served."

"Okay. I'll go get her." Hope smiled and exited the kitchen. She found Jolie sitting on the back step, chucking stones viciously across the dirt path into the trees.

"Hey, your mom told me to call you. Dinner's ready."

"I'll be there in a minute," she answered tersely, her interest in the gravel at her feet increasing. Hope sat beside her. "You'll mess your skirt, the step's dusty."

"It'll brush off." Hope was unconcerned. Still Jolie wouldn't look at her, so she continued. "You sulking because you killed a pie?"

"No," she mumbled defensively. "Wasn't my fault. I just walked past and the stupid thing fell off the counter. It was perched right on the edge."

"And they banished you."

"So they could clean. I was going to do it, but Mom chased me out. She hates having me and Andre in a kitchen. Something always goes wrong…or missing." Her voice was tight and sullen.

"So. What broke your smile, then?"

"Nothing broke it." Another small stone was lashed across the dirt and rattled into a bush. There was a moment of silence as they watched it disappear in a small puff of dust. "You."

With that she stood and stalked off into the trees.

"Me?" Hope's question rang after her but was ignored. Hope sprung to her feet and chased after her.

"Me?" She grabbed her arm.

"You," Jolie repeated moodily, trying to free herself.

"You've got some nerve blaming me, when you're—" Her words

were cut off as she was pushed roughly back against a tree. Jolie's dark, flushed face thrust into hers.

Hot breath brushed across her cheek as Jolie snapped, "You can't do it. I won't allow it."

"Do what?" Hope was confused, and a little bit intimidated, but refused to show it. Instead she masked it with a look of angry belligerence.

"Carry his cubs."

"Cubs?" Now Hope was completely confused. What was Jolie so upset about? But before she could process the weird twist and turns of their conversation, Jolie covered her mouth in a hard, rough kiss. It was bruising and clumsy. Hope's head banged against the tree, and her teeth gouged into her own lip.

"Ow."

Jolie pulled back instantly, her face scarlet, her eyes huge wells of embarrassment, anger, and something else. Distress. Hope sank into the open look, plunging into the exposed soul of the woman before her. It was a raw, instantaneous moment. She was for one eternal second completely connected to the irrational complexity of Jolie Garoul's heart. Involuntarily, Hope reached out to touch her.

"Jolie? Hope?"

Patrice called from the back porch; dinner was ready. Jolie abruptly broke away and bounded back toward the cabin, her long stride opening up a gap Hope could never close.

"Hey," Hope called after her. "We've got to talk," she told the swinging kitchen door. Jolie had gone. *And this would have been the perfect time to do it.* Sighing, she brushed herself down and followed.

Hope's mouth felt crushed and numb. Her chest was constricted. Air had to squeeze into her tight lungs. She forced herself her to breathe deeply. Any sensible and rational conversation would have to wait it seemed. But she knew something she'd never even thought about before. In that rough, clumsy, totally amateurish kiss, and in that deep baleful gaze, she spied a world of longing. A world that surprised and intrigued her with its intensity, and she wasn't sure what to do with it.

CHAPTER FOURTEEN

Hope was surprised to find herself not sitting next to Jolie, or even Andre. It seemed Marie and Patrice had split the seating arrangement to encourage mingling and conversation around the vast dinner table. Hope found herself between a lanky teenager, who introduced himself as Paulie, and Connie Fortune, which amazed her. She had been a fan of Connie Fortune's work for several years, especially her wildlife series. And now she was sitting beside the reclusive artist at a Thanksgiving dinner. They happily chatted away for several minutes, allowing the Garouls to descend on the serving bowls like a swarm of starving ship rats. When everyone's plates were eventually piled high, they filled their own, all the while chatting about Connie's portfolio and art and nature in general.

"Thank you for the praise. It's always nice to meet someone who likes my work. Before you go home you'll have to visit my studio. It's a little cabin set back from the others. About a half mile past where you and Jolie are staying."

"This must be a wonderful place to work. How did you come to live in Little Dip? If Jolie hadn't been driving, I'd never have found it. It hardly leaps off the map."

"Well, for the most part I've been working with Marie and Garoul Press—"

"But you were a well-known wildlife illustrator long before that."

"Wow, you do know your stuff." Connie looked pleased that Hope genuinely was interested in her work, especially the earlier pre-Garoul phase. "Actually, I was on a hiking holiday in the mountains following a tip that rough-legged hawks were nesting in Little Dip. So, naturally I trespassed, and met the formidable Dr. Marie Garoul. It's a long story. One day I may tell you all about it, but I'm much more interested in you and Jolie. It's wonderful that she brought you along to meet us."

"Oh, let's just look on it as a business trip first and foremost, shall we? Jolie won't relax until we get the finance presentation over and done with." Hope carefully slipped out from a potentially embarrassing conversation. She didn't want to promote the misinformation floating around. But curiously, she didn't want to be the one to expose it either. Jolie's clumsy kiss out in the backyard had clued her in to the subtle complexities of the situation. Hope knew she didn't have a full picture of what was happening, but she was prepared to wait a little longer to at least try and speak to Jolie about it.

Her gaze slid down the table to where Jolie sat quietly concentrating on her dinner, not bothering with the conversations flowing around her, as stoic and unyielding as a riverbed rock.

"Work schedule or not, it's lovely to meet you, Hope. Patrice and Claude were so excited when Andre told them Jolie was bringing her girlfriend along for the holiday," Connie continued with a smile, unaware of the small detonator she had just set off under her dinner companion.

Andre? Andre is behind this whole mess? Why am I not surprised? Of all the lame-brained, idiotic… Hope glared down the table. Several places to Jolie's left, Andre had Amy in hoots of laughter, unaware of the hot look roasting him from afar.

At last it became abundantly clear where the mix-up had come from. Relieved that it would all soon be set to rights, Hope sat back and enjoyed her meal. Across from her, Patrice was chatting animatedly with Paulie's mom, Shirley. Marie, Leone, and a cousin called Angelique were having a heated debate about an opera they had seen recently. Between these small groups were several others, consisting of Garouls whose names Hope could not immediately recall. All had grinned affably and shaken her hand when she arrived for dinner. The atmosphere was hopping with laughter and raucous talk. It was a happy family gathering of industrious and intelligent individuals, bound by more interests than mere family gossip.

Claude sat nearby, chatting with Godfrey and Paulie, who Hope noticed absolutely adored his uncle.

"Do you go hunting with Claude a lot?" she asked.

Paulie blushed brightly as he answered her. He was at that age where he was still crushingly shy. But his eyes sparkled with enthusiasm for his subject.

"Oh, yeah. He teaches me all kinds of stuff. Not just about hunting and fishing, but about the woods, too. Because we own the valley, we have to learn how to manage it."

"I never thought of it that way. I always assumed trees just took care of themselves." Hope was immediately engaged. Something about Paulie's awkward but honest love for what truly mattered to him reminded her of Jolie. Was she looking at a callback to Jolie's own youth?

"No, the woodland needs managing. And the roads and parking areas, too. My dad"—he indicated a man Hope knew as Robért—"maintains all the cabins and the compound area. Well, he has help, but he heads it up."

"It's like a little cottage industry your family has going on here. But I suppose it's a small price to pay for the luxury of having a holiday homestead of this size and privacy."

He nodded. "That's what it's all about. The privacy. You have to work hard for that."

Despite the earlier calamity, there seemed to be more than enough fruit and pumpkin pies for everyone, even for those who wanted second or third helpings. Hope had never seen a family with such appetites as the Garouls. Food just disappeared. It was effortless for them to clear every overflowing dish on a table that had practically groaned with the amount of food placed upon it.

"Okay, before the cleanup team begins, we quickly need to tweak the sleeping arrangements," Marie announced to the table as after-dinner coffees and port were poured. "We have to reshuffle a little, as Andre and Godfrey managed to arrive today. The boys are in one of the larger two-bed cabins and are sharing with Pierre and Mandy." She looked across at a young couple who smiled happily at the arrangement. "And, Paulie, I'm afraid Angelique has called dibs on your room, so you're on the bed settee in Jolie and Hope's cabin. Is that okay with you guys?"

"Okay with me." Paulie seemed happy enough.

Hope blinked in dismay and quickly looked over to Jolie, who had a similar look of muted panic on her face. She sat staring at the table, frantically twisting her pinky ring until Hope thought her finger would start to smoke. Then another emotion swept across her features, one of shame and inevitability. The time for truth had arrived.

As angry as she was with Jolie's recent behavior, Hope's heart went out to her. Jolie cleared her throat, and a frown creased her brow. Already Hope could see the red bloom of embarrassment of her cheeks. Jolie's eyes became guarded, as if a shutter had been drawn between her real self and what she was now compelled to announce to her family.

"Hmm, about that." Jolie cleared her throat again in preparation for her own denouement. "There's been a misunder—"

Hope interrupted. "It's no problem at all." Her voice rang out loud and clear down the table to Marie. Jolie looked up startled, and Hope held her gaze with a cool, level stare before turning to Paulie.

Jolie sat glued as Hope chatted amicably to Paulie, organizing his move up to their cabin. What did it mean? Why was Hope doing this? Was it some new form of torture? Because Jolie had already more than her fair share today. She was still sick to her guts thinking of Andre asking Hope to carry his cubs. Tired and confused, and so out of her depth with this entire situation, she shifted her gaze to her father. He sat impassively watching her. Then his whiskers twitched and a broad smile broke over his face, like the sun coming out, bathing her in warmth. He tilted his head to one side and gave her a sly wink before rising to leave.

"Come here, son," he boomed down the table to Andre, indicating they should go for a stroll together. Andre looked surprised but happily followed his father. With a cheeky grin, he blew a kiss to Godfrey, who was left to pick up his dishwashing duty.

❖

"Jeez. What happened to that rabbit?"

"That's Tadpole. And he's not a rabbit."

Jolie couldn't help but grin at the conversation drifting in from the living room as she quickly shuffled her bag into Hope's bedroom. She stood and looked at the huge double bed with its bright patchwork quilt.

I'll be lying on the floor all night. Who'd have thought I'd miss that lumpy old couch? Maybe she should just sneak out and go hunting? She sighed. Confusion and misery sat on opposite shoulders whispering sweet nothings about her inadequacies into each ear.

The door swung open and Hope entered. The air in the room reduced quicker than sauce, and congealed in Jolie's lungs. She stood planted at the foot of the bed and waited. Hope perched a hip on the edge of the high mattress and sat facing her.

"The things I have to do to get you to talk to me," she murmured. Jolie watched her silently. "And maybe it's still not enough?"

The silence stretched like an elastic band. Hope decided to see what would snap first. She wriggled herself into a more comfortable position. Jolie still stood ramrod straight. Hope picked some imaginary lint off her skirt while Jolie's eyes darted around the room in a shifty little dance. Hope relaxed back against the headboard and watched her, a small smile playing on her lips. *And three…two…one…*

"I didn't mean to kiss you. But you can't do it," Jolie blurted in a tight voice.

Bingo. "Do what?"

"Have his cu—babies. You can't. No. I won't allow it."

"Is that because he's your brother, or because I'm your mistress?"

"Ack." Jolie choked.

"Excuse me?" Hope calmly regarded her, hands folded on her lap. Jolie's ears flamed and high spots of color brushed her cheekbones, accentuating the dangerous glitter in her eye.

"Sit here." Hope patted the quilt beside her, misreading Jolie's heightened color as understandable embarrassment. Jolie slid onto the bedspread and they sat facing each other.

"I'm sorry you're upset. I really don't know where the rumor came from. I never said anything. I didn't start it," Jolie said. *But I want it, and everyone knows it but you.* "I told Dad the night we arrived and were given this cabin. He said he'd sort it out. I was going to ask him after dinner what was going on, but he disappeared with Andre." She felt angry, powerless, and exposed. It was bad enough her inner fantasies had been ripped apart for everyone in her family to see, but now Hope was peering into the open wound as well. For Jolie it felt unbearable and shaming.

"I kind of guessed there was a misunderstanding somewhere, and it turns out Andre got everyone's wires crossed," Hope said in a kinder voice. "I know now you're not responsible, but I came here as your guest and employee, Jolie. It's a mess, and you and Andre have to clear it up. I can hardly look your parents in the eye without feeling like an impostor. And it feels terrible because I really do like them."

Jolie's body actually ached with all this. Every way she looked at it, it hurt her. She was upset that Hope was socially embarrassed at being perceived as her lover. Worried that her pack would be disappointed, because they genuinely liked Hope and Jolie knew they approved her as a suitable mate. And most of all she was embarrassed for herself. This whole extraordinary situation was a mockery of her newly discovered need to claim Hope for her own. And it had been publicly exploded before she'd even realized how deeply it ran.

"I'll kill him." Her whole face darkened at this news of Andre's involvement.

"Please wait until after the board meeting." Hope sighed and rubbed her forehead as if her bosses were the biggest headaches ever. "And for the record, about that surrogate mother thing, Andre was teasing you in his own bizarre, cruel twin way. It's not going to happen."

Jolie's whole body jerked with relief, then tensed with further anger at Andre's meddling.

Hope watched her curiously but said nothing more on the subject. Jolie needed to be defused before she incapacitated Andre for the foreseeable future. Carefully, she changed tack.

"Okay. Disaster recovery time. Let's just get this presentation behind us. It's what we came here to do. This mess can be tidied up after we get back to the city. A few phone calls and all will be well."

A small nod greeted her idea. "I'll sleep on the floor tonight." Jolie stood and moved away as if to add emphasis to her statement.

"Are you doing that because you kissed me? Because if so, it's a little late for token gallantry."

Jolie's face scorched again. She squirmed in her shoes.

"I'm sorry about that. I was angry and I don't know why I did it," she mumbled, looking slightly to the left of Hope, refusing to meet her gaze.

Hope nodded, deciding to let her off the hook. She didn't know what to make of it any more than Jolie did. For the moment she was content to wait until she could process it further. So far, it had turned into a truly ludicrous day. She needed to let the last twenty-four hours pass over her. Tomorrow and the next day she would do her job, and then she'd go home. Only there would she find the space to think about Jolie Garoul and her clumsy kisses. The tip of her tongue played with the small gash inside her lower lip. A reminder of Jolie's headlong, passion-filled exuberance. Sucking on the tenderness, Hope made up her mind.

"It's a big enough bed. We can share. We've both slept with other women before without leaping on them." She gave a hard glare, remembering the biting incident. "I'm sure we can contain ourselves for the next few nights."

Jolie was dubious. She had never slept in a bed with another woman who wasn't a Garoul. She had never done *anything* in a bed with another woman. It was a thing of myth for her. Mating was a bond for Jolie: all or nothing. There was no space in between for anything else. She had waited a lifetime for someone she didn't know she was waiting for.

Jolie watched Hope stand and straighten the bedspread. The irony was not lost on her that her "someone" didn't know she was being waited for, either.

Hope glanced up and misinterpreted the befuddled, distressed look. "I swear, Garoul, you sleep-bite me again, and I will be the biggest nightmare you've ever had in your entire sorry-ass life."

❖

"So," Andre's father asked as they trudged along the creek path, "what do you make of her?"

"Hope?" Andre couldn't think of anyone else so central to his parents' thoughts at the moment. "I love her to bits. She's been a good friend of mine for years and years."

His father seemed to approve of this news. "Is that why you told your mother they were a couple, because you liked the idea?" he growled in a woe betide you if you get the answer to this one wrong way. Andre gawped at him.

"What?"

"You heard."

"I did hear, and what?" They stood looking at each other. "Dad, what are you talking about? I never told Mom that. I said Jolie was bringing Hope down with her to help with the presentation."

"Did you?"

"I…I…think so. Shit, what did I say? I can't remember." He was speaking more to himself than his father as he tried to recall the exact conversation. He shrugged. "Well, that's what I meant. I can't help it if Mom got the wrong end of the stick."

The fact they both knew Patrice Garoul could grab the wrong end of any stick and twirl it like a baton of confusion did not lessen the glower on his father's face. Andre swallowed hard.

"You didn't answer me."

"Sorry. What was the question, Dad?"

"Do you think they're right for each other?"

"God, yes. Yes. I'd love to see that happen. I'll do everything I can to make it happen."

But his father had heard enough. His arm fell across Andre's shoulders and they turned onto the path home.

"Dad? Why didn't you say something if you knew there'd been a misunderstanding?"

His father smiled. It beamed out from under those magical whiskers and lit up the cloudy day.

"Because I've no doubts at all that this is the one for Jolie. As far as I'm concerned there is no misunderstanding, just a little mistiming, maybe. That's all. Hope came here to Little Dip as the intended mate for Jolie, and I see no reason why she shouldn't leave the same way."

"I'd love for Jolie to have someone like Hope in her life. That's why I had them work together. You have no idea of the struggle Jolie put up—"

His father gave him a hard squeeze that momentarily took the air from his lungs. Andre blinked, suddenly transported back to an age when he barely reached his father's belt loops, and a particular homeward trek in the evening dusk after a hard day's logging. He had worked so hard that day, and had been so tired out, but then, as now, he felt his father's love and pride wrap around him like a warm blanket.

"I love my family, Dad." It came out a little tight, a little moist and emotional, and he felt embarrassed because his butch gene was such a wuss. His father's arm tightened around his shoulders again.

"I love you, son."

CHAPTER FIFTEEN

For most Garouls, Thanksgiving ended with an early evening. Jolie, Hope, and Andre had a last-minute strategy session to confirm they had everything more than covered. Through his profuse guilt at being the creator of evil misinformation and cruel conjecture, Jolie suckered Andre into doing loads more than he'd originally intended. But accepting for once that Jolie had the moral high ground, he complied with only the merest bitching. Satisfied with the re-jigged schedule, they retired to their respective cabins.

"Where's Paulie? He out late?" Hope asked as they returned home. Jolie had a good idea exactly where Paulie was—out patrolling the valley with her father as wolven. And she couldn't help but envy him the simple pleasure. She hoped that after the meetings were over she, too, would have a little time to stretch her claws.

"Oh, he'll be back. We'll leave the door unlocked for him."

"Okay." Hope took Tadpole out for his evening toilette. He still refused to explore more than five yards from the steps. On a brave day he made it as far as the tree line, but mostly he snuffled around the porch, raising his whiskery snout every so often to give a concerned sniff at the breeze blowing in from the forest. Hope was convinced he was feeling poorly even though he still ate like a small pony and had fallen in love with the ham bone she had brought back from dinner as promised.

Jolie got ready for bed while Hope saw to Tadpole's supper. She was loitering awkwardly in the bedroom in her large T-shirt and sweatpants when Hope returned.

"Can you put Taddy into his bed while I get ready?" Hope asked, grabbing her nightwear and disappearing into the small bathroom. Tadpole and Jolie swapped an evil-eyed look.

❖

Her face was washed, her teeth brushed. Now came the part she was still coming to terms with. Taking a deep breath, Hope popped her prosthetic eye and rinsed it under the tap, removing the day's dirt. She examined her face in the mirror dispassionately. It wasn't too bad. Lord knew there were people out there with worse disfigurements. She should be grateful. Her fingers manipulated her upper and lower eyelids as she examined the empty socket. The flesh was healthy, red and vibrant. Just another part of the inside that not many people get to see. She knew she was one of the lucky ones. It could have been a whole lot worse.

"So, where do we go from here?" she asked her reflection. It seemed she was slowly getting over the initial shock of her prognosis and the operation. Life went on and she had moved with it. She was managing at home and in work; she had kept up her friendships and her social interests. She'd done everything right according to the hospital's recuperation handouts. But she was still only partway there. She looked at the empty socket.

"I've got more than one void still to fill." With a sigh, she popped her eye back into the socket.

Her confidence was slowly being restored, thanks to her friends. But a huge part of the process had been her initial tussles with Jolie. Talk about finding her feet fast! If she hadn't, she'd be on the floor on her ass, for there sure as hell wouldn't have been a chair to sit on.

Hope smiled when she thought of Jolie and her antics. But this latest nonsense about being Jolie's girlfriend? Well, that was too preposterous. It amazed her that anyone would believe that. And yet they all had, even Godfrey and Andre.

She blinked hard several times to ensure her prosthetic eye was snug, and then gazed at herself curiously. *People didn't blink an eye when they imagined me with her.*

Quickly she turned away from the mirror. Hope didn't want to imagine it either.

"So, where do you sleep, runt?" Jolie muttered to herself, "Come on, hound. Outside with you." Tadpole followed her out onto the porch where she looked around for his sleeping blanket.

"Where the hell is— Oh no." Her eyes locked with his brazen beady ones. "Please don't tell me you sleep with her. Ugh."

With a shudder she stomped back into the cabin, the dog at her heels. His tail wagged endlessly as he rushed to overtake her and lead the parade to his bed in the corner of Hope's room.

"Good." Hope appeared behind them resplendent in flannel pajamas. "We're all accounted for." She scrambled onto the tall bed and shuffled over to the side farther away from Jolie. "Can you get the light?"

Jolie nodded dumbly and flipped the switch. Under cover of darkness she pulled off her sweatpants but left on her underwear, and crawled in beside Hope. She lay beside her as stiff as Tutankhamen and stared fixedly at the wooden ceiling beams. Hope fluffed, and flipped, and finally got comfortable.

"G'night," she mumbled, shifting onto her side, her back to Jolie, and drifted off to sleep effortlessly. Jolie still lay at attention, eyes wide open. How could Hope do that? Just sleep? As if this was the most normal thing in the world. Jolie was mystified. Hope smelled nice. Of strawberries. *No biting.*

❖

Hope's belly was about ready to pop with cubs. Big, and round, and alabaster. It looked delicious. Then suddenly they were there! Everywhere, black, furry little werecubs, toddling on two legs every which way. Jolie had to catch them, had to round them up before they hurt themselves. But they increased speed. No longer wobbling, they took off in all directions, giggling and squealing. No matter how fast she ran, or how many of the wriggling, squiggling little varmints she swooped into her arms, another dozen ran through or around her legs. She was running in circles trying to catch them, like a sheepdog trying to herd them up, like a tired old sheepdog trying to...a sheepdog... dog...Woof!

Her eyes flew open. *I was sleeping?*

Hope was sitting straight up in bed beside her, glaring at her. Even Tadpole sat bolt upright, both ears quivering on full alert.

"What?" Jolie asked, struggling to sit, trying to piece together her dream world with Hope's accusing stare.

"You awoke with a 'woof,'" Hope said.

"I did not." Jolie was incredibly offended. "I do *not* bark."

"You've been scrabbling around in this bed for over ten minutes. You look like Tadpole when he dreams he's chasing rabbits. Then you went 'woof.'" Hope continued to glare. "You know, for a project manager and the vice president of a global software house, you have the stupidest dreams ever."

"I can't help what I dream," Jolie defended herself hotly. "I'm stressed."

Hope settled back down. "What are you stressed about, the presentation tomorrow, or should I say today?" She checked the bedside clock. It was after one in the morning.

"No." *I'm stressed because I want to lick you all over.*

"Is it just general stress, then?"

Jolie wished Hope would just let it go and fall back to sleep. Then she could slip from the room and run herself ragged in the woods until dawn. Anything to relieve this tension in her gut.

"Yeah. General stress. Let's try and catch some sleep. I'll promise not to chase rabbits," Jolie grumbled and turned away.

Hope regarded the broad back thoughtfully. It felt good to sleep in its lee. It made her feel sheltered and secure. Hadn't she fallen into a deep sleep the minute her head hit the pillow? Usually she lay awake for hours fretting about life and death and mortal coils, and how close she might be to the end of hers. In daylight hours and in doctors' waiting rooms she could rationalize the whole universe away, cordially and calmly. But alone in the dark she became a little girl again, afraid of the hereafter, the great beyond, feeling small and inconsequential in her own lost life.

Her initial struggles with Jolie had actually been invigorating. They had rooted her back into a work routine. She could see that now. In fact, she had enjoyed getting the upper hand in their little office power struggles. It built her confidence again. And in time she had come to notice something else lying just under Jolie's abrasiveness. The simplest things made Jolie Garoul happy, like a pastry in the morning, or fresh coffee partway through a manic day when there was barely time to draw breath. At first she was recalcitrant, but Hope persisted, until it became apparent that Jolie was simply not used to registering, never mind catering for her own needs. So slowly, over several weeks, Hope had begun to look after those needs for her clumsy, awkward boss.

Snuggling under the covers, Hope mulled over the complex, yet strangely childish woman beside her. She probed the soft welt in her lower lip with her tongue. She liked Jolie and felt that Jolie liked her back, and also in a particular way. Jolie had become so raw and energized since they arrived at Little Dip. She was definitely more subdued, more controlled in the city. It was as if her city-slick veneer was wearing away out here in the mountains, and her true needs and wants were surfacing. Were they the kind of needs Hope would also want to look after?

The rumor that they were a couple— Hope was bemused at the thought of being Jolie's lover. Did she like the idea? And was she even ready for that type of interest? She knew she was still hesitant about reclaiming that part of herself. And even if she did, did she want to reclaim it with Jolie Garoul?

While she would be the first to admit Jolie was gorgeous to look at, there were more than enough "peculiarities" to warn her off. Deep down she knew Jolie would be more than a handful, and Hope knew for certain she didn't have that sort of energy to give away. The cancer had depleted her on so many levels. Her confidence was at an all-time low, but slowly rebuilding itself through her successes at work. Hope was still very unsure about her attractiveness and her private life. Finding a girlfriend, dating, having fun and even sex again all seemed insurmountable obstacles. She was safe and cozy in her circle of friends. Was she ready to venture out further? She didn't think so. Common sense dictated she wait a little longer, go a little slower. Her libido, however, at least where Jolie Garoul was concerned, seemed to be in one hell of a hurry.

❖

About an hour later, Hope surfaced from sleep to find her nose pushed against the side of Jolie's breast. Jolie was now flat out on her back, hands flung above her head, hair draped across the pillow. Hope had wormed in under her arm and settled there, safe and warm and perfectly content. She should move away, but didn't. This felt like the right place to be. Her eyelids fluttered, and she fell back into a deep, restful sleep.

Soon after that, Jolie felt pressure on her bladder, then her belly, then her side. She slowly awoke, looking straight up into Tadpole's deeply dismayed eyes. He sat in the middle of the bed right between Jolie and Hope, as tightly as he could wedge.

Jolie next became aware of Hope's soft hair brushing her throat. Her arm lay heavily over Jolie's rib cage just beneath her breasts. And a leg had slithered across Jolie's thigh, pinning her to the mattress in a delicious act of claiming. A huge grin crossed Jolie's face, despite the little dog's disgusted stare.

See? Suck it up, Rathole. Told you she was mine.

❖

The financial review came right after Andre's CEO report, to be followed by his business development update, which would end today's meeting. Financial reports were second nature to Jolie. She ate, drank, and slept these figures in her Portland life. Today, however, it was the financial plan for the upcoming year that had her anxious.

Andre had already given his honeyed spiel about expansion and a new directive to engage with other old European families. Acutely conscious of Hope being in the room, he had not labeled the other wolven clans as such. Rather he had called them potential partners. Technology made the world smaller, he had stated. Jolie agreed with him that it made perfect sense for some of their common ancestral knowledge to become globally available to other packs and vice versa.

Hope sat and listened to the possible work situation for the company far into the future, and it excited her. Ambereye, Inc. already had a hit game on the market—Wolfbane: Firstborn. Hope had only seen fragments of it in test and development. It was marketed at teenagers and seemed to allow them to take on the persona of a werewolf and learn how to survive and pass as human in a modern city setting. She thought it was an intriguing idea. On a weird level, she was never quite sure if it was designed to allow kids to imagine they were monsters or if it was supposed to teach them how to behave in a more civil and humane manner out on the streets. She wondered what the next game idea was going to be and why Andre had to sell it to the board.

"Hope?" She glanced up from her minute taking to see Andre looking over at her. "Would you mind if we had a few moments, just the family?" he asked almost apologetically.

"No, not at all." She rose to leave, wondering what the mystery was. But she could do with a cup of coffee, so an unscheduled break was welcome.

Andre waited until the door closed quietly behind her before turning to the long table. "We debated the Lykous proposal last year. And we need to decide now if it's a go for Jolie to draw up a diagnostic on the overall investment and return. Can we put this to a vote, Aunt Marie?"

"We can, Andre, but it's a moot point. The pack elders have all agreed to accept an amalgamation of coded information with the Lykous clan. Over time we want to build a global depository of all the wolven families' traditions, culture, and knowledge. This is a good starting point with our Greek cousins. They are as ancient as we are, if not more so. But for propriety's sake we will put it to the vote. All in favor?" Every hand rose. She winked at a beaming Andre.

They concluded the meeting not long after that. Coffee and sandwiches followed, and soon Jolie and Hope were wandering up the trail to their cabin, relaxed that the first day's work was over and had gone well.

Neither had mentioned their start to the day. Hope had finally roused to find herself entangled with Jolie's long limbs. She had merely removed Tadpole and stretched, as if waking up wrapped around Jolie Garoul was an everyday, natural occurrence. Jolie had lain still, pretending to still be asleep for decorum's sake. Until Hope slapped her on the belly.

"Come on, snooze-hound. It's the big day. Up and at 'em." Another playful belly poke to make sure her bed companion was fully awake and Hope was off, grabbing the bathroom first.

Jolie slid from the bed with burning ears and flushed cheeks. Hope obviously didn't understand how torturous her easygoing actions were, or how close she danced to a dangerous precipice. Self-control was strangling Jolie; the sooner this weekend was done with, the better. She could cope better in the city, gain distance, and maybe ask Andre to take Hope back as his assistant again. It might be better for both of them.

Now, after the triumph of the opening meeting, Jolie felt once again the miraculous high of working so seamlessly alongside Hope. They were so good together as a team, and it saddened her that her own preposterous wants were eventually going to destroy this new experience for her. Why couldn't she just get it right for once? Why did her bestial craving to claim Hope have to ruin everything? Jolie was slipping into a deep pool of self-loathing.

They were halfway to the cabin when a breathless Paulie jogged hurriedly down the track toward them. He skidded to a halt in the shale.

"I was just coming to find you. Oh, Hope, I'm so sorry—"

"What's up?" Jolie was immediately alert.

"What is it?" Likewise Hope was concerned.

"It's Tadpole," Paulie gulped. "I was playing ball with him on the front porch and threw it too far. He took off into the woods after it, and I swear—I can't find him. It's like he disappeared."

CHAPTER SIXTEEN

They split up and spent nearly an hour checking the immediate vicinity for the little dog. Hope was becoming more and more distraught as each bush and tree root failed to produce a timorous Tadpole. Jolie, too, was getting concerned. Neither she nor Paulie, even with their wolven senses, could pick up his pampered, city-dog scent. The cousins quietly discussed this anomaly as Hope investigated the vegetation on the other side of the cabin.

"Has the little bugger gone underground? Down a hole or something?" Jolie cursed out loud, exasperated that this wasn't turning into a quick fix. Paulie looked over, startled.

"He's not that bad. I like him. He's just suffering a little jealousy because Hope likes you."

"She does?" Jolie's ears pricked up at that.

"Looks like he's not the only one," Paulie muttered, continuing to scour the ground. "This is near where he was last seen. Look, there's his ball. It's as if something else distracted him and he wandered off—"

"What do you mean? How do you know she likes me? Did the runt confide in you, Doctor Dolittle? All stretched out on his little therapy blankie?" Jolie snorted. Then realizing she genuinely did want this information, she continued more cordially. "Seriously. Hope likes me? How do you know?"

"Look. He's rolled about here. I can see some ginger hairs. And I can scent him, but not clearly."

"That's because he's rolled in raccoon dung. Smelly little weasel. As if he didn't stink enough. No wonder he's so hard to sniff out."

Jolie scowled at Tadpole's deviousness and bad hygiene, then turned her attention back to Paulie. "Seriously. Hope likes me?"

"If you paid more attention, you'd see what I mean." Paulie sighed. "Dogs are very simplistic animals. They operate on a need-to-know basis. Hope was his universe, until you came along with your wolfie smells and sly mating rituals. He's not stupid, you know."

"What sly mating rituals?"

Now Paulie snorted and refused to answer. He turned back to the cabin, Jolie clipping his heels.

"Hey. What sly mating rituals?"

"Any luck?" Hope walked up to meet them, a picture of distress. Paulie and Jolie shook their heads.

"Oh." Hope kept walking, straight into Jolie's arms, and clung to her. Jolie was shocked but quickly enveloped her in a hug.

"Oh, Jolie." Hope sniffled into Jolie's shirt buttons. "I can't bear to think of him out there, all alone and frightened."

Jolie tightened her arms and found herself crooning reassuringly. "Don't worry. We'll find him if I have to rip this whole valley apart."

Over Hope's bent head Paulie raised his eyebrows at her mockingly.

"Those sly mating moves," he murmured in a voice soft enough that only Jolie's keen hearing could pick it up.

❖

"Okay, listen up, team." Jolie called the Garoul search party to attention. Any of the family with spare time had volunteered to help look for Tadpole. She stood on the top porch step and addressed them all with crisp military precision, as if she were organizing the last stand at the Alamo.

"Marie and Connie, take the logging road as far as Big Jack, searching east and west of the track. Leone and Patrice, you take from the parking lot to Leaper's Bluff. I know it's a long shot, but he might have tried to head back to the Jeep. Andre and Angelique, the central compound and surrounding area up to the Bluff and hook up with Claude, who's on the eastern rim. Paulie, you take from Connie's workshop to the Portland turn-off, and I'll go in the opposite direction toward the Lost Creek road sign. Okay? Any questions?"

"Where will I look?" Hope asked, moving forward. Jolie turned and tenderly cupped her shoulder.

"I need someone to stay here in case he comes back. It's getting dark and he'll be thinking of heading home soon," she lied through her teeth. "Godfrey will help you make one last sweep around the cabin before nightfall."

What she really wanted was Hope tucked away so the rest of them could transform into werewolves and get on with it. Several wolven could cover most of this valley in a couple of hours. Godfrey understood this, and he would stay with Hope as they waited for the searchers to return. To be honest, none of them, bar Hope, thought there'd be much chance of finding the little dog in one piece. He was a walking pretzel for most of the residents of this forest.

Hope nodded quietly and stood back. Jolie turned back to the search team. "Okay. He's a small, ginger mongrel, yea big, and he smells like raccoon poo—"

"He does *not* smell like raccoon poo," Hope blurted out, hurt and indignant. Jolie reached over and stroked her arm.

"In this instance he does, sweetheart," she said, surprising herself with the endearment that fell so naturally from her lips. She didn't want Hope to think she was taking a cheap shot at her missing pup. "We'll find him, don't worry."

"Here's a picture." Hope offered up the screensaver of her cell phone. Jolie handed it over and the Garoul clan gathered around it to look at their search objective. There was silence.

Finally, Marie managed, "My, he's a handsome chap, isn't he?" This was enthusiastically supported with nods and incoherent affirmations before they all broke up and headed off to their allotted areas.

"Jolie?"

Hope's call held her back.

"Will you be okay?" Jolie asked anxiously. Hope seemed so upset.

"I just wanted to say thank you." Hope reached for her hands. "I know the odds are against him out there. But thank you for trying so hard. He's everything to me. When I got home from the hospital he just lay down beside me and rested his head on my hip as I cried, and he never moved until I was done."

Hope was crying now, and Jolie's heart turned into a big pink marshmallow. It oozed into every spare inch of her chest cavity, choking her, suffocating her. She couldn't bear to see Hope cry. It was the purest pain she had ever known.

"After losing the eye I was so scared, but he was with me every step of the way. He loved me no matter what I looked like or how monstrous I felt. Total, unconditional love." This came out as a strangled sob. "And I love him back."

Jolie squeezed her into a warm, reassuring hug.

"I'll find him. I promise I will," she whispered. She knew it was a silly, perhaps impossible vow. But she damned well intended to track him down come hell or high water. Dead or alive, he was now the most wanted dog in the west.

❖

Rolling in raccoon poo was not the smartest thing for Tadpole to do. In Little Dip raccoons were even lower on the food chain than city dogs. Jolie could see where he had tried to circle back, but something was between him and where he wanted to go. Something slithery and rustley, no doubt, that probably regarded him as dinner.

Carefully, she circled, testing the air, the dirt, brush, and bark for his faint scent trail. He was terrified, she could tell by the astringency of his smell. She padded on, on quiet paws until she found him in a small clearing, wedged under a rotten log, his beady eyes nervously flitting from leaf to leaf, branch to branch. He was so focused on the bushes that he didn't notice her until she was about ten feet away from his hidey hole. She crouched low and slowly drew near. He let out a tiny welcome whimper. She rumbled back in a deep growl. His tail rose and fell in a single thump of friendship. She gave another rumble, slightly warmer this time, then raised her head and howled into the skies. Tadpole shrank down into the moist soil as answering calls came echoing through the trees from distant parts of the valley.

Jolie growled again and waited as he scrabbled out from under his log. He ducked in close to her heels and stuck there like glue as together they headed back en route to the cabin. Nothing was going to hurt him now. Not while he had the biggest, baddest wolf in the forest for a friend.

❖

Tadpole lay content before the wood stove as his squeaky-clean, fluffy fur dried out. His belly was round with the hero's meal he'd eaten. He had been kissed and hugged and bathed in bubbles by Hope, who now sat on the couch looking at him, amazed he had been returned safe and sound.

"I just couldn't believe it when you walked up the path with him under your arm," Hope said for the umpteenth time. "You know, I just knew you'd do it. I somehow felt it deep inside, that you would go out into that forest and find him." She shook her head, mystified at her own conclusion. "It's like you know these woods inside out. That's twice you've saved him. Oh, Jolie, I'll never be able to thank you enough."

"It was nothing. He hadn't gone very far." She resolved to never tell Hope she had decided to wait and watch the forest predators, and follow whatever one looked like it was on the trail of a really stupid raccoon. In the end a fox had led her to the fallen log. And now, here they were, sitting together relaxed on the couch after a big steak dinner, watching the flames dance. It was bliss. The best reward in the world as far as Jolie was concerned. They sat on in contented silence.

"Okay." Hope eventually broke the spell. "Tomorrow's another working day for us. The last one, and then it's Sunday and home. Let's go to bed."

The simple domesticity of the statement blew Jolie away. It was pure fantasy for her, yet it was also true. They were going to go to bed, and together, after a homemade evening meal and a few hours by the fire. She was so in love.

She froze, her gaze fixed on the flames without really seeing them. She was so in love. The thought had come out of nowhere, and hit her like a rocket. In the chest, because that's where it hurt most, in the chest. Now she understood those valentine hearts with arrows pierced right through them, except it should be missiles with fiery tails exploding on impact into painfully pulverized hearts.

She became aware she was sitting alone, both hands clutched against her pulverized heart. Hope had headed off to the bedroom, and Tadpole was out for the count before the wood stove. Slowly she rose to follow, still stunned at her discovery. Realizing this love had been tucked away in her heart, her mashed-up heart, all along, waiting for her to look and find it. Why had she never looked there before? Why had she just concentrated on and worried over her wolven instincts rising up to engulf her?

It was so obvious now. This was more than an instinct to mate; this was everlasting, life-bonding love. This was the emotional force that combined the dualities of her existence, the human and the wolf. Hope was the living, breathing epicenter of her life. Now that she'd shaken it all to pieces.

❖

Again Jolie stretched out beside Hope as if on a morgue slab. All her actions in preparing for bed had been slow and deliberate as her mind frantically scoured the small print of her heart's secret contract with Hope. She was looking for a loophole in some sub clause that would let her slide out of these painful, unmanageable feelings. To return to the safe blank her life had been before this woman appeared at her office door. If there was a loophole, she couldn't find it. She lay there tight and terrified as Hope snuggled down comfortably for the night, resolving to sneak away and hunt when she was sure Hope was asleep.

"Jolie?" The whisper fluttered in the darkness.

"Yeah?" she murmured back, her voice thick.

"Thank you again."

Jolie smiled bitterly into the enveloping gloom. "I told you I'd get him. I'll always keep my promises to you."

There was more shuffling, and suddenly Hope was leaning over her. She held Jolie's gaze intently before closing her eyes and slowly, and surely, lowering her mouth to gently kiss her.

Full lips cupped Jolie's in an exquisite, moist heat. The soft pressure on her mouth stole her away for a heart-stopping moment. She was mesmerized by the shyness of Hope's kiss. Jolie's lips parted in a small gasp of wonder and the pressure was increased. Jolie was being thoroughly kissed.

Hope knew what she was doing. She knew how to kiss, and she wanted to kiss Jolie very much right now. She also wanted to test something out for her own satisfaction.

"Mmm," she hummed happily as she finally broke away. "That was very, very nice. I think I like kissing you."

"Again," whispered Jolie, totally spellbound, "again."

And she melted into Hope's arms.

CHAPTER SEVENTEEN

Hope was flat on her back. *Oh my God, what just happened?* Her hands, buried in Jolie's thick hair and pinning her mouth to hers, was probably a clue.

"Again," Jolie had sighed and turned into her arms. So she had kissed her again. This time harder, longer, trailing her tongue tip across Jolie's upper lip. She had teased her, glorying in the trembling, raw emotion pouring off Jolie's body.

This was what she wanted to know. What it would be like to hold Jolie Garoul, to touch her, to savor her like this. And she'd known Jolie wanted this, too. She had known since that clumsy kiss in the trees.

For Hope this was a momentous decision. This was the first time since her anesthetized libido had shaken itself awake, that she felt brave enough to take a chance. Her cancer diagnosis had seized her with crippling fear and cold dread. Now she was en route back to her old life, and she wanted Jolie to show her the way. She felt safe with this dangerous, enigmatic woman. She knew her moods and was sensitized to her bizarre ways. Hope wanted to be sexual again. She wanted that part of herself back. It used to be such an important part. Now it was time to reach out and reclaim it, and Jolie Garoul was her chosen lover. So she'd kissed her, and found herself being passionately kissed back.

At first Jolie's kisses were clumsy. She seemed even rustier than Hope. But with gentle coaxing and learning by example, Hope soon had her kissing her just how she liked it, sweet and slow, with tasting and sucking. And little nips all along her jawline, down to her shoulder to that sensitive spot that made her shiver right through to her backbone. *Mmm. Good girl, Jolie.*

Jolie was a very quick study and in no time she had Hope clinging to her neck, moaning in her ear. She pushed Hope onto her back and lay over her to drop kisses all over her face. Jolie became conscious of the soft swell of breasts pushing up against her chest. Hope had full breasts. Jolie had noticed them that first day when she hadn't cared who the newcomer with Andre had been. Hadn't realized this was her new assistant, not some passerby to secretly ogle. Now those breasts cushioned her, soft and sensuous. She kissed down Hope's throat to her cleavage, as far as the pajama top allowed. Hope crooned approval at the silken trail. Jolie hesitated, her lips sucking lightly on Hope's breast bone. With nervous fingers she fumbled with the tiny buttons on Hope's flannel top, and froze as the material tore slightly. She cast an anxious look up to Hope's flushed face.

"I never liked these," Hope murmured, uncaring about the ripped button. She shifted slightly to help remove the top. Jolie ripped the garment into shreds and sent it sailing to a distant corner in seconds flat.

"Oh," Hope blinked in surprise. Her pajamas weren't quite ready to be dust rags either. Jolie stripped her own T-shirt over her head, kicked off her panties and lay nude over Hope's body in one quick, choreographed move.

"Oh." Hope gasped again as her skin bloomed against the flushed heat of Jolie's flesh sliding across her breasts and belly. Her curtain of long, dark hair delicately flowed over Hope's throat and shoulders.

Jolie realized she was living her dream from the other night. She fell onto Hope's soft warmth, encased by her arms and thighs, but she had to be careful not to bite. The kisses and licking and sucking were transporting her out of her body with delight. Jolie wanted to possess Hope in every way possible, to take her and hold on to her forever. *No biting, no biting.*

"Ow! Stop biting."

"Huh?"

"They're nipples, not gumdrops."

"Oh. Sorry," she mumbled shamefaced into the valley of Hope's glorious breasts. She raised her head. "It wasn't really a bite," she said earnestly. Then she growled as Hope's scent filled her and she was once again lost.

It was hard to control her beast side; her need to mate with Hope was overwhelming her. Again Jolie latched onto a wondrous pink-tipped gum drop and she drew it into her mouth, unable to resist nipping, just a little. Hope moaned and arched. Jolie smiled around the plump strawberry nipple, smug that she was learning all Hope's secrets. She rolled her tongue and flicked, and was rewarded by another gasp. Jolie was addicted. She moved from one breast to the other, tugging with lips and teeth, soothing with long, lazy sucking. Jolie was just beginning, just savoring the taste. She had waited a long time to find her mate, and now she had all the time in the world to enjoy her.

Hope was hot and writhing, liquid and befuddled. She hadn't foreseen this. Yes, she'd wanted sex, but sex as she remembered it. Not this crazy explosion of her insides into hot Jell-O that oozed out of very interesting places. Jolie was inexperienced, Hope knew, because she was just the opposite. And yet here she was, on fire under Jolie's mouth. And now her hands were on Jolie's shoulders pushing her down to where she so needed her to be. Jolie was shaking, struggling to hold back a tremendous carnal energy; it sparked from every pore of her body. Hope knew she was cradling a hand grenade, and she had already pulled the pin.

"Please, Jolie. I need you to touch me there…" she murmured, somewhere in between coaxing and begging. She didn't really need to do either; her pajama pants soon went the way of her top, ripped from her body and tossed aside. Hands cupped her bare buttocks and raised her off the bed and Jolie burrowed between her thighs with a contented growl that hummed all along her flesh. Then a long, firm tongue speared her, beginning a slow, delicious torture, and the hand grenade went off in Hope's head.

Her first orgasm was heavy and deep. It came too fast and almost frightened her with its intensity. She cried out, bucking and twitching, impaled on the tongue that flickered and pulsed inside her.

Jolie clung to her, her fingers biting into Hope's bottom. She wasn't going to let her go anywhere. Exhausted and sweaty, Hope twisted and turned, trying to pull away.

"No. Done," she rasped, "all done." Her answer was another deep growl that vibrated through her sex up into her belly and out along her trembling thighs. Jolie moved to hunt out Hope's timid clitoris, latching on to its base and nuzzling it, until it swelled to meet the tip of her tongue.

"Oh." Hope's head collapsed against the pillow as her clitoris took control of her universe. "God, I'm gonna die..." But her hips were pushing hard against Jolie's mouth, demanding more and more.

This was not the way it was supposed to happen. Her fuzzy thoughts tried to make sense of the whirlwind her bed had become. She had no control over anything. Jolie was on a rampage all over her body. She came again, quicker than she'd ever managed before from clitoral stimulation. She wasn't sure if these flash-flood orgasms were a cheat or a mercy. Again, it wasn't an issue as Jolie dipped her head and proceeded to lap at her sex.

"No, no, please, Jolie, you're killing me." Hope pulled at her weakly but insistently. Jolie slowly crawled along her body and stopped inches from Hope's face. Nose to nose, Hope could inhale the musky scent of her own sex on Jolie's lips and breath. Her chin and cheeks shone with it.

"More." Jolie's eyes glinted as she lowered her mouth for a long, deep kiss. Hope clung to her. Very slowly and steadily, two long fingers pushed through Hope's outer folds, sliding inside her in one long, easy thrust. Hope gasped into Jolie's mouth, and her inner muscles spasmed around the intruding fingers as Jolie began to fuck her. The crushing kiss swallowed sighs and cries until Hope had to break away for air. Then her moans filled the room and Jolie moved her mouth down to a full, heavy breast, pulling the nipple into her mouth and sucking on it roughly. She moved from one pinched tip to the other, swathing them with the flat of her tongue, nipping the areola, gorging on the abundant, silky flesh. Hope rocked easily on Jolie's fingers, so she added a third and pushed harder to fill her. Hope's clitoris proudly popped again, demanding attention, and Jolie stroked it gently with her thumb.

Hope crested, her inner walls clutching Jolie's fingers in a death grip. She arched with a ragged cry as wave after wave crashed through her, finally beating her back down onto the mattress, totally spent. She lay there sweating and gasping for air.

She managed to croak out a sincere promise. "If you touch me again, I swear I'll hit you with the bedside lamp."

"I want more," Jolie whispered, her breath hot and sticky in

Hope's ear. "I want all of you. Forever." Her words came out low and harsh with raw emotion.

"There's no such thing as forever, and you've got all I can give." Hope was exhausted. Even as she murmured the words she was slipping into a semi-comatose sleep. In seconds she was dead to the world, replete and content, and thoroughly blissed out.

"I want more," Jolie told the dark.

"I came five times last night," Hope happily declared the next morning. She giggled as Godfrey choked over his coffee. They were holed up in the kitchen together while the Garouls sat in the next room. Another family ballot had shooed her from the meeting and into the kitchen for an early coffee break where she was pleased to find Godfrey loitering.

She watched him try to compose himself as he formulated at least a dozen questions in his head while mopping his chin.

"Were you alone?"

"No, I wasn't," Hope blustered indignantly. "As if I'd tell you that. I was with Jolie," she confessed, shy now after her earlier brag.

"I knew it. I just knew it. Andre owes me fifty bucks."

"You bet on it? I am hurt and appalled, and you owe me a cut."

"Deal. I only bet that you'd fall for her charms here in Little Dip, not that you'd go on a sexual marathon. Talk about a comeback."

"I had no idea it was going to turn out like that either, or I'd have run from the room after the first time."

"There's something about this place makes 'em more...virile." Godfrey gave Hope a lascivious wink and they both dissolved into giggles. "So spill. Who started it?"

"She did. No, well, I did. But she's the one who wouldn't stop. I swear she nearly killed me—"

"Oh my God," Godfrey trilled. He loved a good bodice ripper.

"I ache all over. I can hardly move. I don't know what I started, Godfrey. I'm not sure how much I can take."

"Oh, you can take it all, baby. This is great news. The old horny Hope is back."

"The old horny Hope was begging for mercy. I swear I never had sex like it in my life. Do you think it's because of the cancer and I'm still below par?" she asked, very seriously.

Godfrey frowned. Obviously Hope was unaware of the lycanthropic link with the Garouls. It made them very intense, devoted lovers.

He tried to make light of it. "Too much for you, huh?"

Jolie had to be the one to enlighten Hope as to what kind of mate she had taken. Though part of him thought it might have been better if Jolie had prepared Hope before leaping on her, he had no doubt Jolie was incredibly attracted to Hope and cared deeply for her. She probably had right from the start, if she'd had a name for what she was feeling back then. Perhaps it would have been better if their emotional bond had been allowed to develop before they moved so frantically into the physical. But then emotions had never been Jolie's strong suit, and here in Little Dip she had been coiled tighter than the spring in a detonator.

"Did she blow your little socks off?" he continued to tease.

"If I wore socks they'd be in orbit right now and NASA would be calling a press conference."

"Trust me, hon." He wrapped an arm around her and they moved out to the back deck. "These things take time. Your body has been through a lot and you need to remind Jolie of that. You have to take control and make this what you want it to be. Believe me, she'll follow like a little lamb."

Hope snorted. "Yeah. Like that will happen."

"She really cares about you, Hope, anyone can see that. And you wouldn't do this unless you trusted her and wanted her, too, right?" He raised an eyebrow and tried to look stern, brooking no nonsense from her. Hope gave a little half-smile and came clean.

"Well, you have to admit she's a big hunk o somethin' else. And you know how it is now, Godfrey. It was wonderful to have someone like her be attracted to me, especially as I feel so insecure about my looks…my entire self, in fact." He nodded and let her continue. "And to be honest, I missed my sexual self, and I was never sure if that ole buzz would come back. If I was ever going to have sex again, or even want it. I felt safe with her. She made me feel good about myself."

"But what about her? I'm hearing how you feel about you. And it's all good stuff, hon. Great stuff. But how do you feel about her?"

"I don't know about that yet. I like her. She's gorgeous, and a bomb in bed. Do I need any more than that right now?"

Godfrey nodded in understanding. But inside he was uneasy. He had a suspicion there was a terrible imbalance of expectation and investment between Hope and Jolie already. Tomorrow they would return to the city and normal living. What that turned out to be was anyone's guess.

CHAPTER EIGHTEEN

Andre hunted Jolie down soon after the meeting ended. Godfrey had grabbed him and imparted the news and his view of the situation. After a quick confab Andre was dispatched to find his sister and relay some desperately needed, but subtly disguised advice. He and Godfrey were heading off on their ski trip later that day, and he wanted to catch Jolie before they left.

"So, you and Hope, eh? For real this time." He smiled, careful not to sound too jocular, yet show how happy he was for them.

Jolie's face scorched.

"How'd you know?" She was suddenly fearful that she'd been an open book all through the meeting. She'd tried to keep calm and composed, not wanting to steam up every time she looked at Hope. Had she been transparent as glass?

"Hope told Godfrey, and Godfrey told me, and now I'm gonna hire a big billboard and tell Portland," he said, swatting her arm. "I'm happy for you, Jolie. I think the world of Hope. And I love the idea of you two being together. Can we talk properly when I get back from vacation?"

"Sure. I'd like that. I want to ask you some things—"

"Like maybe how to tell her the Garouls are werewolves?"

"Some pointers on that might be helpful," she answered dryly.

"Tell you what. Hold off till I get back. Go slow. Try wooing her with dinner, and fine wine, and the theater. Do nice things together," he advised without his usual bossing and fussing. "Remember she's been through a lot health-wise, so don't exhaust her. Keep it fun," he added sternly.

Jolie nodded enthusiastically. "Sure, fun."

Andre gave her a big hug. "It will be all right. Make the emotional connection as strong as the sex and she'll be your mate for life," he whispered in her ear.

"Okay." Jolie watched him leave as crippling anxiety slid around her, squeezing like a hungry boa.

"Fun," she repeated out loud to herself. The word sounded foreign to her.

❖

"Dad, how did you tell Mom you were a werewolf?" Jolie found her father heading out of the compound and fell into step beside him.

"Ah, the age-old, universal question." He smiled contentedly. "It's a beautiful day. Let's go for a stroll, sweetheart."

They walked along a back track in companionable silence.

"Hope's been hurt?" he asked out of the blue.

"Cancer. She lost an eye. The left one."

"Ah, I sort of wondered."

"It's hard to tell. I didn't realize until she told me."

He nodded. "Then it made sense?"

"Yeah, then it was sort of obvious. Her balance, the way she moves, looks at me. Sometimes she's very self-conscious, other times I can tell she's almost forgotten about it. She's adapting more every day, and coping in a new environment like Little Dip has been a good morale boost, too."

He smiled. "So, all the little things added up and began to make sense."

She nodded. "Yeah, the little things."

"But in the end those things make no real difference because you love her? Isn't that right?"

Jolie blushed. "Yeah. I'd love her no matter what. I just want her to be healthy and happy."

"Hope's a clever girl. What makes you think all the little things about you aren't adding up for her?"

Jolie was shocked. "You mean she might already know?" Panic flooded her voice. She hadn't considered this.

"No," he said. "I mean she has some of the clues already. She just needs a reference point. Something that will bring it all together and make sense."

"A reference point? How can I give her a reference point?"

"That's something that will just happen, hon. Some little thing you'll say or do will have her wondering. When you spot that moment, that's when you start talking."

"Talking?"

"Yeah. But you can't just dump it all on the girl. You've got to let her start to figure it out for herself. Make it feel like part of a discovery. Make her feel involved and included. It's all part of the bond."

"Okay," Jolie said, but felt far from okay. She was worried Hope might already have suspicions that meant Jolie would have to react in a calculated and sensitive way. She'd have to make Hope feel part of the secret. Part of what Jolie was—wolven.

"Come and look at this tree with me. I think it needs to be felled." Her father moved off the track and down into the trees.

"Why not wait and see if it lasts the winter? Then cut it down next spring if it's still standing?" She followed him and together they walked on, talking woodsmen talk. It seemed the subject was closed.

I'll ask Mom. Somehow Dad made her feel included enough for her to actually become a werewolf like him. Mom will know what it's like from Hope's point of view. Yeah, Mom will help.

❖

Jolie found her mother sitting on the top step of the porch surrounded by seed trays and paper bags. It was late morning and she'd just come back from her walk with her father. Jolie hunkered down beside her to help sort out the seeds and bulbs for spring planting.

"Mom, how did Dad tell you he was a werewolf?"

"Ask your father, dear."

"I did, he just smiled and told me Hope probably already had a good idea and I was to be prepared with all the answers. But, Mom, I'm not sure what the questions will be." She watched as her mom sorted seeds into paper packets, labeling each as she went.

"But you love her enough to want her to know?"

"God, yes. I want Hope to be in every part of my life."

"To feel that way about her, you must be pretty sure of her and how she'll take the news."

That was just it. Jolie was not confident at all. Maybe it was too soon to tell Hope. Maybe she should wait. Keep her away from Little Dip and all these "clues." Jolie was becoming more and more unnerved by the whole process. She wished there was a pamphlet she could just hand out. "Congratulations on your new werewolf. Please take the time to read this brochure and familiarize yourself with its feeding and grooming habits. Your werewolf comes with a lifetime guarantee. The Garoul family wish you many hours of enjoyment with our product. If you have any further questions, do not hesitate to call Little Dip quality assurance on—"

"Here." Her mother handed Jolie a pencil and a dozen or so packets.

"What are they?" Jolie twirled her pencil.

"Look inside."

Jolie popped open the envelope and peered in. "I still can't tell."

"Is there a scent?"

She sniffed. "Nope. Nothing that tells me anything."

"My. Guess we'll just have to plant them and take a chance."

"Okay. What will I write then? A question mark?"

"No. Write, Jolie and Hope, and then the date. That way we'll always remember this conversation."

Jolie shrugged but scrawled the names and the date across the packets. "Why?"

"Because I want to see what grows between you both. You've planted a seed, Jolie. It's germinating in Hope's head even as we speak."

Jolie felt weak. Now she was planting clues left, right, and center. And she felt so unprepared for what she had started. Maybe it was a sort of secret rite of passage each Garoul had to figure out for themselves when they brought a mate into the clan. So far it was going well. Everyone seemed to approve of Hope. All Jolie had to do was get Hope to approve of *her*…for a life-bonded werewolf partner.

"What are we having for dinner tonight, Mom?" She changed the frightening subject. "I'm in the mood for fish."

❖

"Hello? Anyone home?"

The call brought Hope onto the cabin's porch. Jolie had gone to see her folks while she had begun the laundry.

"Connie," she cried out, delighted. "Come in. It's wonderful to have you visit."

"I was wondering if you'd like to wander up to the studio with me. It's a lovely afternoon for a short walk."

"I'd love to. I think even Tadpole's up for it." Tadpole was dancing around Connie, his tail wagging crazily, begging for attention and a quick ear scratch. Connie laughed and bent to oblige.

"He seems none the worse for his big adventure."

"If anything, he seems more confident. He wandered outside this morning and came back in quite happily. Before, he'd never let me out of his sight, and he'd never venture anywhere near the trees. Now he wants to go everywhere with Jolie. She had to sneak away from him this morning."

Hope was pleased and bemused at the change in Tadpole. She'd finally slid out of bed and Jolie's arms that morning to find him contentedly curled up in the crook of a sleeping Paulie's knees. Tadpole had given her a bleary look and a limp tail wag before settling down for a further snooze.

"Just let me set the laundry dial and grab a coat."

Soon they were wandering along the track to Connie's studio with an excited Tadpole at their heels.

❖

"If I ever come back here, I'm going to start bird watching. Just looking at these illustrations makes me want to see the birds for myself," Hope said.

They had spent the last half hour going over a series of bird illustrations Connie had produced for an ornithology magazine. Hope loved the delicate detail and vivid colors, and had found it hard to believe each and every specimen was a native of the valley.

Connie laughed. "Good, that's what the magazine's all about. And you'll definitely be back. Time and again."

"I really hope so. I love it here." Her answer drew a strange look from her host.

"So, how long have you known Jolie?" Connie asked, handing her a coffee cup.

"I've known Jolie longer than she remembers. I've been a friend of both Andre and Godfrey for many years. In fact, I'll go so far as to claim to be their matchmaker. I met Jolie several times at different social events before Ambereye even started, but was obviously instantly forgettable in those days. It's only recently, since we started working together, that she even notices I'm alive."

"Really? I'd hazard a guess she not only knows you're alive but counts every breath you take."

Hope blinked in surprise. "Oh? Well, until she saw me as an effective assistant she never paid me the slightest bit of attention. I had to buy her pastries to bribe her to share her work diary."

Connie hooted with laughter. "That sounds so like her. You haven't been together very long, then."

"Not even forty-eight hours," Hope answered honestly. She felt shy at her revelation. Connie blinked in surprise, so Hope rushed to explain. "Andre got into the mix, and somewhere along the way Claude and Patrice thought we were a couple rather than just work colleagues."

"Ah." Connie nodded. "But that's not the case now."

"No. We've moved along since arriving here."

"That can happen in a place like this. It's magical. What do you make of the Garouls and the valley?"

"I'm very happy to have made the acquaintance of both." Hope smiled warmly. "Jolie has a wonderful family. And I can see they love and support her as much as she deserves."

"She's the quietest of them all. I remember her growing up as if it was yesterday. We always thought it was because Andre was such a show-off. You know how it is with twins. But now I believe it's because Jolie is an observer of life. She rarely jumps in. I'm glad she met you. I don't think you'll let her sit back and watch the years waste away. Somehow I think you're the type to grab life by the scruff and shake every last ounce out of it. You'll be good for her."

"I've always tried to be—at work, I mean."

Hope was a little overwhelmed; they'd only slept together once and she felt married off. She wished Godfrey was still around. She could have talked to him about it. He always had time to listen and gave the best advice.

"The thing with the Garouls, Hope, is you never get quite what you think you will. They really are something else." Connie smiled at her with such warm confidence Hope felt her stress float away and evaporate somewhere above her head.

❖

"Hey, Hope."

She was halfway home when Amy called out a greeting.

"Hello, big boy." Amy tickled Tadpole, who squirmed at her feet.

"Hi, Amy. I've just left Connie's. She showed me her work for the bird magazine. It's fantastic. Do you share that studio with her?"

"For the moment. But Leone's building us a cabin with a studio attached. Like Connie's setup, only bigger. We want to live in it year-round and go up to the city for work only when we have to."

"That sounds wonderful. But I would miss the city after a while. I like it here, but I don't think I could live here all year."

"There are a lot of Garouls who think like you. That's why most of the cabins are for vacation purposes, and only a handful are for year-round living. I know Jolie wants to build here. She's already got dibs on a lovely spot further up the Silverthread. Get her to take you there sometime. It's a lovely walk along the river."

"Maybe, if we have time."

"Oh, she'll make time. I'm surprised she hasn't shown you already. Probably too busy with the board meetings and stuff, I guess."

"Is it near here?"

"Maybe an hour along the south river trail. It's easy to find. It's been cleared, and she has a sort of fishing shack on it where she and Claude barbecue and have a beer after a day's fishing."

"Where are you going now?"

"I'm heading up to see Connie. Hey, I'll catch you later tonight at Claude and Patrice's."

Hope blushed at the reminder. She'd thought it lovely of Jolie's parents to host a farewell dinner for herself and Jolie. They couldn't make her feel more special or welcome. The Garouls were truly lovely people.

Waving good-bye to Amy, Hope hesitated on the track. It was still early afternoon. It wouldn't be dark for some time. The river winked at her through the trees and she knew she could find the southern trail quite easily. Maybe she should take Tadpole for a real walk. He hadn't had one for ages. And maybe they could swing by Jolie's shack. It might be nice to have another little insight to her quiet lover. *Lover?* A hot flashback from the night before blazed across her mind of Jolie's tongue lazily tracing the crease under her right breast. Hope could feel her face burn hotter than ever.

Yes, no doubt about it. A lover. She mulled over the word. She had a lover now. Weighing it in her mind, she tried to get a feel for its balance in her new post-op life. Was there space for a lover? Was this a wise thing to do? She could almost hear her logic falling over in despair at her recent emotional behavior. She'd taken Jolie Garoul as a lover, deliberately so. So why was she slowly freaking out because Godfrey, or Connie, or even Amy, was telling her how great Jolie was, and how wonderful that she was building a cabin, and what a great hideaway this valley was, and…and…

Claustrophobia crept over her. She took a deep breath. *Come on, Glassy. You've been around the block. So you got a sexy new lover. Okay, so she's your boss. But you're going to leave her department in a few weeks anyway, and go back to your old post. So chill. It's a fling, and you need it. It's all part of the recovery process, remember that. You are not married to her. This is just fun.*

Her rally speech didn't really work.

CHAPTER NINETEEN

In the end, curiosity made her lead Tadpole along the Silverthread. It was an easy, level trail to walk and the afternoon was bright, the river burbled merrily, and winter birds sang out to one another. Hope was enjoying herself.

She wished Jolie was there with her. Apart from going over documentation before the meetings, a few meals and, of course, fucking until the mattress exploded, they hadn't done that much together that weekend. Jolie had gone off to see her parents right after Andre and Godfrey left for their ski trip. Now Hope missed her.

She would have liked Jolie to show her where she wanted to build her own cabin. She was glad Jolie had plans for her future that didn't involve slaving away at Ambereye until she mummified in her office. This cabin dream was an interesting insight, and Hope supposed it was why she was walking along this meandering path by the riverside. She was intrigued and interested. On some level she was still putting together the puzzle of Jolie Garoul, and there were vast chunks missing.

They'd been wandering along happily for over an hour when Tadpole suddenly took to his heels and ran ahead, barking madly. Startled, Hope made after him calling his name, but he plunged through the underbrush and disappeared from view. She heard him yapping around the next bend and increased her pace as fast as she could manage.

"Stupid pup. The squirrels are probably teasing him senseless," she muttered, anxious for him after his last escapade. In some ways it was easier having him skulk around the cabin than thinking he was the king of the forest.

Hope rounded the bend and found herself in a clearing with a little wooden shack. It was really no more than a roof with three sides. It housed a bench table with wooden seats and a small grill. Some cast-off clothing was heaped on the table, and the front wall lay totally open to the riverbank. Hope froze in disbelief. There, in the river, standing thigh deep in the water, was the strangest and most intimidating animal she had ever seen.

It was tall, and stood upright, but wasn't a bear. At least it was not like any bear she knew of. Tadpole stood on the bank barking at it, much to her horror. Even as she watched, the creature plunged long arms with vicious claws into the water and swept a large steelhead trout up into the air. It landed on the bank close to Tadpole. He scrabbled over and pranced around the flopping fish barking excitedly, but keeping a safe distance at the same time.

Hope couldn't understand what she was seeing. Another fish landed nearby, and Tadpole raced over to begin another round of yapping and dancing around this one. Hope could see several fish floundering along the bank. She pulled back and hid in the shadow of the trees. She was anxious. She didn't want the creature to see her, but she couldn't run away without Tadpole, who seemed totally unaware of the danger. In fact... Hope took another peek just as a trout flew through the air and landed splat on top of Tadpole, setting off another frenzy of happy barking. Were they playing?

Tadpole's tail wagged madly, and he kept darting down to the water's edge, waiting for a new fish to be thrown at him. The creature growled and playfully splashed water at him. It was a game!

Hope didn't know what to do. She was frightened. Just looking at the creature terrified her on a primal level. Every instinct she had told her to flee, but she couldn't leave Tadpole. Once again she withdrew around the bend in the path and fretted. Finally decided on a course of action, she filled her lungs and took a chance.

"Tadpole!" she bellowed as loudly as she could. "Here, boy. Here."

Either she had just brought that devilish beast down upon her, or Tadpole would come running, and they could continue like that all the way home. That was the extent of her plan—shout and run. Some plan.

"Taddy!" she yelled again, and took a timorous peek through some branches to see if she could locate him and the massive creature he thought was a playfellow. To her surprise the river was empty and Tadpole stood barking like a fool at the tree line on the opposite bank. Had the creature run off when it heard her call, knowing she was nearby? *Please let it be an ugly, timid bear.*

"Taddy, here, quickly." To her relief Tadpole came scurrying toward her. She took a few tentative steps into the clearing to collect him in her arms and get the hell out of there when something drew her attention. The heap of discarded clothes in the shack. The red check of the shirt caught her eye. It seemed familiar.

The eerie silence from the surrounding forest halted further investigation. It was beginning to freak her out. She was unsure when the birds had stopped singing, and she had the awful feeling of being watched. She lifted Tadpole into her arms and turned to hurry back the way they'd come. She had no inclination to explore the clearing or the shack. She just wanted to get back to their cabin as soon as possible.

❖

When she finally got back there was a note from Jolie on the kitchen table. "Paulie and folks headed home. Gone to help Dad cut logs. Back in time for dinner. J. Miss you."

It was nearly dinner time anyway, so Hope laid clean clothes out on the bed and went for a shower. She was toweling herself dry when Tadpole's welcome bark alerted her to an arrival. Wrapping her bathrobe tightly around herself, she left the bathroom to find Jolie stripping off in the kitchen, shoving her clothes directly into the washing machine. Tadpole sat beside her, his tail thumping on the floor.

"Hi." Jolie smiled at her, seemingly unconcerned about her nudity. "Did you have a nice day?"

"Mmm." Hope felt her cheeks heat as her eyes swept over the tall, tight body. Her stomach clenched as memories of last night came flooding back. Not that they'd been that far from the surface. Since relaying her news to Godfrey, she'd been reliving delicious moments of it all day long.

Jolie approached slowly until she stood before her. Carefully her fingers pulled at the tie holding Hope's robe closed, loosening it. Her eyes never left Hope's, hypnotizing her into acquiescence. The robe fell open and, gripping each side, Jolie gently pulled Hope forward until their naked flesh fused together. It was electrifying, the coolness of her own skin, still damp from the shower, brushing against the sweat and spicy warmth of Jolie's. With a low rumbling growl Jolie dipped her head to nuzzle Hope's neck, making all her senses brim over with delight.

Hope's skin goose-bumped at the touch of Jolie's lips. It amazed her how her body locked into Jolie's; they fit snugly together on a very physical level, and it alarmed her. She'd never felt so content with a new lover so quickly, as if she was drowning in molasses, too overcome with the sweetness to recognize the danger. She pulled back as far as Jolie's arms allowed her.

"Oh no, you don't. I've just got myself clean. Get into that shower now, Garoul, or we'll be late for your parents' dinner." She delivered a playful slap to a lovely buttock, and again thrilled at the casual intimacy they shared. They were a parody on honeymooners.

"Shower with me," Jolie rumbled in her ear before gently nipping an earlobe. Again, Hope tingled at the warm breath caressing her ear, and the red-hot rush that sexy, growly voice sent through her. She felt almost programmed to fall to the floor and have sex each time that particular low growl rolled from Jolie's throat and vibrated through her body. With great effort she peeled herself away, shaking the lusty images from her mind.

"Having a shower with you would be like stepping into a liquidizer. I'm on the verge of collapse as it is. There's no way I'm doing another round with you." Deftly she stepped away and retied her robe with a firm double knot.

Jolie looked a little put out, but allowed Hope to set the pace.

"I can wait. I've been waiting for you forever." She tenderly rubbed Hope's nose with her own. "Your nose is wet. You must be feeling healthy." She smiled at her joke.

Hope pulled back and wiped at her face. "It's the shower. I need to get my hair dried. I wish a wet nose was all I needed to be healthy."

Jolie gathered her in her arms again. "Don't let your worries stop this, Hope. You need love in your life. Love will heal you, through and through, and I have tons for it for you."

"You're crazy. I can't just expect you to—" But Hope's words were smothered in Jolie's embrace.

"I'll always look after you. I love you so much, and believe me, I'm not going to lose you now I've found you, Hope Glassy. You're my mate…for life."

Hope pulled back slightly. "That's a big thing to say this early on, Jolie. Don't steamroll me into this. Let's just see what happens day by day, okay?"

Jolie swallowed hard and nodded. She had to go slow. Andre and her parents had all succinctly told her to go slow, and she would.

"I'm going to take you to the theater when we get back," she blurted, anxious for Hope to know she knew the right things to do. How to woo her, as well as care for her.

"Not if you smell like that. Theater stalls are not stable stalls. Go wash, or we'll be late."

"And wine and dine you, too," Jolie added. But Hope was pointing firmly at the bathroom door. Jolie complied, determined to show restraint when asked.

Shaking her head, Hope watched her leave. Part of her wanted to jump in that shower and arrive late and disheveled for dinner. But she was tired and ached all over. Last night she had been bitten in places piranha couldn't reach.

If they called it biter-cise the gyms would be packed, she mused as she crammed her damp towel into the washer with Jolie's things. She hesitated, touching the sleeve of Jolie's work shirt. It was a familiar red plaid. It reminded Hope of the one she had seen in the shack. But what did that mean? It was a common flannel pattern; a million work shirts sported it. And those clothes could have been abandoned there for ages. Hope hadn't taken the time to look properly. She'd just wanted to get away.

Damn, I forgot to ask Jolie about bears. It would have to wait until later. They were already running late. Hope moved back into the bedroom and grabbed her hair dryer.

❖

"Are there many bears in the valley?" she asked as she passed the bowl of green beans to Leone sitting next to her. This was greeted with a general hesitancy that made Hope wonder if bear talk was inappropriate at the Garoul dinner table. She felt a flush of embarrassment.

"Not usually," Claude answered carefully. He was sitting opposite her.

"If one comes in it never stays long," Leone added. "Why do you want to know? You'll always be safe here."

"Do you think you saw one?" Jolie asked anxiously. The congenial atmosphere over dinner quieted a little. Hope sensed she had hit a nerve with her hosts, but she couldn't understand the delicacy around her question. She'd have to ask Jolie later.

"I'm not sure. Tadpole was barking at something and from a distance it looked...sort of like a bear—"

"Sort of?" Leone pressed her. Jolie shot a worried glance at Claude and shifted in her seat, ill at ease. Again Hope frowned. Why was everyone so awkward about bears in the valley? Had a bear attacked someone before?

"Well, I didn't get a good look. Tadpole scared it off, but it looked like a bear to me. Only—ugly?" She shrugged, trying to make light of it and close the conversation. Her embarrassment was growing to the stage she'd rather have admitted to seeing a UFO hovering over the treetops. It inhibited her from relaying every detail about her trip to the river.

"Ugly?" Jolie looked incredibly offended.

"Tadpole scared it?" Leone snorted loudly.

In fact, several giggles were quickly stifled around the table. Hope didn't get it.

"Yeah. Ugly in a Bigfoot kind of way, maybe." Again this was greeted with muted laughter by all but Jolie, whose face bloomed several shades of red. Hope was getting annoyed at being the butt end of an in-joke.

"Nah. No Bigfoot around here. Just some bear from over the bluff, I bet." Leone grinned evilly across at Jolie. "Wait till I tell Andre that you spotted an ugly old bear. He'll be very interested to know that. It's so rare to see them in Little Dip."

Jolie glowered back, and again Hope wondered what the big joke was.

"This trout is delicious." Marie diplomatically pulled the conversation away from bears, ugly or otherwise, and onto their meal. There was a general round of agreement. Patrice had cooked a wonderful dinner.

"All courtesy of Jolie," Patrice answered happily. "She caught dozens of them down at her shack this afternoon."

"There's some great fishing along that stretch of the river," Marie said. "When will you begin your cabin, Jolie? You've got a great spot down there."

Claude was the one to enthusiastically answer with talk of plans and materials and possible start dates. Jolie sat silent, her gaze locked with Hope's wide-eyed stare, reading every shock wave as it rolled off her body.

CHAPTER TWENTY

They walked home in silence.

Jolie was lost in troubled thoughts, unsure where to begin the conversation they needed to have. Had Hope realized the truth about the Garouls? It had been a close call this afternoon by the river. Tadpole's appearance should have warned her, but the little squirt had taken to following her everywhere possible. She'd assumed he'd tagged along after her, finally sniffing her out—not that he was actually accompanying Hope on a walk.

It had been fun watching his hysterical reaction to the flopping fish. She'd enjoyed playing with him, but it had distracted her. She hadn't caught Hope's scent on the wind. She should have noticed that; it should have been an alarm signal. But she had missed it because she still had Hope's scent all over her, a strong mating musk that clung to her, elating and comforting all in the same instance. Something soap and water could never remove. It was secreted in her pores, her sinuses, her taste buds, her head, and in the very chambers of her heart. Everywhere. Hope swam in the swirl of her fingerprints like the tide over rippling sands.

Deep in her gut she knew Hope had her answer. How long would it take for her to compute, to accept, to ask? Jolie wanted it out in the open before they left the valley and hopefully began their new life together. She wanted Hope to understand and to love her anyway. To love the real Jolie Garoul.

God, how she wished Andre was here. She gave a heavy sigh.

"What's wrong?" Hope asked.

She came back too quickly. "Nothing's wrong. It's perfectly natural for a Garoul."

"Sorry?"

"Huh?"

"You sighed and I asked what was wrong."

"Oh." Jolie was a little flustered at her misunderstanding. "I miss Andre is all."

"I miss him, too. And Godfrey. I wish they were both here."

"Yeah," Jolie murmured. They continued on in silence.

❖

In bed Hope turned her back to Jolie as soon as she slipped under the covers.

"I'm really tired," she mumbled and lay staring at the wall with a knitted brow. She was lost in a myriad of confusing, circular thoughts. There were dots everywhere in her head, but none were connecting properly. And the few that did presented such a fantastical picture, she automatically rejected it. The red shirt lying abandoned in the shack. The huge creature in the river that ran when it heard her. Yet Tadpole knew this creature—he had played with it. And all those fish that ended up on Patrice's dinner table? Hope's head hurt. She decided to blame it on the wine. One thing was for sure—the Garouls had a secret. From their amused reaction at dinner they knew about the bear creature.

Oh, how she wished Taddy could talk. He would tell her what was happening. He wouldn't let her worry.

Jolie lay on her side and watched Hope's shoulders rise and fall. She was not sleeping, her breathing told her that. It also told her Hope was tense and worried, and on a deeper level, scared. Jolie stole in behind her to spoon, her arm curving protectively around Hope's waist.

"I said I was tired." Hope stiffened even further.

"Can we talk? Just a little? I know you want to sleep, but I think we need to talk."

Jolie was terrified of the "talk." She never opened up about herself, her feelings, or her secrets. Yet here she was inviting it, initiating it even. She knew Hope was feeling insecure and probably trying to suppress her unease with huge dollops of logic. Instinct told Jolie if she allowed that to happen, then she would have missed an important opportunity to reveal the truth to the woman she hoped was her life mate. In fact, had determined was her life mate.

There was silence for a moment, then Hope whispered hoarsely, "I don't know what to think, never mind say."

"Anything. You can say anything. Ask anything." Jolie's heart lurched erratically at Hope's words. She was terrified.

She cupped her body closer, hoping to give them both a little comfort, and nuzzled through Hope's hair to find a thumping pulse point. It trembled under her lips and she closed her eyes to savor the desire flashing through her. She was so dedicated to Hope, so in love. But was she a creature who could be loved in return? Her family was living proof that it could be that way. But did Jolie deserve the same? Could she expect that from Hope?

"You can ask me anything," she whispered into the soft flesh of Hope's throat, eyes closed against her fear.

There was a hesitation. A quiet intake of breath before Hope's quiet question exhaled into air around them.

"What am I in bed with?"

❖

Jolie threw another log into the wood stove before settling back onto the couch opposite Hope. They both sat curled up, nursing the cups of cocoa Hope had made as Jolie stoked up the fading embers. Now fire glow was the only light in the room as Jolie began her story.

"Remember I told you before how the Garouls arrived in America in the early sixteen hundreds. Well, at least Yvette Garoul did. She was exiled from the ancestral family lands of southern France and sailed for the New World. She dressed as a man and became a tracker and fur trader along the Hudson, then moved out west."

"I remember. Why was she exiled?"

"She stole her brother's wife. They fought over the infidelity and she lost. That's how the story goes."

"Her brother's wife? She was gay?"

"Her twin brother. And yes, she was lesbian. A high proportion of Garouls are gay. We think it's so we don't overbreed."

"Wow. Why can't you overbreed?"

"Let's stick with one story at a time. I don't want to muck this up." Jolie plucked fretfully at a loose thread on the thick Wallowa blanket covering Hope's knees.

Hope encouraged her. "Okay. So Yvette Garoul came to America disguised as a man. God, what an amazing story."

"Well, in those days it was survival of the fittest. And Yvette had a big advantage…" Jolie looked over at Hope, who hung on every word, captivated. "She was a werewolf. From a long line of werewolves, in fact."

"Werewolves," Hope repeated flatly. "You had me up to that point. I was enjoying the story until you turned into the Brothers Grimm."

Jolie shifted uncomfortably. Was this the way it was meant to go? She hated all this talking. Much better to chase Hope through the woods, drag her to the ground, strip her naked and bite her. Simple. The old courtship ways were best. She tried a more immediate approach.

"Hope, what did you see in the river this afternoon? Do you really believe it was an ugly bear?"

Hope shifted uncomfortably. She didn't answer. Jolie stood; the firelight flickered across her lean face and played in the depths of her eyes.

"Do you want to see it again? The creature? I can call it from inside me. I can change. But when I do, Hope, I'll want to lie with you; I won't be able to stop myself. I can smell your scent, and I know you're ready to mate with me."

Hope's face flamed. She remembered the marathon session from last night. She knew her body well enough to realize she had been simmering all day with lust. Her libido had returned with a fearful vengeance, totally ignoring her logical self as it screamed at her to slow down and think things over. This latest "ugly bear" shock had brought her brain to an entire standstill. Everything she'd taken for granted about Jolie, the stoicism, the steadiness, the sanity, had just gone up in smoke with this wacko werewolf story.

"*You* are going to change into an ugly bea…a werewolf? And ravish me?" Hope stared at Jolie long and hard. "I don't think so. This nonsense has gone on long enough. I'm tired, you're insane. I'm going back to bed."

She needed a good sleep, and to wake up refreshed. Then she'd pack and get the hell back home. She had made a mistake sleeping with

Jolie Garoul. A big mistake, plain and simple. She was in recovery. She was on strong medication and off tilt. A mistake, that was all. No need to beat herself up. At least not yet. She could do that next week, when she was back in the city and Candace was in full "I told you so" mode.

"What did you see at the river? Tell me." Jolie's voice sounded rougher, deeper.

Hope became obstinate. "I'm not sure. I didn't get a good look at it. All I wanted was to grab Taddy and get out of there." She didn't like or want this conversation. She didn't want to be forced into saying what she thought. Well…sort of thought. *Werewolves!* It was just too preposterous, but Jolie was making her nervous, and that in turn made her angry.

"Jolie, stop creeping me out. We're not teenagers at camp."

She started as Jolie pulled her T-shirt over her head and kicked off her panties, standing nude before her in the firelight.

"Damn," Hope muttered, disconcerted as her libido kick-started itself and roared into life on all four cylinders. Was it a trick of the firelight, or were Jolie's eyes flashed with amber? Hope was tired. Her prosthetic eye was sore and her real eye vision was blurring.

Jolie's face seemed to flow before her, wavering and reforming, like long grass flowing in a breeze. *How much wine did I drink?* She found herself staring at a feral version of Jolie's dark features. Her eyes gleamed, her lips curled back, she gave a short snap with sharp, white teeth. Hope felt her temperature plummet. Her intellect didn't understand what was happening, but her guts did. They wanted to heave in fright, and her feet wanted to flee. Even Tadpole had wormed in under the table, watching them both with a look of frightened fascination.

"Jolie? Stop it. You're scaring me now."

Jolie stooped, hunching over, growling into her chest. Her spine popped and cracked. The calcified snapping brought Hope to her feet.

"Jolie. Stop it. Stop it now." But she was backing away as she spoke.

Jolie glanced up at her from under her brows. Her eyes glinted devilishly, hair disheveled. Her jaw sockets cracked, and she panted with pain. It was too much. Hope turned and fled for the bedroom.

Jolie leapt over the couch and followed on her heels, bursting into the room after her. She grabbed Hope and tossed her onto the bed as if she were no more than a doll. She pulled her over onto her back and leaned over her so they lay face-to-face.

"Don't hurt me," Hope whimpered.

Jolie froze.

"I'll never hurt you," she whispered hoarsely. Her teeth clicked as she snapped her mouth shut.

"Promise?"

"I'll always keep my promises to you." Jolie lowered her mouth to Hope's pulse point. She growled and sucked on the quivering heat pouring off Hope's throat. If she bit down hard, would Hope turn? Would she have a wolven life-mate? Would Hope survive it? Jolie didn't know these things. She was scared. Scared to change fully. Scared of hurting Hope. Scared of being rejected for what she was. Her father had said all the little things would make sense. Her mother told her to plant seeds and see what would grow. She had no real idea what they were talking about. She was acting on pure instinct now.

"You're in bed with a werewolf, Hope. You've taken a werewolf for a mate," she murmured into the sensitive spot just below Hope's ear. "And you are *my* mate, now and for always." Her teeth snapped near the ear lobe. She was hungry for her. She wanted her.

Rocking her hips, centering herself heavily on Hope's sex, spreading her legs farther apart, she could scent Hope's arousal, taste her fear. Both inflamed her. She pulled back, growling. "Roll over."

Hope's mind was shutting down. Disbelief clouded her thoughts. *Werewolves?* It had to be a joke, one big prank. Yet here in the wilds of the Little Dip valley it seemed very possible. She struggled to rationalize what was happening.

Jolie was pulling at her, her movements clumsy and fevered. The sharp amber glint in her eyes had softened, all the hard edges of her face now blurred to softer curves. Hope was pushed over onto her stomach. Rough hands circled her buttocks in a swirling caress, and with a deep purring rumble Jolie lowered her head and bit the soft flesh. Hope gasped and jolted at the sharp nip, only to find herself pinned by Jolie's weight. Her bottom was sharply nipped several times, and then a thick tongue bathed the reddened flesh. She cried out and wriggled in discomfort. Her face flushed, her breathing labored, she squirmed under the intimacy of Jolie's attentions. This activity was taboo for her.

She had never encouraged it with any previous lovers, and now she felt she was being given little choice but to submit to Jolie's wishes.

No. No, that is not what we are going to be about! Twisting back on herself, she turned to face a crouched, growling Jolie. Her eyes still shone pale and eerie. Her demeanor, while still disheveled and wild, held none of the earlier dark menace Hope had sensed under the surface. All Hope could see was sexual arousal. Jolie was fevered with it.

Hope was still uncertain at what Jolie truly was…what she claimed to be. But Hope was not a plaything. She glared with a mixture of trepidation and alarm into those shining eyes. They confused her, a prism to so many things: bestial lust, primal energy, and a blazing love light that burned her up, that scared her. She drew back her hand and delivered a hard, stinging slap.

Startled, Jolie sat back on her heels holding her cheek. Hope registered her shock and spoke quickly. "Don't touch me. You promised not to hurt me, but you will. I need time to think, and to rest. Leave me alone, Jolie. Sleep somewhere else tonight."

"You're sending me away?" Jolie gawped, her voice a shallow pant.

"Yes. If you really cared, you'd understand why."

"But…"

Hope stared at her silently.

"I love you." Jolie spoke in that soft growl that made Hope's insides melt. "I'd never hurt you. Don't do this. Don't send me away."

"I need to do this. I need time." Hope held strong to her resolution. Jolie held a strange power over her. She made her care, she made her want, she made her confused.

"If I go will you still be here in the morning? You won't leave?" Jolie whispered, her eyes two large pools of hurt.

"Where would I go?" Hope shook her head, more impatient with herself and her quagmire of emotions than with Jolie. She needed space. She needed time. Most of all, she needed her sanity restored. "Please, Jolie. Leave me alone to think this out. You can't just dump something like this on me, contort into a…thing, and expect sex. Jesus! Get out." Her initial shock was turning to anger. Jolie reached out to touch her.

"Stop it. Don't touch me." Hope struggled upright. She was close to tears now, and shaking as she pulled the bedclothes up protectively.

"Don't cry. Oh God, I love you so much." Jolie crawled up the bed and tried to hold her but Hope shrugged her away.

"Jolie, you can't love me. You don't even know me. We had sex, that was all, and it was a mistake. Even our sex drives are a total mismatch."

"No, no. I can ask Andre or Leone how they do it. We can get in balance as a couple. It's possible," Jolie said anxiously. "Don't be scared. You're safe with me. It's just a shock—"

"Andre and Leone?" Hope blinked at her in dismay. It had never occurred to her that the others were…afflicted too. How had she missed that salient point? Jolie had said Yvette Garoul was…was a…

So obviously all the Garouls were. *Shit. I'm so stupid. Jesus, what am I going to do? I think I'm going mad.*

"Jolie, is everyone here a…werewolf?"

"No. Amy isn't, and Shirley, Paulie's mom. Mates are usually human."

Hope stared at her in shock. "Why not them?"

"They choose not to. Humans have a choice. The Garouls are born to it."

"So anyone can become a werewolf."

"We prefer the term wolven. And it's hard on the human body. Not everyone survives. Some of the Garoul mates choose to cross over. We help them, and all have thankfully pulled through. But it's risky. It's a hard process without the proper support."

"Oh God. So Marie? And Connie?"

"Yes." Jolie nodded. "What did you think I was trying to tell—"

"Paulie?" Hope looked horrified.

Jolie nodded again. "He's just maturing into his wolven side. It happens at puberty. My dad usually helps the young ones get—"

"Oh my God. Your parents? Oh no."

"Of course my parents. How do you think me and Andre were born wolven if at least one of our parents wasn't a werewolf?"

Hope looked at her stupidly, her shock cresting close to unmanageable levels. Jolie continued, trying to enlighten her. "Both my parents are wolven. My mom decided to change after she bonded with my dad. If both parents are wolven, then they always have twins. My cousin Jori and his girlfriend, Elicia, are going to have twins next April," she said matter-of-factly.

Hope paled. She lay down and stared at the ceiling.

"Godfrey?" She suddenly jerked upright.

"Nope. He wasn't interested, though Andre would have liked him to."

"Oooh." Hope moaned and lay down again. Her world was falling apart around her. Godfrey, her Godfrey. And Andre. Both friends of hers, forever. Both with this massive secret.

"Are you okay? I know it's crazy, but I wanted you to know before we went any further. Except, well, I already have...all on my own." She looked anxiously at Hope, who seemed fixated with the roof beams. *She doesn't care I'm in love with her. She doesn't need it.*

"Jolie." Hope's voice had shrunk to a very small whisper. "When you brought me here, to this valley...did you plan to...eat me?"

Jolie couldn't help but snort. "No. We had turkey, remember?"

She reached out and this time was allowed to stroke Hope's shoulder. She did so carefully.

"We came to present the financial report to the board of directors. And everyone thought you were my mate, and I realized I liked that idea. That I had feelings for you for some time. Back in the city. I think I fell in love with you somewhere in the city." She let her simple truth fade away into silence, watching thoughts flit and cloud over Hope's face like weather formations.

"Hope? Are you okay? Can I get you anything? And then I'll go. I promise I will."

"I'm exhausted," Hope murmured. "And probably insane. I think my head is going to explode."

"Can I get you some tea?"

"Tea? Tea. Are you being surreal?" Hope's voice had an edge of hysteria to it.

"No. If you want some I'll make it." Jolie sprang from the bed, glad to be moving, to be helpful, to be doing something other than talking. Other than digging her grave with her spade of a tongue. "I'll be right back."

When she did return, carefully carrying a hot cup of chamomile tea, she found Hope fast asleep. Her body had reacted the only way it knew how to this mind-numbing overload of bizarre information. It had surrendered to the sweet rest and recuperation of sleep.

Jolie set the unwanted cup on the bedside table and tucked Hope's blanket under her chin, bending to steal a light kiss to her forehead. She breathed in her scent and held it in her lungs, fearful it might be the last time she was ever this close. In the morning her fate would be sealed. Hope would have processed the information, her body would have moved beyond shock, and she would be in a position to make up her mind.

Jolie already knew the answer. She could sense it—the intellectual detachment, the struggle for logic over this quirk in reality. The craving for a comfort zone that did not include the supernatural. Hope would walk away.

And then there was the matter of the heart. Her own heart was too big, too greedy where Hope was concerned. She knew Hope's heart was not returning the same amount of need, or passion…or love. Hope was still healing. She had other, more important places to put her emotional energies. Jolie had moved too fast, and too recklessly. She had allowed the valley and the Garoul expectations to set her pace. Hope's body was recovering from cancer and enucleation. She didn't need this. She didn't need her. Hope was right; it had all been a mistake. They had both made them, but in different ways. Hope wanted to feel whole again, like her old self, and had taken a lover as part of that. Jolie wanted a life mate and had pounced, blinded by her own desires, not seeing Hope honestly but rather as she wanted her to be.

Jolie wanted to crawl onto the bed and wrap herself protectively around Hope while she slept. To simply hold her. It would be heaven to hold her, probably for the last time. But she had made a promise, and she would always keep her promises.

Instead she moved out onto the porch and looked at the night sky. Naked, she walked into the forest; she would change and hunt, ruthless, quiet, and stealthy. She would stretch bone and sinew, bunch muscle, snap with cruel, curved teeth and drive her quarry to the ground. But she wouldn't howl. She was ashamed of the desperation and the loneliness her wavering cry would reveal.

CHAPTER TWENTY-ONE

Hope woke to a cold, gray morning. She blinked, and snuffled, and reached to the other side of the bed as if expecting something. But that half was empty. She raised her head off her pillow. It was obvious she had slept alone. Lying quietly, she watched the dawn chase shadows from the ceiling.

Werewolves. The Garouls were all werewolves—or wolven, as they preferred to call it, because branding is *so* important. And their spouses could choose whether to become the same, or remain human. Brilliant. She had obviously been made privy to a big family secret. A humongous family secret. Would they let her leave knowing it? Or would they eat her alive, unless...unless she became one of them? Became Mrs. Jolie Werewolf?

Hope mulled over Jolie's confession in the cold light of day. It still left her reeling. She needed Godfrey like never before. It was hard to believe he knew all about this. Was part of it, even. God, how had he kept his mouth shut?

She felt so lost in all of it.

As she lay there swathed in confusion and contradictory thoughts, something else became clear. The person she *most* wanted to ask questions of, to help clear her muddled head, was not Godfrey, or Andre. That particular person was not lying in bed beside her, either. She had gone away as promised, and now she was missed. What was all that about? Hope didn't like waking up in the wide bed alone. She wanted Jolie there beside her. All this werewolf talk had blown holes in her head. Hope had no idea where to go with this situation.

She began to unravel the tight knot of feelings that bound her.

Okay, so, first thought on waking was... Missing Jolie. *It's a mess. I'm a mess.*

Next came the stupendous disbelief in what she had been told, followed quickly by upset and confusion as she began to accept it. She didn't want the people she liked, and especially those she loved, being different. Being wolven and having this bizarre secret—wait a minute, loved? Sure, she loved Godfrey and Andre. They were her best boy buddies, for heaven's sake. Jolie was...well, Jolie. She didn't love her. She was her weird boss. Okay, so she'd slept with her. Once. Just once, she'd had sex with her. Well, okay, there was a whole lot of sex in that one night. *And* it was the best sex of her freakin' life.

Hope's toes curled under the quilt at the memory, followed quickly by a scowl as she realized her body missed Jolie. It was acting as an entirely separate entity from her reason, logic, and plain common sense. It tingled and glowed and ached, and wanted. And it was more than lust. This need burned deeper. There was something else— Hope sat up in a flurry, eyes wide with dismay. All the biting! She was infected with lust for Jolie Garoul. That's what all the biting was about. She was contaminated with wolven mating bites!

"Well, what can I expect from someone who steals my stapler. And God knows what else," she muttered and scrambled out of bed. She scooped her feet into her slippers and dragged on her bathrobe. Marching into the living room, she fully expected to see Jolie sprawled out on the bed settee now that Paulie had returned home. She drew up short. The couch had not been slept on. Tadpole was also missing. Usually he came scurrying to greet her as soon as she stirred.

"She's even stolen my goddamn dog."

A delighted bark came from outside. Hope strode over to fling open the door on Jolie and Tadpole playing on the porch steps. Jolie listlessly threw his rubber ball and Tadpole charged into the surrounding shrubbery to retrieve it. His tail waved with ferocious pride every time he triumphantly returned with it in his mouth. In contrast, Jolie looked dejected, sitting in a plaid shirt and jeans, her shoulders slumped. She seemed to have little enthusiasm for the game. Turning expectantly at Hope's arrival, her whole body language changed, her back straightened and her face opened up.

"Hi. Did you sleep well?" she asked.

"Yes. No." Hope scowled at her and collected the squirming Tadpole in her arms, where he dropped sloppy kisses on her cheek and chin.

"Yes, no?"

"Well, what did you expect? After news like that?" Hope looked away. "It's not every day…" Words failed her. She had absolutely no reference point for lycanthropy. She set the dog down before she dropped him, and watched him run off after his ball. "When are we leaving?"

"Um, we can stay another day or two if you want to. I can swing it with Andre." Jolie was nervous. She'd been rehearsing these simple sentences all night. "I could show you a little more of the valley. If you'd like?"

"Jolie." Hope hesitated, and then plunged on. "I can't stay here. I want to go home."

"Okay. I understand."

"No! You don't understand. I'm recovering from cancer, Jolie. I need to look after myself. Eat well, gets lots of rest, not become depressed, keep life interesting and stimulating…but not like this! Not with…with werewolves, for God's sake." Panic entered her voice.

Jolie reached for her but Hope shied away. "You're my mate, Hope. My chosen. I'll love and protect you forever—"

"No. You don't get it, do you. I'm meant to be the one on the outside. Part of my face is missing, I'm not pretty anymore, I'm not *me* anymore. I'm less. I've changed. *I'm* the monster." Hope turned her face away to hide her tears. "Then you came along…"

"And out-monstered you?" Jolie said softly. "Hope, you're beautiful to me. You're beautiful to your friends. You're *more* because of your illness. You're stronger, wiser, more determined. Don't be afraid of the future. I want to offer you a long and happy one. Please reach out and take it."

"Jolie." Hope shook her head and took a deep breath. "I want to work with Andre when we finish this project. I think we need a little space. Things have gone very…peculiar between us. We should step back and think about things. I'm not even sure if Ambereye is the place for me anymore."

"Oh." This was no surprise. Despite her pleas Jolie had seen this coming a mile out. She had desperately hoped a few more days at Little Dip might help Hope get over the shock. Now it seemed far more serious. Hope might leave her, leave Ambereye. Now it was frightening. Jolie was panicking. She had seriously fumbled the outing of herself and her family.

She had no doubt of Hope's integrity. In fact, part of feeling an attachment to a potential mate was knowing that the wolven secret would be safe with that person. It was an instinctive thing. But it would have gone so much better if Andre had been around for her to consult with. He had told her to wait, but that was before Hope had seen her in the river. She'd totally blown it.

"Okay then. Okay." She found herself rushing to appease Hope's wishes, so contrary to her own.

They stood in silence for a second that seemed to stretch into a century.

"So. When can we go?" Hope asked again. Her gaze swung from the tree line, to the porch post, to the clouds above. Anywhere but at Jolie.

"Whenever you want. As soon as you're packed. Just say." Jolie looked away, embarrassed that Hope couldn't even meet her eyes, so deep was her discomfort around her. She felt her presence was unwanted. "I'm going to go and say good-bye to Mom and Dad. Then I'll pack my stuff. I won't be long, just twenty minutes or so. Is that all right?"

"Would…would you say good-bye from me?" As cowardly as it was, Hope couldn't face Claude and Patrice. Her upset would show on her face and she didn't want to hurt them. They had been lovely to her. Everyone had. Another wave of confusion washed over her. What was her real problem here? What was going on? All Hope knew was that she had to get away. Had to grab some air clear of this valley and its peculiar inhabitants.

"Sure. Sure I will." Jolie nodded. She turned to leave. Tadpole made to follow her. "No, Taddy. You stay here with your mom."

He waited until Jolie was a few paces ahead, and then followed her anyway, without a backward glance. Hope sat on the top porch step and hugged her knees, watching her scruffy dog glued to Jolie's heels as they both disappeared down the track. What was wrong with her? This was her secret fantasy. Even more so, since the debilitating surgery. Hadn't she dreamed of a committed relationship with someone special? Of settling down, finding her happy ever after. Jolie was a wonderful, eccentric, one-in-a-million girlfriend.

She loves you. She even said so. She gives you screaming orgasms, has you ripping up the bed sheets. You admire her work ethic, her looks, her money, her family— Okay. So you're shocked and scared about her family secret, but before that you enjoyed meeting them all. They were...are, nice people.

Two large tears plopped on to her thigh, soon followed by more. She wiped her tears away, careful of her left eye. Both tear ducts still worked, and soon her cheeks were wet with tears. She was scared. And if she was honest, it was more than just the werewolf thing. Though God knew that was enough. She was scared because her feelings for Jolie were more complex and frightening than anything she had ever known. She'd been trying to find herself—or rather the woman she used to be, before part of her face was removed. Instead she'd disappeared completely into the weird world of Jolie Garoul.

The trill of her cell phone surprised her. The reception in the valley was poor to say the least, and she thought she'd turned it off. But then she remembered turning it on to show the search party her screen saver photo of Tadpole on the night when he'd disappeared. Now she scrambled to her feet, lunged into the cabin, and pulled the phone from her coat pocket. She checked the caller ID. Godfrey!

Beloved friend above all others; he was psychic, gifted, missed. Hitting the button his cheery voice floated into her ear. "Hello, beautiful. How's things in valley of the dolls?"

"Wolves! There'll all wolves, and I'm gonna kill you, you motherfu—" The phone cut out. "Damn. Damn. Damn. Damn. Damn," she screeched, tossing the damned thing onto the couch, where it immediately bounced off, landed on the stone hearth, and fragmented.

"Damn." This came out as a snuffle, followed by a flood of fresh tears.

❖

"Can't you drive any faster?" Godfrey hissed in frustration. Andre's Lexus was slowly negotiating the narrow country roads. "This is an emergency, we need flashing blue lights, for God's sake. Not Miss Daisy at the wheel."

"No. You'll have us all killed and or arrested. I'm going as fast as I can, given the road conditions and the speed limit. I am *not* breaking the law because of your hysterics."

"Hysterics." Godfrey was livid. "Hysterics was our friend crying down the phone because that bonehead of a sister of yours can't handle *any* situation with *any* sensitivity whatsoever."

"Well, I'm doing the best I can," Andre snipped back, not denying that Jolie had probably royally stuffed this one up. Damn it, he'd told her to wait until he and Godfrey got back to Portland. What was she thinking of, terrifying Hope like that?

They passed a signpost that said twenty miles to Lost Creek. From there it was only another ten to Little Dip. The road under their wheels was slick with a thin layer of fresh snow. They should arrive in under an hour if the weather stayed clear.

Above them the skies looked ominous. Larger snow clouds were gathering thick and fast. They had been lucky so far this year, with moderate snowfall. It looked like the good times were over. Those clouds looked vengeful. Andre sneaked his speed up, just a little bit. He wanted to be at his parents' before snow began to fall. It was bizarre. That morning from his ski lodge window he had been scanning these same skies praying for snow; now here he was trying to outrun it.

❖

"I think we were lucky to get away when we did." Jolie looked anxiously at the huge snowflakes landing on the hood of the Jeep. Already the roads were white. "It must've been hours since the snowplow was last down this route. The road's almost gone."

"Do you think we'll make it?" Hope's voice was full of worry.

"Another twenty miles or so and we'll pick up the main road, then we'll be fine."

"Maybe we should turn back?" Hope was feeling guilty now that her histrionics had dragged them away at the worst possible time. She knew deep down she could have survived another night at the cabin—with Jolie back on the couch.

"No. If we turned back, we'd only be snowed in for days. Little Dip gets big snow dumps, being a valley."

❖

"We're snowed in." Andre glumly looked out his mother's window at the whiteout.

She stood smiling beside them. "It's a pity you missed the girls. There must have been only an hour between you. You must have practically passed each other on the way in." She shook her head at the mishap. "But I'm so pleased to have you both back, and so soon."

"It's a regular winter wonderland," Godfrey gushed, nursing his mug of hot chocolate.

"I could have been skiing," Andre said, his mood sinking further.

"So much for our mercy dash. It's a pity Jolie left so soon. I really thought they'd still be here." Godfrey sighed.

"Bitch." Andre huffed.

"That's a bit strong. It's not as if she knew we were coming to the rescue." Godfrey sounded surprised at Andre's attitude.

"I meant you, Florence freakin' Nightingale. You insisted we rush over here to shred linen and boil water—"

"I never did. She's *your* sister. I came here to help our best friend."

His mother rolled her eyes as they began to bicker.

❖

It was very late when Hope finally bustled through her front door and deposited Tadpole on the hall carpet. He immediately took off to see what, if anything, had changed while he'd been away. Leaving the bags sitting in the hallway, Hope moved slowly into the kitchen to brew a cup of tea. She felt a little guilty at not inviting Jolie in for a cup, but it was late and Hope was tired. And she needed space.

Things had been awkward in the car; talk was stilted as Jolie concentrated on the road ahead. The weather conditions had been terrible, but they were home now, safe and sound.

Hope dragged herself to bed, too tired to unpack. She needed to rest. Tomorrow morning would come far too quickly. And even though she had been instructed to come into the office in her own time, she still wasn't sure how she felt about seeing Jolie again in the cold light of their normal, everyday life. Werewolves were not meant to exist outside of fiction. They certainly weren't supposed to be your friends, and work colleagues, and lovers. They were meant to lurk around graveyards and haunted mansions every full moon, and rip annoying cheerleaders limb from limb. They most certainly were not meant to scorch your bed sheets, and brand your heart, and fuck with your head until your reality popped like a bubble.

Grateful to be in her own bed, Hope lay frowning into the darkness. They were in her life now. In every goddamn corner of it. Jolie, Andre, Godfrey, the lot of them. Wait until she next saw Godfrey Meyers; she was going to roast his ears. He knew she had slept with Jolie and had uttered not one word to clue her in or warn her. Some friend he turned out to be. And as for Andre, well, he would hide behind Godfrey like he always did when Hope was pissed off at him. What a pathetic creature of the night he was. She knew for a fact he was terrified of bees.

And Jolie. She sighed and turned restlessly. Jolie. What was she going to do about Jolie? She was angry with her for…for… What? Making her toes curl? Loving her? Being different?

Hope's head was beginning to hurt again. Why couldn't Jolie have kept things simple? Why couldn't she just have been a rich, doting, brilliant lover who made Hope feel like a million dollars just by looking at her? That was all Hope needed——to have fun. To feel sexy, and wanted, but not loved. Never loved so intensely, so deeply, so unconditionally, despite her sight, despite her illness, despite the cloud over her future health.

Damn it, Jolie. Why bring such raw emotion into it? Why peel open each other's hearts and look inside? As if it wasn't hard enough. Why did she have to go and be a freakin' werewolf?

Hope slid further into a whirling morass of confusion until she finally fell asleep. Her dreams were full of dark forests and darker eyes, and kisses that made none of it matter anyway.

CHAPTER TWENTY-TWO

Jolie slowly drove her Jeep around the block for the umpteenth time. She noted the lights in the little house were finally extinguished and guessed Hope had gone to bed. The snowfall had lessened considerably as they had driven toward the city. Now it blew along the pavement and over the lawns in light flurries, piling up in sheltered pockets, turning trees and shrubs into Christmas card images. Peering through the wiper tracks on her windshield, she made one last sweep of Hope's house, ensuring herself that all was well. At last she turned left instead of right at the end of the street, and headed homeward.

Home. But it wasn't. She didn't want her home to be a sterile apartment, furnished with the stylish things Andre and Godfrey picked out for her. She wanted to live in the little house with the yellow door. With the woman who made her heart do flips, who cared for her in little ways, little pastry ways. With coffee just how she liked it. Who knew about the job she did, and her sad addiction to it. Who coped with her awkwardness and borderline sociopath behavior, and who, despite it all, kissed her until her brain buckled, and her knees turned to mush, and she could howl at the moon like a lunatic, forever.

It had all been going so well, hadn't it? She had waited such a long time for this connection. Watched her brother and her cousins succumb to its mystery one by one, wondering and worrying if her turn would ever come. And now it had, and she had fucked it up. And worst of all, she wasn't sure how she'd managed to do it so goddamn thoroughly.

"I should have wined and dined her first," she muttered in self-hatred. She pulled into her parking space. "And took her to the theater."

She grabbed her bag and strode to the elevator. "Bought her gifts. Like chocolate, and jewelry, and"—she scoured her mind to think what else she'd seen paramours given in the movies—"yachts."

Maybe she still could buy these things and try to woo Hope back? She'd ask Andre's advice tomorrow; he should be back from his skiing trip. He would help her rescue the situation.

❖

Jolie sat and gazed morosely at Hope's empty cubicle. Then she glanced down to her pastry-less desk, and back up to the cubicle again. She missed Hope, she missed their morning routine, and she wanted to turn back the clock to before Little Dip.

She had told Hope to take her time getting in this morning. Now she was fretting Hope might not show at all. Might leave her, and Ambereye, because Jolie was horrible. What would she do if that happened? She would run away, too, and hide in Little Dip and chop wood all day, that's what she'd do.

Next she glared in the general direction of Andre's office. He had still not appeared and it was well after nine o'clock. Jolie had turned up early as usual. But the morning felt empty without Hope. Jolie found her absence disquieting.

A small flurry of activity caught her attention. Her staff were discreetly sidling away from their desks toward the kitchen area. Deciding it was a little too early for a midmorning coffee break, Jolie sauntered over to her door to see what the draw was, and if maybe she could yell at someone. That might make her feel better.

Against the general crush of bodies pushing into the kitchen, Hope pushed out, with two coffee mugs and a plate with a precariously balanced pastry. She headed toward Jolie's office. She'd just arrived with everybody's morning sugar hit.

Hope steadily held Jolie's gaze as she approached. She brushed past her, causing Jolie to start and step back. She set a cup of coffee and the pastry plate on the desk.

"I take it you had no breakfast, again," she murmured as she swung back out to her cubicle and booted her computer into life.

"Mmm, no. Thank you," Jolie mumbled and retreated to her seat. She wanted to say something deep, and thoughtful, and incredibly relevant. But she decided it was best to shut up and eat and cling to the normality of it all like a lifeline. For once, she barely tasted the morning treat; memories of something far sweeter commandeered her thoughts.

❖

"That's a nice sweater," Candace said at lunch. "Is it new?" She reached out to finger the wool on Hope's forearm. "Hand wash only, I'll bet. You sure know how to torture yourself."

"I use the wool wash cycle."

"That's not the same. Why do you think they call it hand wash— wait a minute. What's that on your neck? Oh my God. Is that what I think it is?" She tweaked Hope's collar.

"No. No, it's not. I fell. Had a bad balance attack and fell." Hope felt her face burn.

"Fell on your boss." Candace was not going to be fooled. "Fell on your boss like a sandwich, from the look of it. Jesus, John, and whatshisface. I let you outta my sight for three days, and you come back looking like a shark attack. Spill, woman."

"There's nothing to—"

"Spill. Right now. Or I swear to God, I'm gonna march right into Jolie Garoul's office and ask for the health and safety regulations for staff tetanus injections."

Hope's mouth opened and closed several times; still no sound came out. Candace pushed harder. "Then I'm gonna take *you* straight down to the ER and make sure you get one in your butt. Tell me. Tell me now."

"Well, she rescued Tadpole…twice. And she was so nice. And I liked her…so…we…we slept together."

Candace absorbed the paltry, meager sentences with a stern glare.

"That's it? She saved your flaky dog, and you just gave it up? Thank God your house didn't burn down and the fire department roll up, there'd be a gangbang on the sidewalk. So where are you at now? Are you dating?"

"Well, no. No, we're not dating. It's sort of…well…" Hope squirmed. How to explain she was having a little bit of a drama over her new bed-breaking lover being a werewolf? It was hardly a Dear Abby situation.

"So you went to her family's holiday place for the weekend. Had sex, and now that you're back in the real world it's all cooled down." Candace's voice was hard. Again Hope wriggled in her seat, embarrassed at her implication.

"Look, it was me who wanted to cool it down. I mean… It was good for me to, you know, do it. After my operation, I mean." Her face blazed again and she wanted to fan herself with a napkin but resisted. "What I mean is, I wanted to see if I could feel like that again—"

"And she offered to help you find out. That was good of her." Sarcasm dripped off Candace's tongue. She was obviously not going to give one inch to Jolie Garoul's supposed sexual philandering.

"You make it sound as if she took advantage, and it wasn't like that. It was me who went after her." Hope didn't want to be painted as the victim here. There was no victim, was there?

"Um-hmm. You chased her? You chased Jolie Garoul around the bed and then jumped her? Ha! Hon, I've seen that hungry way she's been looking at you for weeks now. You may think you did the running, but believe me, girl, she was backing up all the way. No wonder you collided with a bang."

"That's a bit dramatic. It wasn't like—"

"Wasn't it? You didn't even *want* to go up there. You wanted a quiet holiday at home. You're still vulnerable, Hope. And when something happened to your little dog you probably went to pieces. And behold, who was there for you to lean on…in bed?"

"No. But…" Hope sighed, suddenly tired of the conversation and all of the thoughts it provoked.

She remembered the situation she had walked into at Little Dip. The Garouls thought she and Jolie were already lovers. Why had Jolie been so reluctant to squelch that rumor? Had it all been an exercise in seduction?

Now she was confused. Jolie was hardly a smooth operator, yet she had an animal magnetism that made Hope jittery and unfocused. An added complication was that she had indeed jumped Jolie. Hope had initiated their whole sexual encounter. She had been vain and insecure, and wanted to see if she still had allure. What she found instead was an awkwardly ferocious lover who made her bed spin.

To make matters worse, she couldn't confide the whole truth to

Candace and get a more balanced point of view from her friend. She couldn't say, *Well, it's different for us because Jolie's a werewolf, but apparently they're very loyal and loving.*

She needed Godfrey's input like never before. But Andre had not shown up to work yet, so they must both be still holidaying?

"Where's Andre? Wasn't he supposed to be back today?"

Candace shrugged. "I can't raise him. He should have been in this morning. Half the world's looking for him, too."

❖

"He's not answering his home phone, and his cell is off." Jolie stomped around her office in a froth. "I even tried Godfrey's shop, but they said he'd taken another week because of his mother." She was fuming at Andre's continued absence without leave. "I mean, I need his input on this report and his approval on these figures." She pointed angrily at her monitor. "Meanwhile, all his calls are being rerouted to me, no matter how many times I tell Candace not to, because I have nothing to say to *any* of these people." Her voice rose as she paced back and forth in front of her desk.

Hope watched impassively, waiting for the storm to pass and Jolie to calm down. The phone rang as if on cue, and Jolie snatched it up, listened for a second before slamming it down into its cradle. She stomped over to her office door and bellowed across the entire floor to where Candace sat,

"Why? Why are you doing this? I can't help *anybody* in Phoenix. Just tell 'em he's *not in*, okay?"

Then she slammed her door in a massive huff. Behind her back Hope could see Candace giving Jolie *the look*, much to the appreciation of the rest of the staff. Candace's looks had a sort of voodoo vibe to them. Hope grimaced, waiting for Jolie to stab herself accidentally with her letter opener or trip on a carpet tile. Thankfully Candace's mojo must have been working on only one cylinder, as Jolie failed to spontaneously combust. But only just.

"What do you think he's up to? Do you think he wants to punish me? Maybe he's conspiring with her," Jolie jerked her thumb over her shoulder at Candace, "to drive me mad."

Hope shook her head slowly. "I have no idea where he is or what he's up to. I can't get him at home, and Godfrey's sister has heard nothing either. I'm getting worried, Jolie. It's not like them to go AWOL."

Jolie exploded again. "It's not AWOL, it's fresh snow and let's bunk off and ski for another few days and to hell with my stupid sister who drove all the way through a blizzard to be in the office for Monday morning. Let her talk to all those nutjobs in Phoenix!"

"Now, that is just not true. It's about your brother and Godfrey being missing. It's not at all like them, despite your paranoid delusions to the contrary," Hope said sternly. She had to keep Jolie in check. She was not having a good day. Apart from all the pressure of Andre's non-appearance, she had mysteriously managed to get coffee, cartridge ink, and grease from the photocopier all over her blouse and suit jacket. Hope's suspicions were alerted when she realized Nadeem and Deepak were involved in all three incidents. She hoped Candace had not spread any idle rumors about Jolie's supposed "love rat" behavior toward her. God knew she had enough on her plate without inappropriate revenge attacks on her behalf. Things were tense enough, but she was managing to hold it all together.

The mini-crisis Andre had unintentionally provided with his absence was actually an ideal diversion from the tension that existed between her and Jolie. As it was, Jolie was channeling all her excess emotion into the Andre scenario rather than the situation between them. That was good, because it gave Hope thinking space, and that was something she desperately needed. Jolie's desperate deflecting showed she needed a little space to vent in, too.

❖

"Guys." Hope stopped by Nadeem and Deepak's neighboring cubicles for a quiet word on her way home. "I'm not sure what's going on here, but Jolie could blow at any moment. Especially with Andre being a no-show. If I were you, I'd be a little less clumsy around her expensive suits. Okay? Otherwise the dry cleaning is coming out of the doughnut fund, get my drift?"

"Well, the cartridge ink was a genuine accident. But the oil stain was absolute genius," Nadeem grudgingly admitted. "It's just we don't like the way she treats you—"

"You don't know the way she treats me. And believe me, if I had a beef with her, there'd be a lot more than coffee and ink stains on her jacket. She's my boss. You cross her, you cross me. Sorry, boys, but it's part of the PA code."

"Okay, Hope. No more boo-boos," Deepak swore solemnly. Nadeem nodded in agreement.

"Good. Thanks for caring, but I'm cool." She smiled warmly at them and headed off, another problem dealt with. And she *was* cool. She'd surprised herself with how well she'd held the day together while Jolie frayed and frothed and fell apart.

Jolie didn't need thinking space to know this week she was damned. Everything had gone wrong since Hope had pulled away from her. Andre, her main emotional support structure, had eloped to the slopes on a fun spree. Typical of him, just when she needed him most. Her parents were incommunicado, probably because of the snowfall in Little Dip. And she was mysteriously cursed at work. Everything was going tits up. Every day there was some minor catastrophe and she emerged from it the worse for wear.

Also, the staff had started glowering at her again, just as she'd gotten used to them not glowering. It was disconcerting. It had gone on for four days now, and she was becoming demented.

It was three a.m. on Friday morning, and she hadn't slept a wink. Out on her balcony, the cold city air swirling over the tree tops made her senses twitch. Maybe a quick run in one of the city parks would cool her heels.

Nighttime was her worst time. Then she lay in a puddle of deep carnal thoughts about Hope, remembering every curve and arc and dip and dent of her pale, luscious body. The warm fluidity of her skin, soft and sweet, like vanilla cream. Her tongue tingled, and the coppery taste of blood marbled across it as her incisors thickened and curved and sliced a new home in her gums. Her change had begun to creep up on her as her desire mounted, and that was not good. It was a distraction, a torment that she was barely able to control at work. In fact, the recent turmoil in the office had acted as a buffer between them. Jolie sensed Hope was grateful for the reprieve. That made her hesitate to initiate the postponed "talk" she had wanted to have the night she had revealed to Hope what she really was.

She threw on her sweats and running shoes and ran like fury to the small park in Sellwood that Hope used for Tadpole's playtime. It was a park forever ingrained in Jolie's mind as a happy place. She had few enough of them in this city.

She leapt the railings at a quiet, overgrown spot, and quickly stashed her clothes safely away. After sniffing the air and ensuring all was still, she crouched and went through her transmutation almost effortlessly, energized to be in a place she associated with Hope. Keeping to the shadows, she tore across the lawns, hugging close to the trees and shrubs, glorying in the freedom of the night and physical exertion. Power streamed off her flanks, muscles bunched and stretched as she loped and spun and pounced and circled under the city skyline.

She realized she was close to the gates that Hope used. She glanced over at the park entrance that led to Hope's avenue. She knew the back way, across the neighborhood yards and gardens. She knew all the shadowy edges of trees and garden sheds, and shrubbery, where a great beast could stealthily slide. It shamed her that she knew them, but her wolven side was gleeful. It drew her through the gates, and the thin layer of night, on toward the honey locust tree.

The little house was so calm and peaceful, all tucked up for the night. The earlier snowfall had blanketed the lawn and flowerbeds, but the paths had been cleared. Hope would be curled up under soft blankets in a big cozy bed. A bed that oozed of her scent and cocooned her soft, slumbering body. Jolie had never seen Hope's bedroom. She wondered what color it was. What it smelled like. How the light filtered through the windows, night and day.

From inside she heard a yapping bark. Tadpole was awake and knew she was there. She stiffened.

Another friendly bark, this time at the back door. He was insistent to get out and greet her. Then she heard Hope murmur, the key rattle, and the door opened a crack allowing a trickle of light to spill out across the yard.

"What is it, Taddy? Pee-pee time?" Hope mumbled sleepily.

Jolie leapt.

❖

Hope stumbled back into her tiny kitchen. The small of her back jarring against the countertop halted her retreat. She froze. The creature had literally dropped before her from out of the night sky. She recognized it from the river.

"Jolie?" she gasped.

It stood upright, filling her entire kitchen doorway. Tadpole jumped up a few times in welcome, but on being ignored he wandered off unconcerned into the garden. The creature advanced no farther over her threshold. Instead it stood motionless, waiting.

"Jolie?" Tension slid from Hope's shoulders, and she took a tentative step forward. Amber eyes cautiously watched her every movement. She could sense no danger, no malevolence. This was Jolie. Her Jolie.

"Why are you here?" she asked in a whisper. "Like this?" She took another slow step forward.

The creature neither moved nor blinked, just regarded her steadily with eyes that held a soft, intelligent glow. Hope reached out a trembling hand and brushed her fingers across thick sable, as sleek and dark as wet ebony. Raw, primal power hummed under her fingertips, raising the fine hairs on her arm. It was beautiful. Up close it was absolutely beautiful.

She examined everything. Her gaze ran over huge clawed feet and hands, powerful limbs and a tight torso, the chest flattened with musculature yet still curiously female, all coated in a thick black pelt. Carefully, she reached up toward the stubby muzzle, lined with cruel teeth. It inclined its head slightly to let her touch its face, thin black lips curling back to further display razor-sharp incisors.

Hope stretched for the feature that most fascinated her. Tenderly, she ruffled a small, furry ear. Her fingertips ran along the rim to the pointed tip with its sparse crown of stray hairs. She smiled in wonder. The broad chest, level with her head, rumbled with a gentle purring growl. The great beast dipped its head for more strokes and petting touches.

Hope ran her forefinger along the damp muzzle and down the crescent of a long fang, delicately resting the tip of her finger on its sharp point. She poised there, holding her breath, stunned at what she was doing. It was so surreal.

A thick pink tongue poked out and stroked the heart of her palm, making her gasp at the hot, moist touch. She pulled back quickly, and it raised its head. Once again she was bathed in the sweetest golden light shining from its eyes.

"Jolie?" she whispered in awe.

With one long, unreadable look it turned and was gone, leaving her alone in her kitchen. The door was now open to only the cold night air and emptiness.

Hope fretfully paced the floor for hours afterward. Was it safe in the city for such a thing to run free? Would it get home in one piece? What if a car hit it or a policeman shot at it? Shot at *her*—not *it*. Shot at Jolie? Her Jolie?

Twice she dialed Jolie's number to make sure she was home safely, only to cut off before it rang, feeling silly, and adrift, and totally unsure of herself and the entire situation.

Eventually she went to bed, glad that she had Friday off. If this was a consequence of having a werewolf as a lover, then she didn't like it. It brought too many anxieties with it. No wonder Amy wanted to keep Leone in Little Dip and not out running the city streets.

She so wished Godfrey would come back from skiing and talk to her about all this. She was confused and upset. How did he look out for Andre? Did he have to worry like this night after night?

She promised herself, first thing tomorrow morning she'd surreptitiously call the office and make sure Jolie had turned up for work, and in one piece.

CHAPTER TWENTY-THREE

I can't believe you slid out of that valley and left me stuck in it," Andre railed. He had arrived into the office by midmorning in one stinking mood, and hadn't let up on how hard done by he had been by his sister, his partner, nature, and the weather. Everything had apparently conspired against him and his skiing holiday. They were both shut away in Jolie's office, supposedly catching up on the working week. Jolie's head was reeling with his constant whine.

"Yeah, like it's been a real jamboree here. Candace is one step away from gutting me with a hole punch, and everybody is shifty and sullen around me, just like the good ole days," Jolie grumbled back.

"How are things with Hope?"

"I gave her today off. She had to work late Monday through Thursday and she's exhausted. It was chaos here. You'd organized all these meetings with half the Americas, and then never showed up. I was beginning to wonder if you'd been buried in an avalanche."

"Yeah. I can see you cried so hard your nose swelled up. I meant *how are things*, doofus."

"What things?"

"Love things, wolf things?" Andre sighed in exasperation. "The last I heard she was having a freak-out because of you. That's why Godfrey and I came hurtling back to Little Dip. Don't you know anything that goes on?"

Jolie stared at him blankly. "Well, I didn't know that. Hope told you she was freaked?" She was hurt. "She told me she wanted space to think, and wasn't ready to talk yet. When did she talk to you?"

"She told Godfrey." Andre looked at her and relented. "Look, Jolie, you gotta be gentle on the humans when you tell them *Homo sapiens* is not the one and only. They don't like not being the most important thing on the evolutionary ladder, never mind top of the food chain."

Jolie frowned. "When did Hope talk to Godfrey?"

Andre sighed. "Godfrey got through to her on his cell phone but was cut off before they could finish. Hope sounded very frightened about the wolf thing. That's why we came back to Little Dip. To help, but you'd already left and we got snowed in. So tell me. What happened?"

"Well, I was going to woo her like you said, and pace myself and everything. But she saw me in the river—"

"Yeah, I heard all about the ugly bear story."

Jolie ignored his jibe. "So Hope asked me what was going on, and I told her, because it seemed like the right time. But she got upset."

"What did she do?"

"She told me to go away and let her think about it and we'd talk later. And that's what I'm doing."

"So you didn't sit down and discuss it then and there?"

"No. She wanted space…and maybe to work for you again," Jolie finished quietly. "If she doesn't leave Ambereye altogether."

Andre digested this. "You let Hope take control at a time when you should have been guiding her through the process of understanding and accepting your wolven side."

"You told me to wait."

"You need to talk about this now," he stated bluntly. "You should never have allowed her distance. With distance comes disbelief, which is great when we don't want humans to believe in us, but crap if you're trying to charm one into becoming a mate."

"But she said—"

"Go talk to her."

"But—"

"Now. Go. Right this minute. Go, find, talk." He practically shooed her out of her own office. "Must I write the script for every little move you make?"

❖

"I can't find him anywhere." Hope's voice quivered with anxiety as Godfrey jogged up to her. They stood together at the park gates looking left and right, anxious for a glimpse of Tadpole.

Godfrey delivered his bad news. "He's not by the postbox either. And that's a favorite spot."

They had been scouring the neighborhood for nearly an hour. Godfrey had called to collect Hope to go for a walk across the park to their favorite coffee joint. They agreed they needed a latte and a massive catchup, with all the juicy trimmings. No sooner were they through the park gates than Tadpole's ears jerked upward, his nose buried itself in the grass, and suddenly he was off at full tilt and soon out of sight. Hope had no idea what had possessed Tadpole, and no amount of calling could halt him or bring him to heel.

"I can't believe it. He's never been the same since Little Dip. It's like that valley's a curse." She was close to tears. Godfrey hugged her tightly.

"Look, let's head back home and see if he's sitting on the doorstep waiting for us. What do you say? If he's not there we'll come back out for a second look, okay?"

"Okay." With one last miserable look up and down the park, Hope turned to follow him.

Their walk and talk had become a disaster. Hope's heart sank. Losing Taddy in the city was just as frightening as losing him in the woods. And this time there was no Jolie to rescue him.

As if on cue Godfrey asked, "Is that Jolie's car?"

He pointed up ahead to Hope's house. Hope looked up from her brooding thoughts. It did look like Jolie's dark green Rubicon. She picked up her pace. As she drew closer a blob of ginger fur appeared at the passenger window. Next an excited reedy bark assured her she was not deceiving herself. Tadpole was sitting in Jolie's Jeep!

"Taddy. She's found Taddy. Wow. They must be superglued or something." She broke into a cautious trot, aware of Godfrey jogging along on her blindside.

Seeing their approach, Jolie slid out of her vehicle, a joyous Tadpole wriggling in her arms.

"Look what I found sitting on my doormat." She offered up her precious cargo.

"Oh, Jolie. Thank you so much, once again. I was worried sick."

Hope scooped Tadpole out of Jolie's arms with a big smile that made Jolie puff with pleasure.

"Your doormat?" Godfrey asked dubiously.

"Yup. Well, the apartment block doormat. How the hell he managed it, I'll never know." Jolie knew damned well that the runt had picked up her wolven scent and had followed his wolf buddy all the way across the Willamette. The real mystery was how he was not lying squashed on the roadside somewhere along the way.

Godfrey raised a cynical eyebrow, and she had the grace to blush slightly. Luckily, Hope was so engrossed with alternately scolding and kissing the dog she failed to notice the exchange.

"You realize that you're on a leash forever, buster. In fact, pull any more stunts like that and it's a ball and chain, okay." Hope was chastising him nose to nose. "Uncle Godfrey and Mommy were looking everywhere for you. Yes, we were."

Jolie rolled her eyes and began to shuffle from foot to foot. Happy as she was to deliver furball safe and sound, and earn some badly needed hero points, she was unsure if she should stay or just melt away. Godfrey's presence was in the way of her heart-to-heart with Hope.

She had gone home to change clothes and to call Hope to see if they could meet for a talk, as directed by Andre. Finding Tadpole sitting, tail thumping, by her apartment stairwell was a real surprise and an added bonus. It gave her the perfect opening. When Hope didn't answer her phone, she quickly guessed Tadpole had been reported MIA and Hope was probably out looking for him. Even better. Jolie would be his deliverer, and she remembered what happened last time she'd saved Tadpole. The memory of that kiss and night of passion had been replayed a million times in her head since their return.

Dressed in jeans and an old sweatshirt, she gathered up her furry little brownie point and headed over to Hope's house. At least the pup sitting on the passenger seat beside her assured her a positive welcome. She wasn't too sure what else to expect, especially after last night's show-and-tell wolven visit. Jolie would happily settle for a cup of tea and hopefully the talk Andre was badgering her to have.

What she hadn't expected was for Godfrey to be there, too. Now she glared at him, hoping he'd get a clue and clear off. Instead he smiled slyly back, knowing damn well the little dog had followed Jolie's wolf scent. Her shoulders slumped. It wasn't cool to prowl around Hope's neighborhood like a lovesick coyote. She hated being caught out and felt like an idiot.

"Let's all have a cup of tea. I'll make it." Godfrey strolled toward the house, Hope following close behind. Scowling even more, Jolie brought up the rear.

"Yeah, Uncle Godfrey, go make some tea," she muttered.

CHAPTER TWENTY-FOUR

Guess what?" Godfrey swanned into the living room, cell phone in hand. "Uncle Andre is coming over for lunch. Isn't that great, Taddy?" He was addressing the dog, but his eyes were firmly fixed on Jolie. She frowned back. What was his problem, and why was he looking at her like that?

"Oh, what will I make?" Hope was on her feet. Godfrey grabbed her arm and pressed her back down into her seat.

"Calm yourself, princess. He's dropping by Giorgio's to collect a mixed sandwich platter. I'll make coffee as soon as he arrives. It's all under control."

Andre arrived twenty minutes later and handed his offering over to Hope with a quick kiss on the cheek. Godfrey and Hope headed for the kitchen to prepare lunch, leaving Andre and Jolie alone in the living room.

"Have you been skulking round this house in wolven form?" Andre immediately hissed in her ear.

Jolie was mortified. So this was what Godfrey's little side glances were all about. He'd ratted her out to Andre.

In the kitchen Hope and Godfrey set about preparing lunch.

"Finally, peace to gossip. So, what's the state of the nation?" Godfrey fussed over individual plates and napkins while Hope sorted out the coffee cups. "What do you make of ole fuzzy ears, now that you know the family secret?"

Hope stopped what she was doing and turned to look at him, a little taken aback.

"It's no joking matter. These people are...werewolves. Like in the movies. Only not. They are here in the city, and at my work, and in my home—waiting to be served sandwiches with little napkin triangles. Godfrey, it's just so unbelievable. Didn't you find it unbelievable at first?"

"What? We live in an age of space travel, moon walks, cloning, laser beams, and painless waxing. All *those* fantastic stories from our youth are now true, now everyday reality. But not the scary monster stories? Are they the only unbelievably fantastic thing that can't possibly come true?" He raised his eyebrows at her mockingly.

"Where do you go for this painless waxing?" She sidetracked away from the difficult thoughts.

"Don't digress. I know all your timid little tactics, girlie. Are you telling me you were absolutely clueless, even after she bit you? And let's not mention the mammoth bonkfest, which you were unladylike enough to brag about, by the way?"

Hope's face burned. "Well, it has been a long time since I attended a bonkfest, and yes, I did wonder a little at Jolie's uncanny stamina." A private smile flitted across her face before she could stop it, earning her a buddy arm punch from Godfrey.

"There ya go," he crowed, "fantastic creature clue number one. Unstoppable love machine."

"But it never occurred to me I was sharing my bed with something a little less than human. Or is it more than?" She frowned.

"Look, hon," Godfrey continued in more sober vein. "It's not going to be a quick adjustment. But you can go at your own pace. The big question is do you want to? Would you like to keep seeing her? Because I'm your friend, and I'm telling you I think you got a keeper there."

Hope looked at him dubiously. "The werewolf thing is freaky. I could barely look Andre in the eye when he came in. It's such a shock. I've known him longer than you, and you never once gave me a clue, you bastard."

"You know I couldn't do that. I bet you've been subconsciously hugging the secret to your chest, too, since you found out. Well, haven't you?"

Hope nodded; she had to admit she'd been curiously protective of Jolie since their return, especially with Candace and the boys in the office. She'd even worried for the great hulking creature that visited her last night. Jolie as a wolf was beautiful, and Hope had found herself fussing, and caring, and worrying about her the same as she did in the office. The line between human Jolie and wolven Jolie was blurring for her.

"I swear, Hope, before he broke down and told me, I had an idea something wasn't adding up with Andre." Godfrey leaned back on the countertop beside her. "I actually thought he was addicted to Viagra or cocaine or something. His energy and sex drive was so crazy. It wasn't until we visited Little Dip and I saw the weird link the Garouls have with nature and that valley that I began to guess. But there was nothing in his city face to give him away. Humans are so wired and stressed in the city. And there are so many wackos out there, too. It's the perfect hiding place for an otherworldly creature. I'd never have figured out if we hadn't gone to Little Dip."

"Yes. I just thought Jolie was a little odd when I first met her. And when I went to work for her, well, I thought she was a nut."

"She is, hon. The sweetest nut on the tree. Trust me." He began to give her his top tips. "They are so easy to manage, Hope. Quite docile really. Loving and loyal. No nasty surprises. But big on energy, especially sexual energy, and very, very passionate. What you experienced, your little bonkfest? That's just a typical early night, after a favorite TV show and a cup of cocoa."

"I don't think I'd survive a week." Hope's face burned at the thought, even as her toes tingled happily.

"Nonsense. All you've got to do is hang on to the headboard for dear life. And feed 'em lots and lots of big, stamina building meals. I'm never done cooking for those two." He nodded toward the door. "See? Look at the fun we're having gossiping about our other halves."

He gave her a big, happy grin, clearly loving that she was now in the know and he could openly share.

"We can hook up with Amy and have some fantastic gossip sessions about our Garoul mates. Think it over, sweetie. I'm telling you, you've got a good person in Jolie. And a very fetching wolven. Talk it over with her. At least do that much, because she's pining for you. And if you dump her she'll fret and begin to lose her hair, and shed all over my carpets."

Hope thumped him playfully. "You're such an idiot, Godfrey

Meyers. But I will talk to her. I do like her, you know, and I don't want to hurt her."

Godfrey smiled. "You don't fool me. You more than like her. You just need to feel a little more secure before plunging right on in."

"Can I help you with those?" The question came from behind Hope as she was loading the dishwasher. The boys had left fifteen minutes ago, Andre offering Godfrey a lift home before swinging back to the office. Now Hope turned to see Jolie hesitating in the doorway.

"I thought you'd gone with the boys."

Jolie shook her head. "No. I was just talking to Andre before he left. I can go if you want."

"Are you not going back to work?"

Again Jolie shook her head. "No. I took the afternoon off. I was wondering if you'd like to walk in the park? Tadpole won't stray. If he does, I'll go after him."

"I have a feeling he'll stick like fuzzy felt when you're around. He followed your trail earlier, didn't he?"

"I'm sorry. I never thought he'd do that. Sometimes I go for a late night run in the city parks. Nothing ever follows me home."

Hope closed the dishwasher door.

"Somehow I think your idea of a run in the park isn't the same as mine." She straightened up and looked out the window at the day still bathed in sharp winter sunlight. "Okay." She made up her mind. "It's still a nice day. Let's go do something positive with it."

They sat on a park bench. Tadpole lay slumped at their feet, exhausted after playtime with Jolie.

"Jolie, what do I do with this secret?"

"What do you mean?"

"I mean am I bound to it somehow, because I know about you and your family?"

"Who are you going to tell? *The National Enquirer*? Ghostbusters?" Jolie shrugged.

"Maybe Oprah?" Hope snipped, feeling silly now. "You know what I mean," she said defensively.

"Oprah already knows. She's one of us."

Hope's head whipped round to find Jolie's eyes dancing with mirth at her gullibility. "Not funny, Garoul."

"Hope, I know you think you've discovered something awful that will change your life. But it's not like that. You've known Andre for years. His friendship for you hasn't altered. Nor has Godfrey's. They still love you. In some ways I think it's a relief for them that you know." Jolie began to fiddle with a small splinter on the seat planking. "I'm glad you know, too. No matter what happens between us," she said quietly. "I wouldn't have told you, or felt like this, if it didn't feel right. If you weren't the one for me."

Hope stared intently at her. "How do you know that?" This was the crux of her problem: how could Jolie be so certain when Hope was still floundering? "You didn't even want me near you when I began working for you."

"Well, you were a pain in the ass. You stole my chair."

"That was *my* chair, and you damn well know it."

"*And* you tricked me out of my stapler."

Now that Hope thought about it, there'd been clues everywhere. Her gaze dropped to the wolf ring on Jolie's little finger. "I gave you the wolf paw one."

"It broke the same day. I was conned," Jolie grumbled.

"That chrome stapler also started out as mine," Hope reminded her. "Is this how it's going to be, Garoul? All of mine is yours?"

Jolie looked up at her, her eyes burned into Hope's.

"Yes."

❖

"I'm afraid it's going to be tofu burgers and savory rice. That's all I got in. Tomorrow I do my big grocery shop." Hope rummaged in the kitchen cupboards. "Oh, and corn, I have a can of creamed corn."

"Sounds great." Jolie lounged by the kitchen door, keeping well out of the way. "Can I help with anything?"

"Pour some wine. The glasses are to your left in the tall cupboard. There's an opened bottle of white in the fridge. I hope it's okay."

Hope was nervous and fussing now. On pure impulse she had invited Jolie to stay for dinner. It was madness since she had nothing in the house to cook with. "Maybe we should just order in."

"Burgers and rice sound good," Jolie reassured her, and passed over a cold glass of Riesling. "But we can order takeout, or even go out if you wish?"

"No, I'll rustle something up."

Hope began preparing the simple meal, aware that Jolie stood watching her every move. Curiously, Jolie's proximity in this little domestic tableau relaxed Hope. She'd expected the opposite.

They ate in front of the TV like couch potatoes, watching a mindless cop show, as if they'd done this a million times before. Then Jolie cleared away their plates and came back to join Hope, pulling Hope's feet onto her lap, rubbing her stocking toes.

"I want us to try. You're right for me," she said quietly, out of the blue. Hope looked over at her.

"How can you be so sure?"

"Mother Nature told me. And she's smart," Jolie said with a wry smile, and tweaked a ticklish toe.

"What did she say?" Hope felt the corners of her mouth lift despite herself.

"She said you need love because love will help you heal. Inside and out. And she told me I'm the one to love you. I'm the best one for the job," Jolie stated with authority, nodding firmly to underscore the correctness of her words.

Hope raised her eyebrows. "Is that a fact? And what do you get out of this stupendous deal?"

"I get to spend the rest of my life with you."

"And I get a werewolf."

"A very loving werewolf. You've been to Little Dip. You met my parents and family, some wolven, some not. You know Godfrey and Andre from way back. You've met Amy and Leone. All mixed couples. These are people who just fell in love, and it doesn't matter about differences. They look at each other and they don't see those things. I want to be with you. I know it can work. I grew up with this. I see it every day when I look at my parents, or my cousins, or my brother and his partner…and you've seen it, too."

Hope digested this. It was true.

"I've got a million stupid questions," she warned. Suddenly it was clear; she wanted to stick around and ask them all. And if each question took a day to ask and answer, that would be approximately twenty-seven thousand years.

Jolie shrugged. "I got all the time in the world for you and your questions."

"Okay." Hope bit her lip. "Question one, will you stay the night?"

Jolie's head jerked and she looked expectantly at Hope.

"Yes," she replied a little breathlessly. "I'd love to stay."

"Told you they were stupid."

CHAPTER TWENTY-FIVE

Godfrey was so right. The thought ran through Hope's mind as she clung to her headboard. *If you turn 'em on, you better hang on.* Her gaze fixed on the dark head nestling between her thighs, filling her body with such delicious, nerve-stretching sensations that she cried out, again, and again.

She had led Jolie to her small, neat bedroom. They'd tremulously kissed as clothes whispered to the floor, encircling their feet. Then, when they were both naked, flesh to flesh, Jolie cradled her in her arms, and laid her on the bed. Starting at Hope's toes, she kissed every bare inch of her body, contentment singing in her croons and growls, and showing in small nips and tender sucking.

Jolie was happy to take her time, to explore, delighting in the goose bumped skin that heated and flushed under her lips, the muscles that quivered under her tongue. Hope's scent filled her head and heart, rich, unique, and much loved. Hope's pulse fluttered in the hollow of her throat, her inner wrist, the dent behind her knee; Jolie found and savored these satin points with the tip of her tongue. She rolled Hope over and kissed the nape of her neck, slowly trailing down along her spine. She lingered over the buttocks, covering them with gentle kisses until she felt Hope relax before continuing down the back of her thighs to finish at the toes again.

Carefully, she covered Hope with her own long body and bit gently where her neck met the shoulder. Jolie's satisfied growl rumbled through both of them. She rolled onto her side, bringing Hope with her, spooning her from behind, and cupped her breasts, squeezing gently yet persistently. The tips hardened in her palm, and she rubbed them until they tightened even more. Hope was moaning loudly now, her buttocks rocking and jutting back into Jolie's groin. One hand covered Jolie's on her breast, the other reached round to rest on a tanned hip. Jolie's fingertips trailed down Hope's stomach and dipped into damp, dark curls and unerringly found her clitoris. Hope gasped as she was gently caressed. Her rhythm intensified as she pushed harder back into Jolie. The fingers were quickly saturated and Hope's scent rose high between them, exciting Jolie all the more. She moved down Hope's body, turning her, opening her up for her mouth to explore every fold and crevice. Her head swam with scent and sound. The moans she coaxed from her made her heart swell as Hope crested under her tongue.

Hope weakly dragged Jolie up along her body to lie beside her.

"Stupid question number two." She brushed her damp hair from her flushed face. "How will you ever get enough sex from me? I'm not built to cope with this amount of attention."

Jolie grinned and kissed the sweaty forehead. "It's not the sex, it's you, silly. If it was just about sexual fulfillment, I'd have played around all these years. I guess I was looking for a partner, someone special to bond with."

"You weren't looking, Jolie. We'd met before, remember, and you never even noticed me. So don't go giving me the 'you're so special' spiel, because I'm not."

"I sure as hell noticed when you came into my den and rattled my bones—"

"Bought you cake, you mean."

"No. My office was my special space. My city den. It kept me safe, gave me purpose. It sheltered me from the world outside, I suppose. You shook it all up. How could I not notice you? You made everything different. I had no idea what was happening until we went to Little Dip and I realized I wanted you for my mate."

"Why was that different?"

"It made me see things clearer. What was happening to me, I mean. I was becoming possessive of you in the city. I didn't want you to work for anyone else. I wanted to sit in your house all day and drink tea and watch you. I used to spy on you from the neighbor's tree. Weird things like that confused me. I was acting so strangely around you. When I took you to Little Dip, it all fell into place. I wanted you, but I didn't know how to claim you." She nibbled lightly on Hope's shoulder, nudging lower, slyly nuzzling into a pink-tipped breast. Hope grabbed her by the ears and dragged her head up.

"Oh no, you don't, Garoul. Now I know how you all get those pointy ears. We're going to talk right here, right now. Okay?"

"Can I ask a stupid question now?" Jolie asked.

"Yes, your turn."

"Are we together? Can I tell people?"

Hope scrunched her brow in thought. "Tell them…Tell them we've started seeing each other. Is that okay for you?"

Jolie nodded fervently. "We'll go slowly. I know you need time." She tapped Hope gently on her breastbone, near her heart. "And on the inside, too."

Hope smiled at the insight. Her heart did need time. She needed a clear scan two months from now. And she needed to adjust to this dynamic woman in her life twenty-four/seven, not just nine to five. She also needed to relax back into her own body and enjoy that she was whole again, and special…and loved. The future suddenly looked brighter, less fearful if she was brave enough to embrace it.

"You know something?" She traced her fingertip over Jolie's lips. "You've brought joy into my life. At work, in my home, everywhere. You've made me look forward to the future and stop worrying if I'll have one. It's funny, because Jolie means joy, doesn't it…more or less?"

The lips under her fingertip stretched into a smile. "You gave me hope. I didn't even know I had none," Jolie said shyly.

Hope cuddled into her arms. "Let's sleep and see what the morning brings."

"What will we do?" Jolie asked, in wonder that she had a tomorrow with Hope. Hopefully many, many tomorrows.

"Grocery shop. Walk Tadpole. Clear the garden path. Those sort of things."

"I love those sort of things when I get to do them with you." She was rewarded with a soft kiss on the nose.

"Good, well-rehearsed answer. Keep it up and we'll be married by June."

❖

Later that night Jolie woke up, overheated and cramped. A quick assessment found her sandwiched in the bed with Hope snuggled up on one side, exactly as she should be. On her other side, Tadpole stretched out blissfully, taking up most of Jolie's side of the bed. Rather than sneak in beside Hope, he had chosen to bunk up next to his wolf buddy.

Jolie lay and contemplated the ceiling with a drowsy grin. It seemed she had found herself a new pack. A little family all of her own.

Deciding to put up with the cramped sleeping arrangements, she closed her eyes and fell back into a dream of forests and valleys, and a love that wound wider, and deeper, and farther than the Silverthread.

Keep reading for a special preview of INDIGO MOON,
the next book in Gill McKnight's GAROUL Werewolf series.

CHAPTER ONE

The first buck sprinted from her right-hand side and bolted before her car. Isabelle braked and watched it cross the road. It was a magnificent beast. She counted nine, maybe ten points on its antlers.

"Oh, so beautiful."

It was followed almost immediately by another whitetail, nearly as big as the first. Eyes rolling with fright, the deer ran alongside the high snowbanks heaped on the edge of the freshly plowed road. They raced frantically up and down the man-made barrier until the larger animal lunged at the steep bank and began an ungainly scrabble over it. The other followed. Pushing and straining with powerful hind legs, they flailed through snow and brush. Finally they topped the bank and disappeared into the woods on the far side. Isabelle watched until they had gone.

Poor things were spooked by the car. She scolded herself for not grabbing her camera. It was rare for a city dweller like her to get this close to such beautiful creatures. It would be some time before a photo opportunity like that came her way again.

With a tsk of self-reproach, she put the Toyota into gear and rolled forward just as a third deer darted out of the trees. Isabelle yanked on the brakes, thrilled at her unbelievable luck. She reached for her camera, then hesitated. The deer was limping. This buck was smaller than the last two and just as frightened. It stumbled and seemed confused. It hobbled over to the snowbank, following its companions. Isabelle noticed the dark, wet patch on its flank. The churned-up snow under its hooves spattered with drops of scarlet. It was injured, bleeding. A bloody gash ran across its rump down onto the hind leg. It limped to the escape route opened up by the others, and with an exhausted leap tried to follow, but the incline was too steep. It slipped and slithered back onto the roadside, lacking the strength to climb. It tried again and failed. It stood trembling, trapped by the wall of cleared snow and the wound on its leg.

Isabelle grasped the handle but didn't open her car door. What could she do to help? She was in the middle of nowhere with an injured wild animal. Should she even approach a wounded—

A loud metallic crash made her jump. Her car rocked violently from side to side, the roof crunching and buckling over her head. She cried out in fright, but the cry choked in her throat. A huge black beast springboarded from the roof of her car onto the wounded deer, dragging it to the ground. It was massive and vicious and moved with frightening speed, ripping into the deer's gaping wound with huge, curved claws. The whitetail was torn to shreds in seconds. Innards lay steaming on the icy road; partially flayed limbs, strips of hide, its severed head were strewn in all directions. The snow all around was now a puddle of wet, melting crimson. The beast reared upright onto its hind legs, flung back its heavy head, and howled an unearthly, wavering cry. A howl filled with blood-curdling triumph. Then it fell back onto the deer's remains and began to gorge.

Isabelle was horrified. She gripped the door handle, her other hand squeezed the steering wheel. She sat frozen, barely believing her eyes. In less than a millisecond a…a…a rabid bear had just…had just…wrecked her car and…oh God, that poor deer.

A growl rumbled, long and low, and very threatening, right beside her ear. Slowly she turned her head to meet cold, yellow eyes filled with sly intelligence. A second creature crouched by her car, alongside the door, watching her. Its eyes pinned her with a look of calculated malice, as if weighing her strengths and many, many weaknesses.

Isabelle's heart thumped in her throat, almost choking her. Numbing ice water pumped through her veins, shutting down her brain, turning her guts to Jell-O, her limbs into heavy, useless stumps. Isabelle couldn't move, couldn't think; she couldn't even blink. The twisted leathery face was inches from hers with only the window glass between them. Thin black lips curled back in a mocking leer, revealing rows of long, pointed teeth. For a fractured moment in time Isabelle and the beast regarded each other, unmoving. Then it sprang. Fangs snapped against the glass, lathering it with saliva. Isabelle jerked out of her stupor. She screamed and slammed her foot on the accelerator. This was no bear. This was a monster. A monster from her childhood nightmares.

The Toyota lurched, tires spinning on the icy surface searching for grip. The monster flung out a huge clawed hand and ripped off her sideview mirror. The driver's window shattered, showering her in shards of glass. Isabelle screamed again and kept her foot pressed full on the gas. The tires bit and the car shot forward, its back end fishtailing wildly. She had no control of the vehicle, no thought other than fleeing. She struggled with the steering wheel as the car zigzagged across the compacted snow. It shot forward and rammed straight into the first beast, still crouched over its meal. With a hard, sickening thud she bowled it over onto the hood and off to the side of the road. She drove on, squelching the deer carcass into the slush and snow.

The impact slowed her down so much she nearly stalled. From the corner of her eye she saw the stricken beast writhing on the side of the road. It howled in anger and agony. The cold twilight was filled with unearthly howls answering back. Isabelle's ears rang with the eerie chorus echoing through the forest surrounding her. These two monstrosities were not alone! There were more of them out there! She gunned the Toyota even harder.

A black blur hurtled from the tree line and flung itself onto the hood of her car. It crashed onto the windshield, cracking the glass into a million little webbed cubes. Her speed bounced the creature straight back off before it could gain leverage. It fell back onto the road and only just missed her wheels. Through the crazed windshield she saw another beast crouched along the road ahead of her, ready to spring at her car. Another joined it, slinking out of the trees. She saw a third farther along. They were everywhere. Ready to leap at her! Everywhere!

Isabelle's mind went blank with terror. She swung wildly on the steering wheel, trying to swerve past the ambush. The agonized screams from the beast she had hit made her head hurt. A loud bang and her car rocked wildly. One was on the roof! Through her webbed windshield she could see two more racing directly toward her. She was surrounded. Like lions hunting a lumbering wildebeest, they were surrounding her, dragging her down by sheer numbers.

She spun the wheel hard left. The next one to make the car hood would break straight through the weakened glass. She swerved sharply, avoiding the creatures rushing straight for her. She tried to dislodge the one on the roof by swinging hard from side to side. She locked the wheel to the left, but they kept coming. They were right on top of her. The first one leapt. She closed her eyes and hit the gas hard. There was a sickening thud. The windshield popped, showering her with glass. Isabelle opened her eyes. This one had hung on. It was less than two feet from her, massive and deadly and stinking of evil. She screamed and jerked the wheel violently to the right. The Toyota cannoned onto the snowbank, riding up the incline at full speed. It flipped over the top, and in a perfect pirouette landed upside down in a trench on the other side.

❖

Isabelle blinked, waking into an icy world of fear and agony. She was squashed into a corner of her mangled car, curled up in a tight ball. Snow and vegetation pressed through the windshield, burying her in freezing muck and debris. The sickening smell of gasoline hung in the air. She hurt everywhere. Carefully, she tried to assess her situation, twitching fingers and toes, stretching limbs slowly, gently. Everything moved, but the effort was torturous.

The car was upside down and the world seemed broken and disorientating. Her shoulder was pushed out through her driver's window into a bank of snow. If the glass had still been there, her shoulder would have surely shattered. It was quiet, very quiet, as if the crash had stunned the forest into silence. Had she passed out? How long had she been there? She was freezing and in pain. There was blood everywhere, but she didn't know where it was coming from. None of her bones were broken; she could move, but barely. Her body felt as shattered as the shards she was lying on. Isabelle moaned.

Huge, curled claws burst through the empty windshield and swiped around blindly, missing her face by inches. The wild slashing couldn't locate her. Isabelle choked down her scream and shrank back as far as she could, careful not to give herself away.

With a loud, angry snarl the clawed hand inched further forward, reaching from side to side trying to catch her, to hook her and drag her out. Cowering in the corner, Isabelle became aware of more sounds from outside. Low growls and snarling surrounded her. And prowling, lots of prowling. The creatures had arrived at the crash site. They were all around the wreck. Isabelle pressed deeper into her corner and shivered. Her nightmare was not over. It was just beginning.

The muscular, clawed arm withdrew as suddenly as it appeared. Isabelle whimpered and clung onto the bent door frame, waiting for what came next. A second later the car began to shake violently. They were trying to right it, but the Toyota barely budged; it was wedged firmly upside down in the trench. Isabelle shrank into her small niche as the car creaked and shuddered. Small bits of plastic and metal rained down around her. The car groaned in protest but refused to move. After several minutes the shaking stopped. Isabelle waited with bated breath. Would they go? There was a moment of silence, then a frustrated roar and the bodywork was fiercely pounded. It felt as if the car was being beaten into tiny pieces. Soon they would be able to reach in and pluck her out like a lump of crabmeat.

Metal screeched as any loose car parts were peeled away and tossed aside. Cold air blasted through as metal panels were ripped off. Isabelle shivered in her corner. Her heart thumped and her chest hurt. Her body screamed with pain and tension. Why hadn't she died in the wreck? Why had she survived only for these hellhounds to rip her apart like that deer? There was a grinding snap from the rear and the whole vehicle jerked as the trunk lid was torn off. Another blast of cold air whistled through. She could hear frantic scratching as long claws shredded through the rear seat. They were getting in, creeping slowly closer. She cowered in terror, fixated on the rattling rear seat. It was disintegrating rapidly.

Her shifted position rattled the loose glass and gave her away. A huge clawed hand burst through the broken windshield and sank into her left shoulder, deep as a butcher's hook. Isabelle screamed in agony. The claws bit into sinew and muscle, popping her shoulder socket. She screamed again, and everything faded. Massive oily waves of pain engulfed her, choked her, stole all the air from her lungs. There was howling again, distant and hollow. She was dragged inch by inch through the shattered windshield. Her skin was hot with blood and urine; her heart lurched sluggishly in her chest. She was sobbing, she was fading away, dying. Dragged out onto the cold snow, the stones and brushwood rough against her skin, the pillow scratchy against her cheek, damp with sweat and tears. Isabelle opened her mouth and screamed and screamed and—

"Hey. Hey." Cool hands stilled hers as she madly clawed the air. "It's okay." The same hands caressed her face and pushed damp hair back off her forehead. "Isabelle? Isabelle? It's okay. Can you hear me?" A voice whispered near her ear, smooth and deep, and totally reassuring.

Tears blurred her vision. There was a soft glow from a nearby lamp. That voice. How did she know that voice? She blinked several times to clear her tears. They rolled round and plump down her face and onto the cool pillow. Someone hovered over her. Long, black hair brushed against her cheek; dark eyes stared intently, filled with calm concern.

"Hush, Isabelle. It was just a dream."

"A dream," she whispered. She tried to move and winced as pain shot through her shoulder, making her cry out. Warm hands soothed her, held her, made her still.

"Shush. Keep still, now. You'll pull your stitches. It was only a dream."

"A dream?" She blinked again, slowly returning to the real world, but bringing all the pain and fear of her dream with her. A damp cloth was pressed against her brow. She looked up into the shadowed face. Lamplight played across it, playing tricks with golden planes and dark angles. One moment she gazed at the face of an angel; in another, a demon. She blinked again, trying to focus. It was a darkly handsome face…what she could make out of it. A woman's face. She smacked her dry lips and swallowed. Her throat felt raw, as if she'd been screaming all night. Again she focused on the face above. Eyes as black as pitch stared back and noted her discomfort.

"I'll get you some water." She moved to go but Isabelle reached out, her chilled fingers leaching heat from a warm forearm. The woman sat and waited.

Isabelle licked her cracked lips and finally asked, "Who are you?"

About the Author

Gill McKnight moves between Ireland, England, and Greece in an eclectic mix of work, relaxation, and downright laziness. When not scribbling in a notepad or pecking away at her laptop, Gill likes sailing, DIY, puttering about the garden, and running away from wasps.

Books Available From Bold Strokes Books

Magic of the Heart by C.J. Harte. CEO Susan Hettinger and wild, impulsive rock star M.J. Carson couldn't be more different if they tried—but opposites attract in ways neither woman can resist. (978-1-60282-131-6)

Ambereye by Gill McKnight. Jolie Garoul is falling in love with her assistant. The big problem is, Jolie is a werewolf. (978-1-60282-132-3)

Collision Course by C.P. Rowlands. Tragedy leaves Brie O'Malley and Jordan Carter fearful and alone. Can they find the courage to take a second chance on love? (978-1-60282-133-0)

Mephisto Aria by Justine Saracen. Opera singer Katherina Marov's destiny may be to repeat the mistakes of her father when she becomes involved in a dangerous love affair. (978-1-60282-134-7)

Battle Scars by Meghan O'Brien. Returning Iraq war veteran Ray McKenna struggles with the battle scars that can only be healed by love. (978-1-60282-129-3)

Chaps by Jove Belle. Eden Metcalf wants nothing more than to flee from her troubled past and travel the open road—until she runs into rancher Brandi Cornwell. (978-1-60282-127-9)

Lightbearer by John Caruso. Lucifer dares to question the premise of creation itself and reveals that sin may be all that stands between us and living hell. (978-1-60282-130-9)

The Seeker by Ronica Black. FBI profiler Kennedy Scott battles ghosts from her past, deadly obsession, and the evil that haunts her. (978-1-60282-128-6)

Power Play by Julie Cannon. Businesswomen Tate Monroe and Victoria Sosa are at odds in the boardroom, but not in the bedroom. (978-1-60282-125-5)

The Remarkable Journey of Miss Tranby Quirke by Elizabeth Ridley. When love enters Tranby's life in the form of a beautiful nineteen-year-old student, Lysette McDonald, she embarks on the most remarkable journey of all. (978-1-60282-126-2)

Returning Tides by Radclyffe. Insurance investigator Ashley Walker faces more than a dangerous opponent when she returns to the town, and the woman, she left behind. (978-1-60282-123-1)

Veritas by Anne Laughlin. When the hallowed halls of academia become the stage for murder, newly appointed Dean Beth Ellis's search for the truth leads her to unexpected discoveries about her own heart. (978-1-60282-124-8)

The Pleasure Planner by Larkin Rose. Pleasure purveyor Bree Hendricks treats love like a commodity until Logan Delaney makes Bree the client in her own game. (978-1-60282-121-7)

everafter by Nell Stark and Trinity Tam. Valentine Darrow is bitten by a vampire on her way to propose to her lover Alexa Newland, and their lives and love are placed in mortal jeopardy. (978-1-60282-119-4)

Summer Winds by Andrews & Austin. When Maggie Turner hires a ranch hand to help work her thousand acres, she never expects to be attracted to the very young, very female Cash Tate. (978-1-60282-120-0)

Beggar of Love by Lee Lynch. Jefferson is the lover every woman wants to be—or to have. A revealing saga of lesbian sexuality. (978-1-60282-122-4)

The Seduction of Moxie by Colette Moody. When 1930s Broadway actress Violet London meets speakeasy singer Moxie Valette, she is instantly attracted and her Hollywood trip takes an unexpected turn. (978-1-60282-114-9)

Goldenseal by Gill McKnight. When Amy Fortune returns to her childhood home, she discovers something sinister in the air—but is former lover Leone Garoul stalking her or protecting her? (978-1-60282-115-6)

Romantic Interludes 2: Secrets edited by Radclyffe and Stacia Seaman. An anthology of sensual lesbian love stories: passion, surprises, and secret desires. (978-1-60282-116-3)

Femme Noir by Clara Nipper. Nora Delaney meets her match in Max Abbott, a sex-crazed dame who may or may not have the information Nora needs to solve a murder—but can she contain her lust for Max long enough to find out? (978-1-60282-117-0)

The Reluctant Daughter by Lesléa Newman. Heartwarming, heartbreaking, and ultimately triumphant—the story every daughter recognizes of the lifelong struggle for our mothers to really see us. (978-1-60282-118-7)

Erosistible by Gill McKnight. When Win Martin arrives at a luxurious Greek hotel for a much-anticipated week of sun and sex with her new girlfriend, she is stunned to find her ex-girlfriend, Benny, is the proprietor. Aeros Ebook. (978-1-60282-134-7)

Looking Glass Lives by Felice Picano. Cousins Roger and Alistair become lifelong friends and discover their sexuality amidst the backdrop of twentieth-century gay culture. (978-1-60282-089-0)

Breaking the Ice by Kim Baldwin. Nothing is easy about life above the Arctic Circle—except, perhaps, falling in love. At least that's what pilot Bryson Faulkner hopes when she meets Karla Edwards. (978-1-60282-087-6)

It Should Be a Crime by Carsen Taite. Two women fulfill their mutual desire with a night of passion, neither expecting more until law professor Morgan Bradley and student Parker Casey meet again…in the classroom. (978-1-60282-086-9)

Rough Trade edited by Todd Gregory. Top male erotica writers pen their own hot, sexy versions of the term "rough trade," producing some of the hottest, nastiest, and most dangerous fiction ever published. (978-1-60282-092-0)

The High Priest and the Idol by Jane Fletcher. Jemeryl and Tevi's relationship is put to the test when the Guardian sends Jemeryl on a mission that puts her not only in harm's way, but back into the sights of a previous lover. (978-1-60282-085-2)

Point of Ignition by Erin Dutton. Amid a blaze that threatens to consume them both, firefighter Kate Chambers and property owner Alexi Clark redefine love and trust. (978-1-60282-084-5)

Secrets in the Stone by Radclyffe. Reclusive sculptor Rooke Tyler suddenly finds herself the object of two very different women's affections, and choosing between them will change her life forever. (978-1-60282-083-8)

Dark Garden by Jennifer Fulton. Vienna Blake and Mason Cavender are sworn enemies—who can't resist each other. Something has to give. (978-1-60282-036-4)

Late in the Season by Felice Picano. Set on Fire Island, this is the story of an unlikely pair of friends—a gay composer in his late thirties and an eighteen-year-old schoolgirl. (978-1-60282-082-1)

Punishment with Kisses by Diane Anderson-Minshall. Will Megan find the answers she seeks about her sister Ashley's murder or will her growing relationship with one of Ash's exes blind her to the real truth? (978-1-60282-081-4)

September Canvas by Gun Brooke. When Deanna Moore meets TV personality Faythe she is reluctantly attracted to her, but will Faythe side with the people spreading rumors about Deanna? (978-1-60282-080-7)

No Leavin' Love by Larkin Rose. Beautiful, successful Mercedes Miller thinks she can resume her affair with ranch foreman Sydney Campbell, but the rules have changed. (978-1-60282-079-1)

Between the Lines by Bobbi Marolt. When romance writer Gail Prescott meets actress Tannen Albright, she develops feelings that she usually only experiences through her characters. (978-1-60282-078-4)

Blue Skies by Ali Vali. Commander Berkley Levine leads an elite group of pilots on missions ordered by her ex-lover Captain Aidan Sullivan and everything is on the line—including love. (978-1-60282-077-7)

The Lure by Felice Picano. When Noel Cummings is recruited by the police to go undercover to find a killer, his life will never be the same. (978-1-60282-076-0)

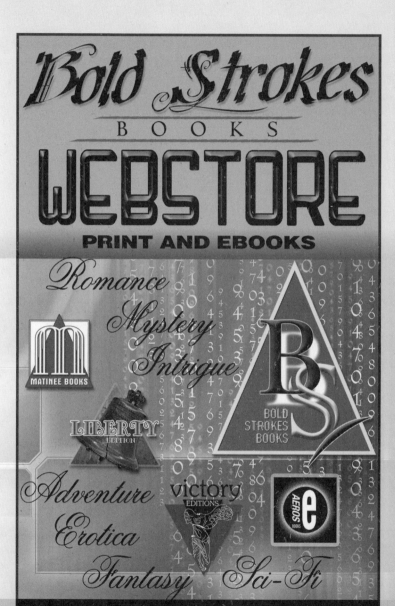